Advanced Reviews for Wavehouse

"*Wavehouse* captures the twists and turns of growing up with sensitivity, humor, and heart-pounding surfing adventures. Fans of Sarah Dessen's beachside novels will enjoy Kaltman's seaside setting peppered with quirky and unforgettable characters. Warning: you may be tempted to grab a board and paddle out to Kendall's Watch once you've finished."

    — Diana Gallagher, author of *Lessons in Falling*

"*Wavehouse* is a much-needed addition to young adult fiction as it centers on a powerful yet painfully shy female athlete holding her own in the male-dominated sport of surfing. Alice Kaltman is able to put readers alongside Anna on her surfboard in a way that only an author who is a surfer herself could. In her descriptions, I can feel the wind through my wet hair, the acceleration of the surfboard beneath me, and the ecstatic terror of entering the shimmering barrel of a wave twice my height.

Delightedly, *Wavehouse* also contains a heart-melting love story and readers will fall hard for the thoughtful and mysterious Men's Junior World Surf Champion Chris Kahimbe. I especially liked how this budding relationship forces Anna to face her disapproval of her mother's over-dependence on men and find her own balance in the feeling of being in love without losing herself to it."

    — Megan Westfield, author of *Leaving Everest*

"A super shy teen surfer braves ten foot waves, a stormy relationship with her single mom and the tumultuous tides of first love in this poignant debut YA coming-of-age story. I cheered for Anna aka The Surfing Siren and readers will too as she faces down her inner demons and overcomes her fears to let her gifts as an athlete and artist shine. A stirring exploration of the sustaining power of a young girl's growing trust in herself, her friendships, and her unconventional family portrayed with honesty, wit and true grit. Bravo!"

    — Laura Geringer Bass, author of *The Girl With More Than One Heart*

Wavehouse

Fitzroy Books

Published by
Regal House Publishing, LLC, Raleigh 27612

Printed in the United States of America

ISBN -13: 978-1-947548-38-1

Cover design by Selene Studios
Cover art by Alison Seiffer

Regal House Publishing, LLC
https://regalhousepublishing.com

Library of Congress Control Number: 2017960264

For Noa, the reader who made me a writer,
and
Daniel, my partner in all crimes.

"So on a summer's day waves collect, overbalance, and fall; collect and fall; and the whole world seems to be saying 'that is all' more and more ponderously, until the heart in the body which lies in the sun on the beach says too, That is all. Fear no more, says the heart. Fear no more, says the heart, committing its burden to some sea, which sighs collectively for all sorrows, and renews, begins, collects, let's fall."

-Virginia Woolf, *Mrs. Dalloway*

Chapter One

Shyness is a disease. It's not contagious, and it's not life-threatening—though sometimes it feels that way. Those of us who suffer from this disease are born shy; we're genetically predisposed to freeze, crumble, or act like panic-stricken rodents in most social situations.

The worst form of the disease is what I call "All-Star Shy Person Syndrome," which means that contact with anyone who has a pulse can make you quake in your flip-flops. It doesn't matter whether you've known them your whole life, or just met them that day. All you want to do is go hide under the nearest rock.

There are some lucky shy folks, I call them "Type A's," who, in spite of their inherent social phobia, can transform themselves into confident alter-egos when on stage or competing in sports. But when they're not scoring goals or hitting pitch-perfect high *C*'s, they're stumbling through life with eyes averted, avoiding as much direct human interaction as possible.

Then there are the less lucky Type B's who, while moderately shy, turn to mush or stone at the mere thought of performing. Type B's aren't always so inept—they can manage a polite conversation with strangers if the situation demands it; plus, they're cool with friends and family, who Type B's think of as gems kept in special pockets, stored and safe. But ask Type B's to perform? To go: "Tada! Look at me! Aren't I great?" Forget about it. There are no comfort pockets for that kind of experience.

If we're lucky or persistent enough, an All-Star or Type B can become a Type A. But no matter what kind of shyness we each have locked in our genetic codes, we all know: once a shy person, always a shy person. We can't will it away, no matter how hard we want to, no matter how hard we try.

When I was ten years old, I still wanted to please my mother.

I thought Sara—as she liked me to call her—was God's gift to womanhood. I aspired to be just like her, even though I knew I was completely different. So when she signed me up for the Montauk Junior Surf Tournament, I didn't consider saying no, even though my shyness antenna was bleeping at full frequency. I tried to convince myself that if Sara liked surfing in front of other people, then gosh, gee, maybe I would, too. Maybe the waves would win me over. Because even when they challenged me, even when they sent me tumbling into places blue, dark, and cold, waves were my best friends. Waves were my watery companions occupying the deepest and most special pockets.

Surfing wasn't a choice for me; it was a calling. Sometimes it felt more natural than breathing. Sara claimed I started surfing when I was two years old. I still have fuzzy memories of lying on the nose of her surfboard, water surrounding us like a cave, with a clear view of sun and sky. When I looked up, I saw Sara standing with her strong calves squeezed around my little kid waist like a vise. No way would she ever let me fall.

If only my wiser self could go back in time and warn that young dummy. At ten, I was deep in an All-Star-Shy-Girl cocoon, avoiding other kids whenever I could, barely lifting my chin to say a polite "hello" to their parents.

I knew something was wrong as soon as we left our home in Kendall's Watch and cruised westward along the one-lane highway connecting Kendall's with the world-famous— maybe even infamous—surf town of Montauk. Staring out the window at the familiar mile markers, dunes, brushy beach plums, and scrubby pines whizzing by, I felt sick to my stomach. We'd driven this route a gazillion times before and I'd never gotten carsick. This was clearly All-Star-Shyness-induced nausea. Soon enough, I was all sweaty palms, shaking knees, and blurry vision.

Sara was oblivious. "This is gonna be fun," she said as she chewed her gum and tapped her hand on the steering wheel. "The waves are gonna be perfect for you, Anna. Trust me. You're gonna have the time of your life."

I did trust my mother—most of the time, anyhow. But not then. Deep in my shy core, I started to understand; there would be no fun at this tournament. There would be no perfection. Instead, I imagined, there would be disaster with a capital *D*. But I kept my mouth shut. *Maybe, just maybe*, I told myself, *you'll get out of the car and this terrible feeling will disappear.*

No such luck. As soon as we arrived at the Ditch Plains surf break in Montauk, I knew I was a goner. Crowds milled about the parking lot; parents unloaded beach umbrellas, surfboards, chairs, coolers, and kids. As Sara started pulling gear out of the back of our Jeep, I stayed glued to my seat and stared out at the beach. From the safe distance of the car, I could smell the sunscreen, sea salt, hot dogs, and beer. Even though it was still only early morning, people were ready to party. And when I say people, I mean *lots* of people. Surfers from all over the East Coast had shown up. And not just surfers, but friends of surfers, parents of surfers, grandparents of surfers, and photographers of surfers. Colorful umbrellas were staked out in prime spectator spots. Little kids screamed with glee at the water's edge as frothy foam covered their feet; their moms stood watch, wearing modest sundresses and drinking pink drinks out of giant plastic tumblers. Teenage girls paraded in tiny bikinis, holding dripping ice cream cones, and a gaggle of old-timers sat in lawn chairs, gabbing away while battery-operated fans blew in their faces.

I hugged my sketchbook to my queasy tummy. Other kids carried ratty baby blankets or stuffed animals around for security. Me? I hauled drawing supplies around wherever I went. Nearby, two girls my age laughed while their mothers gathered beach chairs and umbrellas. One of the girls, a blonde, glanced in my direction, then turned to her dark-haired friend and whispered. They both turned to gawk at me, like two hawks eyeing a defenseless chipmunk.

"I changed my mind," I gasped. "I don't want to do this anymore. Let's go home."

"Don't be silly," Sara said impatiently.

"Please?" I pleaded. "I feel sick. I have a stomachache."

Sara tried the sweet approach. "You're gonna rock this contest,

Anna. I just *know* it. Now put the sketchbook down and get out of the car."

"I can't."

Sara leaned over me, her shell necklace dangling in my face. "Listen, Anna," her voice was low and steady, but oozed irritation, "We've paid the tournament fee already. Plus, we Dugans are not quitters. I'm not going to have my daughter, who is the best surfer under the age of eighteen, bag out of this contest." Sara swung my car door open. "Get out. Pronto."

Hot tears formed in my eyes. The two hawky girls were still staring at me. They could see what a cowardly baby I was.

"Can I...at least bring my sketchbook with me?" I stammered.

Sara stared at the precious sketchbook that I clutched to my chest. I was strong, but about as wide as a blade of grass; it would be hard to pry the book from my clutches. A vein pulsed in the side of Sara's long, tan neck. Her jaw moved as if she had a bunch of marbles in her mouth. Finally she spoke, "Okay, you can bring it, if it makes you happy. But don't get all whiny if it gets sandy. And if other kids want to talk to you, stop drawing and have an actual conversation with them. Deal?"

"Deal," I replied happily. I put my sketchbook back in my canvas tote where my pens and pencils, stashed in a side pocket, were neatly rubber-banded in groups according to color. Scooting out of the car, I forced myself to follow Sara to the sign-up table. A super-stoked boy about my age finished his registration and whooped a big "Oh yeah!" while high-fiving his equally enthusiastic father. Sara and I were fortunately—or unfortunately—next in line.

Panic bubbled up from the pit of my stomach when a freckly woman, with a name tag that read "Alison," handed me a green jersey. She proceeded to explain the rules of the event: "You'll be competing against fourteen other girls, sweetheart. Only five of you will go out at a time. The goal is to catch as many waves as you can in a thirty-minute heat, and surf those waves as well as you can. So it's a combination of quality and quantity. After all the girls have gone, the judges will narrow you down to a group of four. Tomorrow we'll do a second heat and decide on first through fourth place winners in your division. At the end of the tournament, the judges vote on the best overall surfer from among the top contestants. Do you understand all that, hon?"

I gulped.

"How much does she get when she wins first prize?" asked Sara.

Alison looked confused. "How much what?"

"Money, of course," answered Sara.

"There's no cash award in this contest. All proceeds benefit the East End Women and Children's Shelter down in Hampton Bays."

"You're kidding," Sara replied testily. "You mean these kids don't get any payback for their hard work?"

"Sorry, but we're not running this competition as that kind of event. Competing to benefit the children's shelter is payback enough for our kids."

Alison, glancing down at her clipboard, called the next contestant. A whole pack of people now lined up behind us, and some of the grownups had clearly heard our exchange. They looked at Sara as if she had some kind of illness—Greedy Mommy Disease—though I was relieved to see that the kids were oblivious, too jazzed up to pay attention, happily jabbing each other, telling jokes, having the kind of kid-surfer fun that was out of my reach.

As we walked away, Sara grumbled, "La-de-dah. Isn't she the noble one?"

"If you're angry at her, we can just leave," I tried.

"Fat chance. Even more reason for you to win," Sara muttered, yanking me toward the beach. At ten, I was too puny to carry my own surfboard, so Sara carried it for me under one muscular arm. Over her opposite shoulder, she had a giant beach bag filled with the day's supplies: two beach towels, an old Mexican blanket, bottled water, granola bars, gorp, easy-to-peel clementines, zinc oxide for lips and 50 SPF sunscreen for the rest of the body, a floppy sunhat for me, a sexy trucker hat for her. I had a modest tank suit on under my oversized tee shirt, while Sara was in full display in a teeny, tiny bikini barely concealed under microscopic board shorts.

We found a spot on the crowded sand. Kids ran everywhere—the youngest, goofy and unselfconscious, played games of tag and wrestled like puppies in the sand; those my age and older pretended to be chill, but I could tell that some of them were nervous—maybe not quite at my high-alert level, but definitely not as cool-cucumbered as they'd like people to think. One girl chewed her cuticles as if she'd been starved of real food for days; a boy twisted the hem of his rash guard so tight that it looked like he might rip it to shreds. Most of the competitors seemed to know each other, and I imagined that gave them comfort. They looked like they felt right at home while I felt like I'd landed on Mars without a spacesuit.

A stage was set up on the beach, blasting reggae music from giant loudspeakers. A few older couples danced with beer cozies in their hands—clearly soused even though it wasn't even 10 a.m. yet. The whole scene was a giant, chaotic beach party, and shy kids like me *hated* parties. This would be worse than apple bobbing or Pin the Tail on the Donkey. This was a party where kids were competing and showing off. I had no idea how to do either of those things.

"I'm hungry," Sara said. "You want something? I'm gonna hit that food stand over there."

I followed the trajectory of her long arm and manicured finger to a table manned by a couple of hunky surfers. Shaggy blonde-brown hair and biceps; broad shoulders and board shorts. My single mother's favorite kind of food.

"Nah, I'm okay," I mumbled.

Rummaging through her beach bag, Sara brought out a granola bar and a bottle of water. "Well, do me a favor and have these. I don't want you paddling out there without some fuel and hydration in your system."

Sara brushed the sand off the back of her short-shorts and sashayed over toward "the food," leaving me to wait and worry.

I stared out at the ocean. The waves were decent, four to six feet, steep, curling and nicely formed. Normally, I loved those kinds of waves, but on that day I wasn't so sure. My All-Star-Shy-Girl

14

perspective distorted everything, including the surf. Those perfect waves looked as unpredictable as killer sharks who, if hungry enough, might want to eat me in a few swift bites.

The first heat was for boys under seven. They strutted about flexing acorn-sized biceps, jerseys hanging below their knees. One little fellow clung to his father's leg like a barnacle to a rock. *Aha*, I thought, *there's the shy one*. A horn bleated like a hysterical goat, and they all dashed in and began to paddle—even barnacle boy.

My stomach seized and spasmed. Even watching other kids compete seemed to make me queasy. Sketching, I knew, would calm my nerves; I opened my sketchbook and looked through the quirky drawings—Wavehouses from my dreams.

The Wavehouse visions had started when I was six. First, I dreamed only of waves, but in later dreams, the waves became houses. I would wake up, immediately reaching for any scrap of paper I could find, desperate to scribble the Wavehouse before it was forgotten. Life with Sara was particularly unpredictable back in those days, so I suppose Wavehouses were, somehow, my way to control, to imagine, to feel empowered. They fueled me almost as much as surfing did.

Sara became annoyed when every unopened envelope or sales receipt was covered with my drawings, so she went out and bought me a sketchbook. I'd draw Wavehouses that formed on the crests of rolling waves or under green swells, hovering like bubbles beneath the surface of the sea; some were simple cottages tucked behind underwater rock formations and landscaped with eel grass and coral; others were massive mansions with plumes of water spewing from their roofs kept afloat by waves. My Wavehouses were inhabited by mermaids and flocks of seagulls. Fish gathered to form shimmering-scale pathways to underwater doors, or swam in and out of open water windows. Pelicans rested on floating roofs, sunning themselves as Wavehouses bobbed with the tides.

Usually, I never took my sketchbook out in public—no one besides Sara had ever seen my Wavehouses; but this felt like an emergency. My vision was starting to blur with nervous tears. With so much surf-centric activity around me, no one would notice the odd little girl scribbling in a book.

Sara lingered at the food table, laughing and tossing her long mane of jet-black hair while the surf dudes flipped burgers and chugged beers, which meant she wouldn't bug me to hide my book or force me to talk to people. To echo my dark mood, I drew a spooky Wavehouse with a curling mass of foamy white water for a roof and spiky mussel shells for its walls. The windows were jagged and irregular, and the door was lined with shark teeth. I was putting the finishing touches on a slippery stone walkway when a squeaky voice over my shoulder said, "That's really good."

Shocked, I swung my head around, almost giving myself whiplash. The squeaky voice belonged to a chubby girl with curly red hair that surrounded her pale face like a bunch of loose and rusty springs. She wore a puff-sleeved dress, ankle socks, and party shoes. No bathing suit, no board shorts, no towel—definitely not a surfer.

Slamming my book shut, I stared out at the ocean.

"Seriously," she continued, talking to the back of my head, "you're even better than Michael Rindlesmith, and he's our class artist. I go to PS 6, by the way. In the city."

I said nothing.

"I'm in the Gifted and Talented Program," she said matter of factly. "Where do you go to school?"

"Kendall's Watch Elementary," I whispered.

"Huh? I can't hear you." Before I could stop her, she plopped down next to me. "Where do you go?" I'd never seen another person, kid or grown-up, with eyes as blue and as bright as hers.

"Kendall's Watch Elementary," I repeated.

"Oh wow! What a coincidence! I think we're going to Kendall's Watch this afternoon. My parents are looking at houses all over the place. They suddenly want to leave the Upper West Side and live at the beach." she sighed. "I don't want to move, but then again, I sort of do. I'm very indecisive. My name is Myra Berkowitz by the way. What's yours?"

"Anna Dugan," I squeaked.

16

"Pleased to meet you, Anna." Myra held her hand out to me, like a little executive. She was the least kid-like kid I had ever met. *Were all kids from New York City like Myra?* I wondered. I took her hand. It was cool and soft.

"Anna, the artist," Myra smiled. "Do you have any other cool drawings in that book?"

I kinda wanted to show her my drawings, but I also kinda wanted her to go away. I hesitated, and, in that pause, my chance to share disappeared.

"Myra, there you are!" An older version of Myra, wearing a loose, gauzy dress and a wide straw hat, came stumbling across the beach. She was so unsteady in her high-heeled shoes that I thought she might tip over and do a face-plant in the sand. "This may not be Central Park, but you still have to stay close to us. There's stranger danger even in a place like Montauk."

Myra frowned. "Whatever. This is my new friend, Anna. Anna, this is my mother, Judith."

Judith gave me a tight smile. "Pleased to meet you, Anna. Now chop, chop, Myra. We're meeting the real estate agent in ten minutes. Daniel is waiting for us. This beach is a madhouse and it's giving him a migraine."

"Bye, Anna," said Myra with a magical twinkle in her eye. "Good luck with those drawings. Maybe someday I'll see your work at MoMa."

My work at Moe who? Myra made very little sense to me. But I could tell she was giving me a compliment, from the way she talked.

"Bye," I said as she walked away. Wishing she would stay.

Instead, Sara returned with a friend from the food table. "Anna, this is Kurt," she said in a treacly, sing-song voice. "He's from Rockaway."

"Yo, Anna. I hear you're quite the little gromette." Kurt gave me a goofy grin and a surfer's wave, with his thumb and pinky extended and other fingers folded to his palm.

I shrugged and turned away, thinking how much I preferred Myra's business-like handshake.

It was an excruciatingly long time before the "Girls 10-12" heat was called. Meanwhile, Sara and Kurt chatted away about surf breaks and surf stars—surf, surf, and more surf, like waves were the only thing that mattered. I sat on the periphery of their gab-fest drawing Wavehouse after Wavehouse, trying to block out their flirty banter. Then suddenly it was time. I knew this only because Sara shouted in my ear and shook me as if I were a piggy bank from which she was trying to retrieve her last dime. "Come on Anna! Put your jersey on and get out there! *Now!*"

Reluctantly, pulling the green jersey over my rash guard, I picked up my board and stumbled to the water line.

"Um, you might want to attach your leash," the blonde girl beside me said.

"Oh right," was all I could manage. As I bent down to Velcro my leash to my ankle, I could feel her shooting 'loser' rays into my spine.

"Yeah," her dark-haired friend said. "You can't be such a great surfer that you can compete without a leash. Right, Kiara?"

"Right," Kiara agreed. "And that's not allowed anyhow. It's against the rules."

When the horn blew, all the other girls dashed into the water, leapt on their boards, and started paddling out. Immobilized by fear, I felt electric currents running every which way through my body—rigid with performance panic; a complete shyness shutdown. A tornado could have whipped through and I wouldn't have budged. Staring, transfixed, at the ocean, all I saw was blurry blue stuff, and all I heard was a dull buzz in my ears and the *fwump fwump* of my racing heart.

"Anna! What are you doing?" I heard Sara's yell as if she were miles away. "Get out there!"

Stumbling into the water, I started paddling blindly, without any sense of direction. Finally, I made it to the lineup and the only spot left, between Kiara and her nasty friend. I managed to peep out a "Hi," but both girls ignored me. The drift kept pulling me toward Kiara. When my board got too close she snapped at me: "Hey! Stay in your spot. Don't crowd me, you loser!"

18

The other girl giggled, and I felt like a tiny snail, slimy and miserable, trying to steady myself on my board. Then a wave was upon us. It was a clean, easy wave that under normal circumstances I could've ridden with my eyes closed. We all turned our boards to catch it, but I was set up best, closest to the curl, so the wave was 'legally' mine. I could feel the girls' eyes on me, waiting for me to mess up, hoping I would. I felt unable to focus on the coming wave, distracted by the other girls' shiny jerseys flashing in the blinding sunlight, and the roar of the crowds on the beach. The relentless reggae music with its *ska-ska* beats thrummed in my ears. This wasn't what surfing was supposed to be, at least not for ten-year-old me. Surfing was supposed to be my happy place. Surfing was about connection and comfort, but there I was, about as disconnected and uncomfortable as I had ever been.

You can do this, I told myself. *You do it all the time. You love this.* The wave's surface sparkled like a collection of aquamarine crystals, set off perfectly by a turquoise sky and puffy cotton clouds. Feeling a flush of confidence, I paddled with ease as the swell rose behind me in a rolling, smooth tumble. My positioning was perfect, my wave radar in full-function mode. *I'm coming for you, Anna,* I imagined the wave saying. *We can do this!* I imagined how I would carve along the wave once we connected. I would be like a makeup artist drawing a beautiful design all over the face of the wave. The wave was so close, it was go-time. I felt my body prepare, and then—

Nothing.

I never stood up; my tummy was glued to my board. I rode like that all the way to shore, keeping my head down so I wouldn't see the crowds glaring at me, wondering what kind of idiot kid I was. Sara was waiting at the water's edge. The moment my board skittered on to the sand, she, without a word, ripped the jersey off my trembling body. Her eyes blazed like there was a fire in her brain. Unleashing my board, Sara carried it under her arm while she pulled me through the crowds with the other.

I stood and shivered, dripping wet, as Sara stuffed our belongings into her beach bag. She carelessly shoved my sketchbook and pens in with the rest of our gear and stalked over to the Jeep. Everyone stared. Grownups muttered and mumbled; kids pointed and laughed. Making my way through the crowds felt as grueling as traversing the Sahara Desert. Finally, I got to the car and slipped into my seat.

Sara sat white-knuckled behind the steering wheel, smelling like a combination of coconut body wash and sweaty rage. We high-tailed it out of the parking lot, and not a single word was spoken the whole drive back to Kendall's. I don't know who was more humiliated, Sara or me.

Nearly seven years later, not a whole heck of a lot had changed. Yet...

Chapter Two

Anna, wake up." Sara's muffled voice came from behind my bedroom door. "The waves are six to eight feet at Early's. Clean lines. Perfect barrels."

I moaned and turned over in bed, yanking the sheet over my head as I heard the door open.

"Suit yourself," Sara said airily, "but if you want a ride, you've got ten minutes." The door slammed and I heard her footsteps retreating down the hall.

Thanks a lot, Sara, I thought. *For tempting me with ideal surf conditions; for always being impossible to ignore; for making me choose, but broadcasting your own opinion loud and clear.*

The clock clicked over to 6:00—6:05—6:09. Closing my eyes again, I tried to visualize the Wavehouse I had just glided through in my dream. The roof, a green-blue hill of ocean edged with a white curl of foam; the walls, shells, and fish bones. Now my dream dwelling was blurred from memory, replaced by real wave yearnings. *Clean lines. Perfect barrels.*

"Last chance," Sara called from the hallway. I could hear the floorboards creak as she clomped around our tiny house, rummaging through drawers, running water, grinding beans, and brewing coffee. Finally, I heard the squeak of rusty hinges as Sara opened the bathroom door to grab her surf clothes drip-drying on the shower rod.

"All right, all right," I called with exasperation. "Gimme a minute. I'm coming."

So began my own morning ritual of blindly searching through the heap of clothes on my bedroom floor for bathing suit, rash guard, and board shorts. The bathing suit was damp, and after I pulled the wet rash guard over my head and velcroed the equally wet board shorts at my waist I shivered like a scared dog. It was a

21

rude awakening, one all avid surfers knew and none enjoyed.

I stumbled into the bathroom for a splash of cold water to the face, a swipe of a toothbrush to the teeth, and a pass of a hairbrush through the hair. Sara, waiting for me in the kitchen, held a travel cup of coffee in one hand, and a banana in the other. I grabbed both and she smiled, the lines around her eyes crinkling in a way I liked, a way that made her seem her age, almost.

At thirty-five my mother was still beautiful. The local boys who surfed with her every day, who had known her since before they could talk, barely noticed. But the summer surf crowd, the guys who made the four-hour drive out to Kendall's Watch from New York City, those guys gave my mother many admiring glances. Aside from her waist-long jet-black hair, thick red lips, and provocative brown eyes, Sara was a kick-ass surfer, better than all the other women in our town, and most of the guys—not quite professional level, but close. She had a perfect take-off and a perfect body, knew just where the sweet spot was on every wave, and where the soft spot was on every man she hooked.

Sara said that I was "naturally beautiful" and with just a little effort could be a "knockout," but she didn't have too many opinions I could trust. While people often commented that I was morphing into a younger version of her, I couldn't see it myself. My hair, cut blunt at chin-level, was entirely un-sexy but easy to care for. My lips looked like a smashed tomato; add lipstick and I was in danger of becoming a walking stop sign. My brown eyes were too close together, and my bee-sting boobs, and lean, sporty figure made me look more like an adolescent boy than a full-blown sexy girl.

"Come on. Let's rock n' roll before the wind shifts." Sara scooped her keys from the giant junk bowl by the front door and started outside. I followed. As usual.

Our surfboards were strapped to the top of Sara's ancient, barely running Jeep. Sara threw her stuff in the back along with the bars of surf wax, extra leashes, zinc oxide tubes, and musty smelling, sand-encrusted towels.

"You sure you'll be warm enough?" Sara asked. "Marine forecast says the water temp's only sixty-eight degrees."

"I can handle it," I grumbled as I climbed into the passenger seat, belted myself in, and took a slurp of coffee.

"I threw your wetsuit in the back, just in case," said Sara. "You know how easily you get chilled."

"Whatever."

"*Whatever*. You're welcome," Sara sighed as she backed out of our gravel driveway. "I'm gonna need you at the store this afternoon, by the way. The weather is perfect, and tourists will be arriving for their last week of summer fun in the sun, and hopefully buying memorabilia."

Dugan's Shell Shop, started by my grandfather Thomas Dugan, had initially been a small-time gig intended to make a little extra cash after retirement. When I was eleven, however, Grandpa had had a major coronary—a disaster that had required a pricey triple by-pass, nearly wiping out my grandparents' retirement fund. Even worse, at seventy-seven years old, Grandpa had been told that he couldn't do much of anything anymore. Running the shop had become Sara's responsibility. For a local chick with a party-girl reputation, Sara was a surprisingly good businesswoman, and if anyone could make it work in the throes of a global recession, she could.

"Do I have to?" I groaned. I wanted to surf, then go home, and sketch that fish and bone house I had dreamt of the night before.

"Extra hands, extra sales, Anna," Sara snapped. "And we need every dime. I need you and that's that." Sara always liked to drive with the windows wide open, with her long black hair billowing like a dark flag. This was cool—in all senses of the word—on sunny summer days, but a big problem the rest of the year.

That morning, it worked to great effect, enhancing my mother's exotic beauty and ridiculously magnificent hair. The *Sara Dugan*, I thought. *Pirate ship. Prisoners beware. Nothing stands in her way.* Sara switched on the radio, twiddling the dial until she settled on a station that blared Hip-hop. Really? Weren't mothers supposed to listen to classic rock or show tunes?

"Whatever," I sighed. Thing was, she was right. A successful shop always needed more hands. That's where I came in. When I turned fifteen and could legally work, I had no choice but to help out. I tried to spend most of my Shell Shop time in the storeroom, where I unpacked shipments, monitored inventory, cleaned off occasional beach towels that got slimed by a tourist kid's runny nose, or glued shell embellishments back on sunglasses that had been tried on one too many times. Even though customer service didn't completely undo me, I lacked my mother's talent. Instead, I excelled at behind-the-scenes operations. "Don't worry. I'll be there." I always was.

"Hoo-ha, check it out!" my mother hooted as we crested Early Point and the ocean came into view. Perfect white lines were breaking left to right in the cobalt sea. Sara patted my knee in excitement. "Just the way you like them, Anna. Big and steep."

Suddenly I was wide awake and almost happy.

We pulled the car into one of the last remaining spots. A quarter to seven, and the parking lot was already crammed with surfers pulling on wetsuits, waxing boards, or strutting and boasting like a bunch of pumped-up roosters. It was the usual combo of locals and week-enders—mostly guys with territorial testosterone fueling a competitive vibe. Why did guys have to be like that? It was one of the definite downsides to being addicted to a sport dominated by men.

Under any other circumstances, I would've been running for the nearest cave. But when it came to surfing, I managed to ignore the one-upmanship as best I could. Mostly I kept to myself and surfed solo. I kept the lowest of low profiles, while Sara went billboard big. That morning, she pounced out of the Jeep like a lioness and began massaging sunscreen on her perfectly toned arms while several guys in the next car watched and drooled.

"Hey, Anna," someone called as I slid out of my seat—less lioness, more lizard.

It was Jimmy Flannigan, a local kid a year older than me. His family owned the Sea Breeze Motel on the ocean side of Main Street, directly across from the Shell Shop. Jimmy, like me, was a captive who had to work summers to help keep his family business afloat.

While I stacked tee shirts, he stripped beds. Jimmy was a decent surfer and a decent guy, not all macho and brain-dead like most of the boys I had grown up with. He was one of the few kids my age that I felt comfortable around. I guess you could say we were almost friends. Jimmy bounded toward me and handed me a purple flyer. "It's that time of year. I'm totally psyched!"

The flyer advertised the 7th Annual Montauk Junior Surf Tournament, August 27- 28. *Ugh*, I thought. *The surf contest that refused to die.* Every August it came around to remind me of my first public display of complete and total humiliation. And while I no longer considered myself a "Shy Person All-Star," I was definitely not an easy breezy "Type A." I was still, after seven years, firmly in the performance anxiety "B-Group." So, while Jimmy may have been psyched about the goddamn tournament, I was sick to my stomach, and felt as if I had just eaten a plate of slugs.

"This is the first year that the all-round winner gets to keep the prize money. No more charity donations required," Jimmy said. "I think it's gonna be like four thousand bucks! So maybe we'll see you out there?"

Not on your life, I thought. But all I did was shrug.

"Word is there may be reps from the big surf companies coming this year, looking for new surfers to sponsor."

"Reps?" Sara demanded, coming around the front of the Jeep. "From which companies?"

"I dunno exactly," Jimmy said.

Sara looked at me. "So? Maybe this year you'll try?"

Since my surf tournament disaster six years before, all discussions of competitions had been short-lived, exasperated exchanges. Over the years, I had developed a backbone when it came to my mother; at sixteen, I could usually give as good as she gave. What she didn't know was how desperately I wished there were a cure for my performance anxiety, for my brand of shy. If only I could be rid of my Shy-Person-Type-B disease, take on the world, and make my mother—and myself—proud.

I shook my head. "No. No. Triple No."

25

"Oh God," Sara groaned. "You're impossible!" Walking back to her side of the Jeep, Sara resumed her show. The men in the parking lot were clearly riveted as she shimmied into her skintight rash guard and pulled butt-hugging board shorts over her Brazilian-style bikini bottom. I wondered which guy, if any, might score some post-surf-session private time with my mom.

"Sorry," Jimmy said. "I just thought—"

"Whatever, Jimmy," I said. "Thanks for thinking of me."

Chapter Three

The rest of our morning surf session prep passed in stony silence, until Sara cried, "Oh my god! There's Steve Mezzi!" A muscular guy with a gray buzz cut was hoisting a short board out of the back of his slick red convertible. "You remember Steve, the lawyer from Long Beach, don't you?" Before I could muster a response, Sara left in a whiff of heated sunscreen.

Sara was an incredible surfer, and, occasionally, an okay mother, but her guy-centric behavior sent me over the edge. There were times that I wanted to scream, "Why can't you just be normal like other moms? Why do you have to behave like a flirty, love-obsessed teenager?" But speaking my mind with anyone—even Sara—was not my forte.

Offshore winds and warm water meant summer, but so did Sara's surf-seasonal affairs. Few ever lasted longer than a couple of weeks, and only I had to endure the fall-out. To the rest of the world, my mother was easygoing Sara Dugan, a veteran romance junkie, always up for a good time. If only it were that simple.

In younger years, I also got carried away with the possibilities and promises each new romance seemed to offer. I wanted Sara to find true love almost as much as she did—we were both dreamers, Sara and I. But now I was nearly seventeen, and had grown increasingly embarrassed by Sara's constant man-hunting. My dreams, now, were reserved for Wavehouses.

While my mother fluttered and flapped in front of Steve, I grabbed my board and ran down the beach to find my own spot among the waves. The tide was low, which meant negotiating over fifty feet of slimy rocks before the water got deep enough to lay a surfboard and paddle out. Even the best surfers slipped on these rocks at Early's, like clowns on banana peels. "Watching the Falls" was a local tradition, a spectator sport where boards dropped and buff bodies went *kerplop*. Surfers and just plain regular folk sat on the beach to clap and laugh at every fall. I never laughed at anyone, but I had slipped on the rocks a few times. It was a rite of passage—a painful and humiliating one, and every time I had to walk out over those rocks at low tide, I prayed I would make it without a tumble.

In spite of my performance anxiety, I couldn't care less if I messed up on a wave at Early's. Everyone in Kendall's Watch had seen me ripping on waves like an Easy Slide zipper for years, so I didn't have anything to prove. Plus, I surfed so far away from the pack that even if some a-hole did laugh at my rare surf mess-ups, I didn't have to hear it. But on land? On the rocky entrance to Early's? I never got used to that form of shame.

Wrapping my leash around the board, I gingerly tested each rock with the ball of my foot before committing to a weight-bearing step. Avoiding rocks with a slimy, green sheen, and those speckled with sharp mussel shells, I managed to make it to the water without any slips. In thigh-high water, I attached my leash. Lying belly-to-board, I paddled out toward the relative safety of the calm ocean beyond the sizable swells. Churning my arms like the wheels of a steamboat, I avoided a five-foot wall of water about to break over my head.

My surfboard was a narrow teal-blue beauty with a sharp nose and thin rails, just about my size: five feet, eight inches of fiberglass and foam to my five feet, six inches of muscle and bone. Once I'd made it through the swell, I headed toward my own semi-private spot, which I had privately named Surf Siberia. As I passed a cluster of local surfers, I gave a few quick smiles and nods, but paddled rapidly by. While they found comfort in numbers, I was happier by myself, even if the waves in Surf Siberia didn't compare to the A-frames rolling in at the main break that morning. I'd rather ride bumpy, less consistent waves than jockey with twenty other surfers for those perfect peelers.

"Hey, Super Surfer Girl!"

"Hi there, Shredder!"

As usual, certain guys I knew wouldn't let me pass without some kind-hearted grilling. The older surfers in Kendall's Watch—the guys who had grown up with Sara—whose partying days had long since been traded in for wives and kids and tourist-industry jobs, had nicknamed me *Super Surfer Girl* and *Shredder.* The nasty teenage boys—some of whom were these nice guys' sons—called me *Idiot Surfant.* I guess they couldn't relate to my no-frills, no-chatter, no-hype approach. I was a weirdo to surfers my own age—a loner with bobbed black hair, eyes too close together, and monkey arms. But I could out-maneuver them all.

"Yo, Anna! Get your butt over here and surf with us for a change!" Phil Agnew hollered, a powerful shortboarder who had almost gone pro in the 90s, but instead took over his family's landscaping business.

"Put these assholes to shame, Dugan!" Michael Flannigan— Jimmy's dad— yelled.

These men, who had known me since I was a baby, were always inviting me to join them. I guess since I didn't have a father they felt like they had to watch over me. While I occasionally surfed with them in the off-season, in August—when the water was filled to the brim with surfers of every age, shape, size, and ability—I preferred to go off by myself. Besides, Sara, in her tiny board shorts and form-fitting rash guard, would soon be positioning herself in their midst—more than making up for my absence. I smiled, waved, and kept on my merry way.

From Surf Siberia, I could look even farther east toward the unpopulated coastline of Kendall's Watch, to land that had been protected from development since before I was born; with sheer rock cliffs, brush and pine, and the occasional hawk careening out of the trees, the view was beautiful.

Staring out to sea, I waited for the waves. There is a lot of downtime during surfing, lots of time to ponder the wonders of the universe, obsess about your shitty, fabulous, okay, or complicated life, or just enjoy the calmness and serenity of the ocean.

This particular morning, I got into a groove with a nice three-footer coming to me at a go-with-the-flow pace. Paddling for it, I eased to standing, slid down the face of the wave, carved up and down in a whipped design, then cut back deep into the wave—like a knife through butter.

The next wave was bigger, perhaps five feet in height, but already forming a bunch of threatening mini-peaks, like it couldn't decide where it wanted to break. This was typical of waves in Surf Siberia, where the ocean floor was rocky and uneven and the waves responded in kind, often more like whirlpool splash than swell. This one was a big, swirling mess with no clear entry point—a walled-up bruiser about to crash over me in a churlish splat unless I moved quickly. Paddling rapidly, I managed to get to the wave's shoulder where I caught a short but intense drop, and popped up inches away from the foaming lip. I regained my footing, only to be consumed by a gnarly stew that sent me and my board tumbling a short, bumpy distance. The ride had been short and not all that sweet; more like crash and burn.

Losing it, taking chances, and getting creamed were all part of the deal for me. Surfing cruddy waves was often harder, and better practice, than consistently surfing clean waves. Once the mishmash calmed, I hoisted myself back on my board and paddled back to my spot.

Wave number three was a beauty, six feet on the face with a nice peaky lip that would hold me tight. The drop was steep, so hoisting my hips in the air and landing my feet in a solid stance was a snap. This wave was a playdate, not a battle, and, hugging the curl, I trailed my fingers along the inside of my barreling friend, tickling the wave, and reveling in our shared speed. Then, pushing out in front, we played follow the leader, the wave and I. Eventually, however, the wave began to lose juice, as all waves sadly must; I milked it the last stretch with a few carves, shifting my hips one way, my shoulders the other. Then, finally, charging down, I snapped back up over the crumbling face and softly touched down—a falling leaf on a glassy pond. The game was over. It was time to paddle out and find another friend.

Propelling myself through the water, I saw something strange: a surfer at Chompers. Around the next cove to the east, was a really gnarly break referred to by locals as Chompers, named due to the giant teeth-like rocks that threatened to end any decent ride by tearing your board, your body—or both—apart. No one surfed there, it just wasn't worth the effort or the risk; and it was a bitch to get to: a ten-minute paddle against the current from Early's, with no other entry or exit point along the coastline.

That guy is crazy or stupid or both, I thought. *He's gonna kill himself. I'd better warn him.*

Paddling over, I saw a set beginning to form, with telltale humps rising on the horizon. Being in a safe zone, I stopped, but freaked out when I saw the lunatic surfer paddling out for a ride.

"Oh shit!" I cried. "Don't do it!" He didn't hear me; I was still too far away, but could tell by his paddling that he was no beginner.

It was clear this guy had serious surf chops. When the wave jacked up, looking as ominous and hell-munching as any wave at Chompers had a right to look, this crazy man was ready for action. He was a master, managing to catch the steep mess of the wave in a smooth pop-up with a graceful stance that kept him flying. Once in the chomping area, he maneuvered himself between the rocks like a slalom skier, keeping his ride going in zigs and zags, and ending in a smooth, glorious finale slide.

This master surfer then paddled calmly back out—as if nothing special had happened. Then, suddenly, he veered in my direction.

I was a jumble of conflicting desires. The shy me hoped he would paddle past, toward the regular Early's break. *Don't stop*, I thought. *No pit stops in Surf Siberia, please. I don't play well with others.* The Super-Surfer-Girl-Shredder me, who had seldom seen such talent, wanted a closer look at this guy.

The stranger stopped short, just at the edge of the cove where he was still hidden from view of the beach. He was close enough that I could now see him clearly. He looked young, around my own age, with dark skin, wild, curly shoulder-length hair, and white teeth that flashed a broad smile. Raising one arm in a wave, he revealed one of those male torsos that belong in a fancy underwear ad or on a statue in a museum.

31

I sat on my board, totally agog.

He waved again; he must have thought I hadn't seen him the first time. I tentatively lifted my own hand in a tepid, shy girl return.

Resuming his paddling, he headed east, away from me.

Don't go! I wanted to yell—an urge that took me completely by surprise. When had I *ever* wanted another surfer to stay? I watched him until he disappeared behind the next bend in the coastline. It was as if he had emerged from somewhere in the mid-Atlantic and then just as quickly disappeared; like he was a selkie, or a merman, or some other type of exotic sea creature.

Or maybe he was just a loner—like me.

Chapter Four

After recovering from my alien surfer sighting, I went back to my spot in Surf Siberia, catching four more waves—two beauties, and two silly rides to nowhere; each one as good to me as I was to them. I was happy in my carefree zone. But my go-with-the-flow, serenity surf ended with the sound of Sara's high-pitched girl-giggle.

Sound carries across the ocean in a manner that can be disconcerting. Most surfers know to keep their voices low, unless they want their conversation telegraphed all over town. Sara, surrounded by a bunch of guys, was just laughing but her giggles carried all the way to my quiet spot and somehow undid my easygoing time.

When the next set of waves approached, I watched Sara instead of taking off on my own. She was set up perfectly; the first wave was hers, if she wanted it.

My kick-ass surfer mom paddled faster and better than any of the guys around her, went for the wave, and nailed it. Graceful and strong, she leapt to her feet with the lightness of a fairy; but once she got going, she charged like a bull. Her back and shoulders were powerful, and her arms moved with the precision of a Kung Fu master. Many women surf with their butts sticking out—even if they're really good surfers, which makes them look like they're taking a dump. Sara never stuck her butt out. Her back was always nicely curved, her pelvis tipped perfectly forward.

Her ride ended with a typical Sara flourish: turning from her board and swan-diving back into the wave instead of cutting back with her board under her feet. That was Sara, always out for the big effect. As she started paddling back to her adoring fans, I shifted my gaze to my own little slice of ocean.

"Yo, Super Surfer." Jimmy Flannigan startled me from behind. He'd paddled over undetected while I'd been deep in a wave-waiting trance, mesmerized by the undulating surface of the ocean for the bajillionith time.

"Yo, Jimmy," I sighed. "What are you doing over here? Do me a favor and go back to your friends. Leave me to my sub-par waves."

"Just thought I would let you know someone was looking for you," he said.

"Someone who?"

"A scout for the Stella Junior Women's Pro Tour. Dude is asking everybody if they know Anna Dugan, and if so, where he might find her in the line-up. Said he'd heard she was worth watching."

"Yeah, right, Jimmy. You're so funny that I forgot to laugh."

"No kidding, Anna." Jimmy's expression was serious, and he had called me by my real name.

My heart flip-flopped. I swallowed hard. Jimmy grinned. "And everyone's told him it's true. You are worth watching."

"Does my mother know?" I asked.

"I told her just now. She's the one who sent me over to tell you."

I looked back at Sara and her posse. They were waving, shouting my name, hooting, and pointing. Sara, with both arms pumping victory style, was the most conspicuous.

"He's probably here because of your YouTube clip," said Jimmy. "I was gonna say 'way to go' about that in the parking lot, but I could tell you didn't want to talk."

"What YouTube clip?"

"The one of you shredding like the demon beast you are; that YouTube clip. Who shot it by the way? Awesome camera work."

"Jimmy, I have no idea what you're talking about."

"So, you don't know about *The Surfing Siren?*"

"What's the surfing siren?"

"Not *what*," Jimmy said. "*Who.* A siren is, like, one of those beautiful half-bird, half-woman creatures that lured sailors in the olden days with their bodacious voices. Kevin Claussen told me about them. He knows all about fables, and myths and shit."

I stared at him dumbfounded.

Someone had filmed me surfing without my knowledge? It had to have been Sara, or someone she had hired. Squinting toward the beach, I saw the usual combo of dog walkers, surfers, and morning joggers. "Is that scout guy still there?"

"Nah. Dude drove off in his fancy SUV. Couldn't get a good enough visual of you over here in this slosh-fest you love so hard. Said he'd come back *mañana*."

I was trembling. This was too much to take in, and I needed to think. All I wanted was to find a nice big rock to hide under. Or at least a safe ride home. "Later, Jimmy," I said and began paddling back to shore.

"Hey, Dugan. The waves are the other way," Jimmy yelled.

"They're all yours," I called back.

I had to pass my mother and her guys to reach the shore. I wanted to paddle over to her and scream bloody murder; I would have, but for all those strangers hovering around her, shielding her from my fury.

When I got close, I told her, "I don't feel well." But I was thinking, *How could you do this?*

"I knew it. You're cold," she said. "If you want your wetsuit, it's under the blue towel."

"I'm not cold. I just don't feel well." *And it's your fault.*

"Since when?" asked Sara, concerned. "You were fine when we got here."

"Since a minute ago. You stay. I saw Phil Agnew ride one in a couple of minutes ago. He can drop me off at home."

"Is this about that Stella scout, Anna?"

I shook my head. "No. I just feel crappy, that's all."

"But you're psyched about the scout, right?"

The other surfers all bobbed around on their boards, grinning. I felt like yelling, *Don't you idiots have some waves to catch?* In my wildest dreams, I had plenty of snarky comebacks, witty retorts, and the occasional major reaming. In real life, I muttered, "Sara, can we talk about this later, please?"

"I guess," she sighed. "Go on. When you get home drink tons of water. Flush whatever this mystery ailment is out of your system. But I still need you at the store by noon."

How generous, I thought, as I made my way toward shore. I don't know if it was fear or adrenaline fueling my mad dash over slippery rocks up the beach to the parking lot, but I nearly tackled Phil Agnew as he opened the door of his landscaping pickup.

"Phil, can you drive me home?" I panted.

"Sure, Anna. Anytime." He looked at me curiously. "Everything okay?"

"Fine. Fine. Just fine," I jabbered as I angled my board in the back of his truck.

"Something happen with your mother?" Phil asked as I clambered into the passenger seat.

"No, nothing," I said. I wasn't exactly lying. Nothing had happened, yet. But knowing my mother, it was just a matter of time.

Chapter Five

If my mother hadn't been such a romantic, and my grandparents hadn't been such fervent Catholics, I would probably never have existed. The case in point being my one-night stand of a father. Okay, that's harsh. Let's call him my one-week stand of a father. Grandpa and Gramma had been so relieved that Sara hadn't flunked out of high school that they treated her to an incredible graduation present—an all-expenses paid trip to Maui.

I was the souvenir she brought home for them.

In my mind, I referred to my father as CSD, or *Clueless Sperm Donor*, a guy I had never met—supposedly a beast of a surfer who had lured my gullible eighteen-year-old mother with a false name and a bogus background story. CSD led her to believe that he was a local Hawaiian with traditional roots, but on the last day of my mother's visit, he completely disappeared, leaving her with nothing—nothing, that is, except me. In typical Sara fashion, she clung to the fantasy that she would find him, that he would love us and that we would all live happily ever after. Sara spent two years searching for him before giving up, though she still clung to a photo of him, which she kept in the top drawer of her bureau under her thongs and bikini briefs. Throughout my childhood, I would frequently find her curled up in bed, after she'd been dumped or disappointed by some loser, a bottle of bourbon on her side table, a shot glass held precariously in one hand, and the thumb-smudged photo of CSD in the other.

"Come 'ere," Sara would slur, when she saw me in my flannel nightie by the door. I'd run to the bed, climb under the covers, and nuzzle against her side, warm and scented with coconut body wash.

"Look." She'd show me the photo. "Your Daddy. Isn't he hot?"

Clueless Sperm Donor stood in profile, under the shade of a palm tree with a trucker cap pulled low and aviator shades covering his eyes, his smile so wide that his teeth shone like a slash of light across his face. It was hard to tell if he was an ogre or a god; still, I knew what Sara needed me to say: "He's the handsomest man in the whole wide world." For some reason, which to this day I still don't understand, my endorsement made Sara feel better.

I would stay there until Sara fell asleep, then slip out from under the covers, toss all her wadded up tissues in the trash, and carry the shot glass and bourbon into the kitchen. Climbing up onto my Tiny Tots step stool, I would pour the remaining bourbon down the drain and rinse the shot glass. Then, finally, I would go back to my own bed and drift away.

In the mornings, I would wake up to the glorious smell of pancakes. Sara would be in the kitchen, hair pulled up in a high pony, face scrubbed clean. Usually she'd be wearing the ruffled floral apron my Gramma had made her—a silly thing Sara rarely wore, as she rarely cooked; it was, however, after nights like those that she always made me pancakes.

"Hey, sleepyhead," she'd say. "A new day is dawning. I hope you're hungry."

And so the cycle continued. Within weeks, Sara had set her sights on a new target, and little-kid me went hunting with her—seeking replacement spouses, father figures, and knights on white horses. Together we would plan for family life with countless men. The problem was that none of our guys seemed to have the same plan— some just wanted Sara without the kid; others just wanted a good time before they returned to their real lives.

By the time I was thirteen, Sara and I both came to the same conclusion, though we never spoke about it. *I* was a liability. It wasn't cool to bring me along on dates, or talk about "my adorable daughter" fifteen minutes after the guy bought Sara a drink. Her game plan had to change—better not to bring me; or, better still, not to mention me at all.

The distance between us grew even more when I hit puberty and Sara's unabashed passion freaked me out. Now we shared very little. Except surfing—surfing we would always share.

But I had never counted on sharing my surfing with the entire world through the internet.

Phil dropped me off at the postage-stamp-sized cottage I sometimes hesitated to call "home." Our house, built in the 1960s to provide summer workers with temporary housing, had paper-thin walls, unreliable plumbing, a leaky roof, and an ancient boiler that worked in fits and starts. Most of the other worker-cottages in the neighborhood had long since been torn down and replaced by larger, fancier homes. Repairs had been done here and there as we could afford them, but for the most part the cottage remained a nostalgic testament to shoddy construction.

Waving goodbye to Phil, I made my way through the overgrown front yard and wrenched open the warped front door. Without bothering to rinse off, I headed straight to the ancient computer my mother and I shared. I wasn't a big internet person, and got restless staring at any kind of screen for too long. I seldom watched TV other than with Grandpa—who didn't do a whole lot of anything else these days. I wasn't on Facebook or Twitter, or any other social networking site, although I probably should've been, because shy people tend to do well in cyber-realms—no talking, just typing; you can pretend to be someone you're not; make friends with other social misfits by clicking a few sends. But still, it all seemed too weird to me. I preferred to *see* people in the flesh even if I didn't always want to talk to them.

I had heard of YouTube, of course. Every now and then, I had even watched videos of cute babies gurgling at soap bubbles, and dopey tween girls harnessing their inner-pop stars, singing embarrassingly off-key about inane things like their jeans or the days of the week. My best friend and pop-culture advisor sent me the links and insisted that I watch them. Now, in desperate need of her sage advice, I dialed her cell phone.

"Hey, wassup?" Myra Berkowitz said. Myra—formerly of New York City, but now a resident of Kendall's Watch, was one of the few people I couldn't do without. "My mother posted a video of me surfing on YouTube, and now there's some professional scout dude stalking me. I've gotta take this thing off the internet *now*. Like, before immediately!"

"Wait a second, slow down," Myra interjected. "A surf video?"

"On YouTube. I need you to get over here pronto and help me get rid of it before I break the computer. Accidentally or on purpose. I'm not sure yet which it will be."

"Okay. Hold on. I'll be there in fifteen."

While I waited for Myra, I changed out of my soggy surf gear and threw on my standard summer outfit—cotton undies, stretchy bra (no underwire required for my tiny ta ta's) dry board shorts, and plain black tank.

Always true to her word, my pal Myra arrived on time.

Chapter Six

H ey, I'm here," Myra called through the screen door.

"Come in," I hollered, as Myra breezed inside, the screen door slapping shut behind her. "I'm just sitting here staring at the blank computer screen, hoping this is all just a bad dream."

"Okay. Deep breaths. Scooch over." Myra squeezed next to me on the wooden bench.

In some ways, Myra had changed radically over the past seven years—for one, she no longer wore party dresses to the beach. Now, Myra, with her wild red hair, favored vintage clothing and environmental causes; by tenth grade, her baby fat had found its way to all the right places. My grandmother said Myra reminded her of Rita Hayworth—that she'd been blessed with a "Va-va-voom" figure; then, looking at my skinny, curveless body, Gramma shook her head in resigned disappointment.

I'll never forget that October day in fifth grade, when Myra first walked through the door of my classroom and stood in front of the blackboard, grinning from ear to ear while Mrs. McMurty introduced her. Most kids would've seemed at least mildly uncomfortable with a bunch of new classmates scrutinizing them. Myra Berkowitz, on the other hand, looked as relaxed and confident as a professional opera singer practicing scales.

"Class, Myra is brand new to Kendall's Watch. I'd like you all to give her a warm welcome. Now, all together…"

Mrs. McMurty was the only one who chanted "Welcome to Kendall's Watch, Myra," because the rest of us were awestruck, staring at Myra in silent confusion.

I had to admit, she did look kind of strange. Myra was wearing a lavender pantsuit, a pink shirt, and a bright red scarf tied in a bow at the collar; a daisy stuck jauntily out of her lapel. A glittery headband pushed her Brillo-pad hair back from her forehead, but, beyond the band, her crazy curls sprang out all over the place as if she'd stuck her finger in an electrical socket. She wore purple Converse—before they were cool. To top off her eccentric appearance, Myra carried a mini-briefcase instead of a backpack, a habit that lasted until ninth grade when she bought herself a giant shoulder bag.

Pantsuited, briefcase-wielding Myra Berkowitz seemed unfazed by the lack of a hearty welcome. "Hello, classmates. Hello, Mrs. McMurty," she cried. Then, spotting me, she added, "Oh wow! Hello, Anna the Artist!"

"Who's she talking about?" hissed Patrick Corrigan, who sat across from me. Patrick's face resembled that of a pug dog, and, when he was nasty, it got even more squished and ugly. "You're not an artist. You're just weird."

Pam Quinn, Larissa Smythe, Jack Rogan—the other kids in our group—giggled. They weren't as jerky as Patrick, but they weren't exactly friendly either. I stared down at the top of my desk, heat flooding my cheeks, and sat on my hands, waiting for them to get distracted by someone or something else.

While I was busy staring at the fake wood grain—pretending to decipher the scratched messages left by former desk inhabitants—there was a commotion. "Aw, come on. Do I have to?" Patrick whined; then, a scraping of chair legs against linoleum, and a "Thank you, Mrs. McMurty. This seat is perfect," from Myra.

Looking up, I realized that Patrick had been banished to a single desk at the rear of the classroom, and Myra now sat in his seat—smiling at me just like she had that day at the beach: open, ready, and totally happy to see me.

"Okay, let's turn this sucker on," said Myra. She pressed the switch for the computer and slowly the old thing cranked to life.

"YouTube is one word, right?" I asked.

"Yeah. One word."

I typed it in the browser and the site appeared. "So, how do I find myself?"

"Just type in your name here." Myra touched a search bar on the screen with one polished pink fingernail.

Following her suggestions, I laboriously typed 'Anna Dugan.' "Nothing."

"Try just 'Anna.'"

A column of still images appeared—mostly of scantily clad women, babies, and pets. But none of me. "Wait." It suddenly occurred to me. "Jimmy called it something else. *The Surfing Siren.*"

"Jimmy?" Myra raised an eyebrow.

"Jimmy Flannigan. You know, from school. He just graduated."

"Oh yeah. Him." Myra remembered. "He's okay. Kinda cute, actually. Like a modern day Jimmy Stewart but with bigger ears."

Myra was not usually interested in any kids—male or female— from Kendall's. "Don't tell me you're hot for Jimmy? You guys have about as much in common as, I dunno, a sea bass and an orangutan."

"Wait a minute. Who's the fish and who's the primate?"

We were getting distracted, which was not uncommon with Myra, whose brain was so multi-faceted that random comments I made often got analyzed with smarty-pants scrutiny.

"Take your pick," I said. "You can be the fish or the monkey. I don't really care. And yes, Jimmy is nice and sort of cute, but can we please focus on this YouTube thing?"

"Okay, okay. Sorry," she said. "So, type in…I'm sorry. What was it again?"

"*The Surfing Siren.*"

"Cool name. So mythological," said Myra.

"So not cool," I muttered, "but here goes." I typed it in, and there it was—a still of me getting air on the lip of a pretty cool wave. "Ugh. I am going to die here and now."

"Come on. Let's watch it."

"Myra—"

"Come on," she persisted

"I'm scared to."

"Why?"

"I've never seen myself surf. What if I can't stand how I look?"

"Oh, come on, you're amazing." Myra didn't surf, but she liked to watch me and she'd seen me surf hundreds of times.

I stared at the computer screen, paralyzed. "Maybe I'm an okay surfer," I admitted grudgingly. "But you know how self-conscious I am. This could totally undo me."

"What if you're as great as everyone seems to think? Maybe you need to watch yourself to really know."

"I'll just see all the flaws, I know it. No. I can't watch it. You watch it. Tell me what you think." I got up, averted my gaze from the screen, and began nervously pacing.

"All right," Myra said. "Okay. Here goes."

My heart pounded as I heard music swell out of the tinny speaker. "What's going on?"

"It's an added soundtrack. Sounds like a cello. Maybe Bach?"

"You're kidding." *Me* surfing to classical music? I couldn't imagine it.

"Shhh! I'm trying to watch."

It was excruciating waiting, and I shifted impatiently from foot to foot as I listened to the music, interrupted by the occasional gasp from Myra. After a long two minutes, or thereabouts, all fell silent.

"So?" I demanded.

"Wow," Myra sighed.

"Wow, what?"

"Wow, what do you think? It's incredible, you're incredible."

"Oh shit," I cried. I imagined people—those I knew, and those I didn't, hovering around computer screens and smartphones everywhere, all of them watching me surf. *The Surfing Siren?* I knew that was supposed to be a complimentary moniker, but it made me think of the other kind of siren—a loudly blasting alarm crying "STOP!"

"This sucks," I moaned. "We have to get rid of the video before anyone else sees it. Who knows how many have already watched it."

"You can find out how many. Look, it's listed right here."

Sitting down next to her, I looked at the number in bold next to the title: 500 views and it had only been posted for a few days. "Just shoot me now," I groaned.

"Anna, this could be a good thing."

"Impossible." I shook my head.

"Anna," Myra insisted, using her annoying school-marmy voice. "If this is what got that Stella scout to come to Kendall's to see you, this is great. If he recommends you for a spot on a professional women's surfing tour—or even better, takes you on as a client—you could make gobs of money. And you could use that money for college, maybe even art school."

Now that the summer was winding down, and eleventh grade would start in just over a month, Myra was laser-focused on "Life after Kendall's." She talked nonstop about colleges, professions, and dream apartments in fabulous cities. All of it seemed so far away, and—for me at least—far out of reach.

I stared at the computer screen. "You've got my life all figured out for me, haven't you, Miss Guidance Counselor?" I swiveled my butt around on the bench and wedged my hands between my knees to keep both from shaking.

"It's no secret that my major fantasy is for me to go to Brown, with you down the hill at the Rhode Island School of Design."

College was Myra's primary obsession: where she might go, how she would get in, what she would write her essays about, and how she would prep for the SATs. Myra adored academics and loved almost every subject, with the exception of P.E. I tolerated high school, more or less, and was a decent student. Every subject, other than art—which consisted mostly of independent study—I found seriously dull. I managed to get above-average grades, which was better than most of the other kids. But was I college material? I wasn't sure. And art school? Wasn't that where messed-up kids with stretched earlobes and self-drawn tattoos went to school, did drugs, and wore lots of black eye shadow? No way. Not my scene. That sounded more scary than cool.

Nervous sweat gathered in my armpits and a prickly tension worked its way up the back of my neck. I was short of breath for no good reason. "I'm not ready," I moaned. "This is seriously activating intense Shy-Person-Type-B symptoms."

"Ah yes," Myra smiled and rolled her eyes, "your highly scientific mode of categorizing the various kinds of shyness."

"Um, hello? Look at me over here."

Myra looked at me. She got it. Finally. "Oh. Wow. I guess you really are in a state."

"I need to rid the world of *The Surfing Siren*. So how do I delete it?"

"Only the person who posts the videos can delete them."

"In other words, Sara has to take it down?"

"Unless you know her password, yes."

"Well, this friggin' sucks." My mortification rapidly switched to fury. My mother, who had started this whole disaster, was the only one who could now shut it down.

"I think you need Secretspot, ASAP," Myra suggested. "Are you working today?"

"Not till noon. You?"

"They don't need me at the senior center till one." Myra rose from the bench, smoothed her skirt, and hiked the halter straps of her forties-style sundress. "I need to change into a more Secretspotty outfit."

"No kidding." A vision of Myra in her flouncy, bouncy vintage sundress and platform sandals stumbling down the beach momentarily entertained me.

"Hey. No fashion jabs from you, Miss Monotone. I'll meet you at our corner in fifteen."

Chapter Seven

In the late summer—sometime between sixth and seventh grade—Myra and I had discovered an abandoned trail five miles out of town. We'd been walking along Shadmoor Avenue, a semi-private street off the main drag, when we spotted a rusted, collapsed fence among the brambles and weeds. Behind the fence was the tantalizing hint of a path. Curious, we clambered over fallen limbs and rocks, pushing prickly leaves aside and side-stepping poison ivy. We followed the path until it ended at a steep incline. All of a sudden, the sky opened up, the land fell away, and there was the sparkling, crystal blue ocean. Cliffs, like wrinkled paper bags, dropped fifty feet down to a stretch of sandy beach punctuated with massive, surf-smoothed boulders. Best of all, a well-worn gully eroded by rainwater wound its way down, in a natural path, to the cove below.

This land, restricted from development, had been deeded to the town decades earlier, and was rarely visited except by deer hunters in late autumn. One house, however, had been built here before the development was restricted—a modern beach place, all glass and steel beams, that nestled on the edge of the cliff like a resting bird.

The house, despite its new look, had long been the subject of rumor in town. Old ladies, standing in supermarket lines, whispered of "that abandoned monstrosity in the woods"; fishermen, drinking beers after long afternoons on the water, swore they'd seen ghosts fly from its windows; kids of all ages told exaggerated stories about child murders, buried bodies, drug rings, and witches. Other rumors made mention of secret cameras hidden in trees, vicious watchdogs, and a caretaker with a gun. The house, hidden behind a wrought-iron gate, was inaccessible unless you were a scrawny kid who could squeeze between the bars and had some kind of death wish. As far as I knew, no one had ever been up for that challenge.

The facts were far less entertaining than the rumors. The house

47

belonged to some face-lifted movie star from the seventies who was rarely there. A Ms. Ramelle, who spent most of her time in Switzerland or Sweden, I wasn't quite sure which.

From our cliff-side perspective that day, the house looked deserted, and as interesting as it was to see this object of rumor and intrigue for the first time, it was the ocean that really got me stoked. The wind was coming from the north and the swell from the southeast, the combination of which created some juicy head-high waves. And not a single surfer was on any of them. If I had had my surfboard with me that first day, those beauties would have been all mine to play with.

We went home that day with woodsy war wounds—Myra got a gazillion burrs stuck in her gravity-defying hair and I seemed to have attracted every mosquito in a ten-mile radius. We returned the next day and began clearing the neglected path. Coated with bug spray and covered head to toe in old gardening clothes, we armed ourselves with hedge clippers and whacked our way toward the ocean. After an exhausting week of daily effort—with blisters calloused from relentless cutting, knees stiff from crouching, and backs wrenched from twisting—we finally broke through to the shore. We then strategically camouflaged the path's entrance at Shadmoor Avenue with a jumble of big branches and creeping vines.

It was our own private seaside paradise and we named it Secretspot. Not very original, but we liked it well enough and went there as often as we could. Before long we had accumulated a list of Secretspot essentials: books for reading (Myra), books for drawing (me), surf paraphernalia (me), sunbathing supplies (Myra). The waves were all mine, with only the shrieking gulls to distract me. Myra would settle inside the sun-warmed nook of her favorite rock—one with a smooth dip in the center—and read her latest trillion-page Russian epic.

The serenity of Secretspot was exactly what I needed after the double whammy of the Stella scout and *The Surfing Siren*. After Myra left, I tossed sketchpad, pencils, sunscreen, towel, and surf wax into my backpack, downed a quick glass of OJ, and pocketed a handful of almonds. Grabbing my surfboard, I attached it to the rack on the side of my mountain bike. It was an awkward way to carry a board, but without a driver's license, it was the only way to get around. Hoisting my backpack over my shoulders, I took off to meet Myra, who waited for me at the corner of Emerson and Main. Myra's bike was a real clunker, a rusty, old three-speed with a wire basket hanging off the front that she had decorated with plastic flowers. Inside the basket was the huge denim bag Myra took everywhere.

"Yo, Wicked Witch of the West." I slowed my pace to stop next to Myra.

"Greetings, Glenda." Myra waved at me with hexing, witchy hands. It was two miles to the hidden entrance on Shadmoor Avenue; Myra coasted next to me and asked, "So, do you want to talk more about this YouTube, surf-scout stuff, or what?"

"Not really."

"Are you sure?"

"Okay. Here's the deal: I don't want to be a professional surfer, even if it gets me out of this stupid town. Surfers are boring, generally speaking. All they do is talk about waves, waves, and more waves, and I prefer to spend as little time around them as possible." My voice had quickly become high-pitched and mildly hysterical.

"Sorry. Let's just forget about the whole thing." Myra reached over and patted my hand, causing a near collision with my surfboard when her wheel wobbled. "Hey, I know something that will take your mind off the whole professional surf thing, at least for a day."

Uh-oh, I thought. Myra always roped me into her various social, political, and environmental causes. I didn't mind—it made me feel good to help; I just wasn't as committed as she was. And "helping her" usually involved trying to persuade people to donate money. We routinely had doors slammed in our faces and our phone calls disconnected—in short, rudeness galore. And it *always* required salesmanship, with no Shell Shop storeroom to hide in. But Myra was my best friend, so I tried to suck it up and at least give whatever scheme she proposed a half-hearted try.

"Who are we saving this week?" I asked.

"Not who, what," she said. "I'm organizing a beach clean-up for the Kendall's Community Action Group. The storm we had last weekend left all sorts of plastic ribbons and other garbage all over the beach just waiting to strangle some poor unsuspecting seagulls or plovers."

"Okay. Just tell me what to do, boss," I sighed.

"Cool. I'll think of something. Dates to be determined. I'll keep ya posted."

At the Secretspot entrance, I held Myra's bike and stood lookout for passing cars while Myra pushed aside our camouflaging branches and brambles. We rode single file down the path to the cliff-side clearing, where we leaned the bikes against our "Pee-Pee Rock,"—behind which, when nature called, we did our business. It was a dicey climb down to the beach and Myra didn't have the surest of feet, so I hoisted her ridiculous bag over one shoulder and gave her my other arm for support.

"What do you have in this bag?" I asked. "It weighs a ton."

"*War and Peace* and the latest *Princeton Review Guide to America's Top Colleges.*"

"Myra, eleventh grade hasn't even started yet! It's summer time, and we're kids—we're supposed to be chilling. Can't you give this college thing a rest, at least until after Labor Day?"

"Actually, reading about colleges is restful. I like to imagine myself walking past beautiful ivy-covered nineteenth-century buildings, and sitting in seminars with brilliant professors doling out literary tidbits. These are very soothing images." Myra sighed wistfully.

"You're even weirder than me."

"Perhaps, but not likely."

After depositing Myra and her stuff on the beach, I scrambled back up the path for my surfboard. Then I covered my skin with gobs of sunscreen and tossed the tube to Myra. Myra was always trying to get tanned, but she had skin that instantly went from pale and freckly to fried. You would think someone as evolved and as sensible as Myra would let go of the bronzed, beach babe fantasy; but some part of Myra hankered after a fabulous rock star tan, so every summer she pushed the envelope and got at least one wicked burn.

"Hey, paleface. Don't skimp on the 'screen. I can't be friends with a lobster," I said.

"Yes, Mother. Whatever you say, Mother." Myra reluctantly started to smear and I nodded my approval. She was wearing an old-fashioned polka-dot two-piece; the bottom sat snugly beneath her ribs, and the top cascaded in a pile of ruffles over her chest. She looked fantastic—like a glam movie star from the forties.

"You look hot," I said admiringly. "If only Jimmy Flannigan could see you now."

"Ha. Ha. Jimmy Flannigan is probably just like all the other guys in town—they only pay attention to you if you have long blonde hair and a surfboard under your arm, and they prefer to play Candy Crush than read a book, do Jell-O shots, and get trashed on a regular basis."

I shrugged. "Jimmy is usually pretty nice—to me, anyway. In a totally friend-to-friend kind of a way."

"Well, he clearly won't ever be interested in *me*, so maybe you should try for more than friend-to-friend."

"*Ew!* No! When I look at Jimmy, I see him as he was in kindergarten, with his shoes untied and his nose all crusty. He used to sit in the corner and eat paste."

Jimmy might be out of the running for me, but I had had my fair share of crushes on local boys. Unfortunately—or fortunately—inherent stupidity tended to pour forth after they opened their mouths, at which point my secret passion would fizzle.

"Paste, huh?" Myra raised a ginger brow in skeptical amusement. "Well, as fascinating as this conversation is, I've got *War and Peace* to read, so go on. Surf. Rip, curl, shred, whatever it is you do out there."

Finally, board waxed and on the water, I lay on my belly and waited. Usually, I intuitively sensed when and how to join an oncoming swell; knowing where to be had always been second nature, but today something was off. Ever since I learned of the YouTube

51

video, I'd felt paranoid, convinced that I was being watched. Now, I imagined not just one videographer, but crowds with cameras; I imagined writers critiquing my "style" in surf magazines, and felt my heart pound in my chest. Other surfers might find this kind of attention exciting, but it made me want to hurl. I knew that I wanted more than Kendall's Watch could offer—if not now, then eventually. Maybe Myra was right. Maybe someday I could live somewhere else like Los Angeles or Manhattan and do something cool and artsy, where I wouldn't feel like the only shy person in town. But was a professional surf career the only route out of my small town life?

A beautiful head-high wave rose toward me, promising to break in a clean and brisk left-heading line. I barely made the drop, taking off so late that I had to cruise straight down the face like a wild child sledding down a rutted hill. Eventually I got my footing, bent my knees and carved up the center to finish in a nice position inside the curl. Completely respectable, but not up to my normal standards—worrying seemed to be getting in my way.

On the beach, Myra seemed completely enthralled by her epic. The few times I tried to get her attention, she barely noticed. By the end of the hour, *War and Peace* was splayed open on her stomach, and a sunbonnet that resembled a head of wilted lettuce covered her face. It made me happy to know that Myra was relaxing. Usually if Myra wasn't thinking, she was doing. And doing *everything*—working at the library and the senior center; organizing campaigns for her favorite environmental causes while simultaneously taking care of ninety percent of Kendall's Watch old folks. Taking care of me.

In a couple of years, Myra would be off to college—who knew where I would be after high school?—which meant that we only had a short time left to be with each other constantly, in our best-friend, totally dependent way. If I left on a surf tour now, I could potentially spend months away from Kendall's. Myra would have to fend off high school sharks alone—the assholes who made fun of her and disrespected her brains—while I might have to fend off real sharks in Tahitian waters. I was suddenly struck by a fabulous idea, and, excited, paddled back in.

"Hey, Myra!" I yelled, scrambling up the beach. "I just thought of something." Shaking my head like a wet dog, I sprayed Myra's feet with sea spray.

"Hey!" Myra sat up, shocked by the rude awakening. "That wasn't funny," she said—giggling, of course.

"What if you came with me?"

"Came with you where?"

"Wherever I have to go to be a professional surfer—at least until you go to college. You could be my…my…"

"Trainer?" Myra interjected sarcastically.

"Well, not exactly."

"What? Your groupie? Your personal slave? No way."

"Maybe you could do some high-brow intellectual study of surf culture and stick it into your college applications?"

Myra crinkled her nose and shook her head. "I don't think so. Plus, 'intellectual' and 'surf culture' don't usually go together, as you yourself have pointed out numerous times."

"I know," I groaned. "It's just—"

"Get real, Anna. There wouldn't be anything for me to do. Besides, no one's gonna pay for me to follow you around and do nothing."

She was right, as usual. Kneeling in the sand, I felt suddenly dizzy—not spinning-in-a-circle-over-and-over-again dizzy, but weird floating-outside-my-body-type dizzy—the same feeling I had had when Jimmy told me about the Stella scout.

"Anna, are you okay?" Myra asked. "You look like you swallowed rat poison or something."

Get it together, Dugan. "Hmm, rat poison. That sounds yummy. Got any on you?" At least I could still make jokes—even if they were rather lame.

"Sorry, no," Myra smirked. "I left my stash at home. All I have is a bottle of lighter fluid. Want a swig?"

We both giggled. No more needed to be said. Myra gathered her bag and I hoisted my board and backpack, and together we clambered up to Pee-Pee Rock. We cycled back to town singing kiddie songs at the top of our lungs—it was something we often did, when we needed cheering up, or when we had tired of discussing heavy issues. It always amazed me what a rousing rendition of "Itsy Bitsy Spider" could do to lift our spirits.

Chapter Eight

At Myra's house, we showered and changed into dry clothes. Daniel and Judith Berkowitz were in their upstairs office—I could hear them talking about boat rides down the Nile or camel trips in India. They were travel writers, which would be great if you're the ones doing the traveling, but sort of sucky if you're their kid. Before Myra moved to Kendall's, she had spent a lot of time alone in the Berkowitzes' Manhattan apartment with a sullen Australian *au pair* named Gertie. According to Myra, Gertie cried all day and ate some yucky meat spread out of a jar with her fingers.

"Don't all get up at once!" Myra yelled up the stairs.

"We won't," Judith hollered back. "Is Anna with you?"

An actual Daniel or Judith sighting was rare—when in town they spent most of their time upstairs scribbling away. Myra liked to joke that she benefitted from a parenting style of "benign neglect." I wasn't all that sure that this was a benefit, and worried that Myra would really need her parents some day; and, when she did, they would be off in Mexico climbing ancient ruins or testing chocolates in Switzerland—or, even worse, they would just be so immersed in their upstairs office work that they wouldn't even notice she needed them.

"Hey, Mrs. B.," I called.

"Morning, sweetie!" Judith shouted back. "Help yourself to some bagels. Sheila sent the weekly provisions from Zabar's."

There were certain urban habits the Berkowitz family couldn't shake, one being weekly bagels, lox, and cream cheese from their favorite Upper West Side market. Myra's Aunt Sheila, a professor of gender archeology at Columbia—whatever the hell that was—faithfully sent a bagel box that arrived via special delivery every Thursday morning. Judith had declared the bagels from Kendall's Pastry Pantry "an abomination, baked not boiled, with the consistency and taste of Wonder bread." After eating my first Zabar's poppy-with-nova-and-a-schmear, I completely agreed with her.

First, however, I needed to rinse off. Secretspot needed to be kept a secret, and, heading out to the Shell Shop, I couldn't risk Sara suspecting me of surfing somewhere she didn't know about—and Sara could smell salt water a mile away. I scrubbed myself vigorously with a loofah sponge, shampooed three times, wrapped my surf gear deep in a towel, and meticulously wiped my surfboard dry.

Then Myra and I sat at the Berkowitzes' kitchen table and scarfed down our Zabar's treats. Judith breezed down the stairs and into the kitchen.

"Oy vey. Is it hot enough already or what?" Judith was a nearsighted, heavier, clumsier version of her daughter, and Myra secretly joked that Judith was "the perpetual *zaftig* elephant in the room." Since I'd known Myra's mom, she had broken at least ten prized objects collected from their worldwide travels. A stray elbow and *kaboom!*—down went the jade sculpture from Japan. A tripped stumble and *crrrack!*—the Peruvian deity with the embarrassingly long and pointy boobs lay shattered on the floor.

"Myra-doll, Daniel and I need to fly over to Paris for a meeting next week. You'll be okay here without us?" Judith took a big bite out of an 'everything bagel,' sprinkling poppy, sesame, and caraway seeds all over the floor. One of the few things our mothers had in common was that they both insisted we call them by their first names. When I was younger, I had thought it made Sara and Judith really cool; now that I was older, it seemed just another indicator of narcissistic self-absorption.

"Sure. I'll be fine," Myra shrugged.

Judith ruffled Myra's hair with her free hand, like she was shaking out dust from a feather duster. "That's my doll. She's the best daughter on the planet. Right, Ahnala?"

Judith had given me the nickname of Ahnala when first we met; Myra thought it was thoroughly obnoxious and presumptuous—totally faux-Yiddish—but I kind of liked it. I thought it made me sound exotic, ethnic, and a bit above the fray.

"Definitely. The best," I nodded.

"How long will you be gone?" Myra asked.

"Probably only a few days, but it could be longer. Maybe Ahnala will come stay with you if you get lonely?" Judith flashed us a big-ass grin, meant to inspire excitement and childlike enthusiasm—which was sort of lame really, given that we were nearly seventeen years old.

"Whatever, Judith," Myra snapped. "I'll be *fine*." Even my mature best friend slipped into sullen grumpy teen mode every now and then; Judith, however, barely noticed.

"Great! I've gotta get back upstairs before Daniel completely messes up our article. Love you, girls." Judith planted big, squishy kisses on both our foreheads, careened out the door, and raced back up the stairs with the rest of her bagel.

Myra, wiping her forehead, picked off a stray sesame seed or two. "Yuck. She is such a piece of work."

"Oh, come on, Myra-doll," I drawled in my best New Yawkish Judith imitation. "You know I love you, you beautiful bubbala baby."

Myra laughed.

"*Seriously*, you know I'm here, whenever you want me," I reminded her. "Don't get all independent and self-sufficient on me, deal?"

"Deal. Now shut up and let's finish our bagels."

After scarfing down the last cream cheesy bite, I rode to the Shell Shop, arriving just after noon. I stashed my bike in the narrow side alley that separated our store from the bakery next door. Kendall's was the kind of town where you didn't need to lock your bike, particularly if it was out of public view. In addition to perfect parking, the alley also provided perfect smells—intoxicating fumes of burnt sugar, caramel, chocolate, and butter wafted out of the bakery exhaust fan, and every day before work I took at least three deep sniffs. That afternoon I took an extra three deep breaths, prepping myself with extra sweetness before a potentially sour exchange with my mother.

Here goes nothing. I pushed the Shell Shop door open, to the clangy jingle of the "Shell Bell,"—a contraption made by my handy grandfather from clam, abalone, and mussel shells that hung above the entry.

The air in the shop felt cool compared to the humid August heat outside. Sara had cranked the air con up—a ploy to keep sweaty tourists captive in cooling comfort, long enough to sweet-talk them into unnecessary purchases. Sara was rearranging toe rings behind the jewelry case and snapping her gum in time to the country music playing on the radio; she claimed country was good for business, but I think she secretly liked it better than the hip-hop she blasted from the Jeep stereo.

"I told you to be here at noon," Sara said.

"Sorry," I mumbled.

"How are you feeling?"

"Better," I said. "Sort of."

"Did you stay in bed all morning?"

"Nah, I got up around ten and then hung out at Myra's." A half-truth. My life would be ruined if my mother ever found out about Secretspot; she would make it a scene—Sara's scene—bring everyone there, and my private paradise would be ruined. The one thing I had to myself would be taken away. But this particular morning I wasn't thinking about Secretspot—I was ready for war. The battle? The YouTube fiasco. "How could you?"

"How could I what?"

"How could you put that thing up on the internet for *everyone* to see without even asking me?"

"What 'thing'?"

"The YouTube clip of me surfing."

"Anna, I have no idea what you're talking about."

I usually knew when Sara was lying—she tended to shake her head slightly and focus in the general vicinity of my lower forehead, creating the illusion that she was looking me straight in the eye. But now, her eyes were dead set on mine and her head was as steady as a stop sign. Was it possible she was telling the truth?

"That's why that Stella scout was at Early's this morning," I said.

"I just know it."

"Let me get this straight—there's a video of you surfing on YouTube?"

"*Duh.* That's what I just said."

"And, a top scout from Stella has come calling?"

"Yes."

"And this is why you bolted from the water this morning?"

"Partly. I don't want to be scrutinized by some strange scout person. Or five million strangers, for that matter. So you have to take the clip off, now."

Sara smiled, smugly pleased with herself; she looked like the cat who ate the canary. "No can do. I didn't post any videos of you on YouTube or anywhere else. But I have to say, I'm glad someone else did."

"I can't believe this!" I exclaimed, pacing—a difficult feat in the crowded shop where we had sarongs and sporty sundresses hanging on circular displays, and baskets filled with sand toys at my feet. "Just so you know, I'm *never* surfing at Early's ever again, I swear!"

"Come on, Anna. Calm down. No one will give you a contract if you act like a total brat."

"What if I don't want some big professional surfing career? There are other things in life, you know."

Sara groaned in mock dismay. "What? Doodling on a sketch pad in your room, hunched over like some obsessive crazy person?"

"I'm *not* crazy," I snapped. Or maybe I was. I had so many sketchpads that I had had to store most of them in boxes in the basement. When she was in a snitty mood, Sara threatened to throw them all away. It hadn't happened—yet; but just in case, I tore my favorites out and kept them in a separate box hidden under my bed.

"Okay. Maybe not *crazy*," Sara said. "But come on, Anna. You're almost seventeen! You're supposed to be out there having the time of your life, not living like a hermit."

"Gee. It's nice to have a mother who is so supportive."

"I *am* supportive. You're a fierce surfer; you rule the waves. When you're out there, you're out there big—above and beyond anyone else; everyone knows it; everyone sees it."

Out there. I cringed. "Everyone *sees* it. Exactly. Remember the Montauk Junior Surf Tournament? My spectacular performance?"

"Anna, that was years ago."

"Sara, get it through your head. I. Still. Don't. Like. Competing."

It was as if she hadn't heard a thing—"Surfing is a given for you," my mother exclaimed, her eyes bright with enthusiasm. "You could travel the world, make big bucks, surf places I've never seen!"

And there it was. Talk about living through your kid. "Geez. You can't even pretend this is about me. It is so clearly about you."

Sara shook her head in exasperation. "Well, you probably screwed it up already anyway," she said.

"What do you mean?"

"The scout probably gave up on you, and is signing some eager, enthusiastic surfer down in Florida."

"Whatever," I sighed. *Do I even care?* I asked myself. Was I disappointed? Relieved? I couldn't tell. All I knew was the knot in my stomach had eased just a little.

"Well, all this aside, I'm sorry you didn't feel well. You missed an awesome surf session," Sara said, forcing a smile. "Chest-high and clean rights. I was barreled at least five times."

"Oh well, there will be other days." I turned toward the storeroom, feeling my mother's eyes on my back.

"Kelly was out. So was Mindy," Sara called after me.

Kelly Garrison and Mindy Shultz—two of the biggest bitches born this century. Because they surfed—lamely, I might add—Sara assumed that the three of us should be best buds. As far as I was concerned, Kelly and Mindy were worse than the rudest of dudes; they hogged waves, made fun of beginners, and both surfed with territorial aggressiveness I couldn't abide. Nobody owns the ocean—least of all, a couple of sub-par surf snobs with sticks up their you-know-whats.

"Big whoop," I mumbled.

"What's wrong with them?" Sara persisted. "They seem like nice girls."

"Kelly is as much of a snake as any of the guys in the water, and Mindy is a stuck-up, entitled priss."

"You're impossible," Sara sighed. "I just don't get it. When you're not home drawing in your notebooks, you're always with Myra."

"So?"

"So, Myra's okay in a geeky kind of way. But she's not exactly—"

"Exactly what?" My blood began to boil.

"Enough—okay? Myra is not exactly enough."

"You mean she's not cool *enough*. Or pretty *enough*. Or popular *enough*?"

"I didn't say that."

"But you meant it."

"No, I didn't. Anna. News flash: Myra is not enough. You need *more* friends."

"Not friends like Kelly and Mindy."

"Why do I even bother?" Sara groaned. "While you're back there unload the box of Shellys and tag them, please. And it looks like we're running low on Kendall's Watch tee shirts. You need to check the inventory." Sara busied herself dusting the display of picture postcards—old granny heads superimposed on Baywatch bodies with captions like *Everyone feels like a babe in* KENDALL'S WATCH or *It must be something in the* KENDALL'S WATCH *water supply.* Sara thought the postcards were hysterical, and people did buy them in batches. I thought they were the tackiest things I had ever seen in my life, and wouldn't send one to my worst enemy.

Conversation over, I headed to the storeroom and started tagging Shellys—hand-made shell families concocted by Edna McNully, an old friend of my grandmother's and a local nut case. The Shellys were, without a doubt, the coolest things in the shop. Each figure in a Shelly family—mother, father, big kid, baby, and dog, cat, or an occasional bird—was crafted from tiny scallop, snail, and mussel shells, held together with wire; their faces were painted like clowns and they had bright yellow yarn for hair. Edna twisted their little shell bodies in uncomfortable looking poses, and glued them inside wood boxes she called "Shelly Cottages." Edna used dollhouse accessories—some of which I suspect she stole from her granddaughter—to furnish the cottages.

When not making Shellys, Edna walked through town talking to herself and picking up loose trash that she stuck in the deep pockets of her rain slicker. If not for her son John, the mayor of Kendall's Watch, Edna would probably have been carted away a long time ago—that, and the fact that everyone loved the Shellys. After the Kendall's Watch tee shirt, with its psychedelic wave logo designed personally by Sara, the Shellys were our biggest sell.

After Shelly tagging, I checked our Kendall's Watch tee shirt stash. We were definitely low on inventory. Sara needed to call the distributor and order a big shipment ASAP. I left the storeroom to tell her, and found her busy, way busy, with a customer.

Sara leaned over the display case of ankle bracelets and earrings, pouring her body toward the man standing on the other side of the counter. She twisted a lock of hair with one hand and absent-mindedly tapped the display glass with the fingernails of the other. Her target was tall and thick—like a former football player whose glory days were over. His hair was long, dark and shaggy; his suede jacket uber-hipster, and totally unnecessary in the eighty degree weather. He wore Ray-Bans and flipped an iPhone around in his right hand while grinning like a fool at the local goods—namely, my mother.

"Oh!" my mother chirped when she finally saw me. "There you are. Anna, meet Rusty Meyers. Rusty comes all the way from San Luis Obispo. He's staying at the home of an old college buddy off Shadmoor."

Rusty Meyers flipped up his glasses, and held out a blocky hand. "Awesome to meet you, Anna." His eyes were blue and piercing, and the way he looked at me would have been blush-inducing sexy on a guy half his age, but from a forty-something-ish dude it was just disturbing.

Then, I panicked—what if this Rusty was the Stella scout? Instantly I looked down and away, focusing on the price tag of a striped beach towel marked down from fifteen dollars to ten. There was nowhere to hide and I could feel Sara watching me like a hawk; I swallowed the lump in my throat, and reluctantly reached out to shake Rusty's hand. His palm was sweaty. I put my hand behind my back afterwards and wiped it on my shirt.

"Anna," Sara snapped. "Cat got your tongue?" As if a person, shy or otherwise, would ever let a cat anywhere near their tongue! I vowed that if I ever encountered a silent kid, or grown-up for that matter, I would never, ever utter those words.

"That's okay, Sara." Rusty turned his killer gaze back toward my mother, who returned it in full force. Sara looked like she wanted to eat him alive. The charge between them was as powerful as a nuclear reactor, and it made me really uncomfortable. I had thought buzz-cut-Steve was Sara's summer target; obviously he now had competition. Or maybe Steve had already been totally eclipsed? Who could keep up with these things?

Sara leaned closer to Rusty, squeezing her arms together, plumping her already un-ignorable cleavage.

I cleared my throat. "So, pardon me." *Pardon me? I sounded like a grandmother. Get your foot out of your mouth, Dugan! You're desperate to know, so force out the frigging words.* "You're...um...not from Stella?"

Rusty broke his ga-ga gaze lock with Sara and looked at me quizzically. "Stella? Who's Stella?"

"Anna, you silly girl," Sara giggled as if someone were tickling her with a feather. "Rusty doesn't surf. We met last night at The Castaway." The Castaway was a high-class bar and grill down in Easton, the upper crusty enclave between Kendall's Watch and Montauk. The Castaway was one of the many haunts that my mother liked to frequent, searching for wealthy, attractive guys. "Rusty's a venture capitalist. He invests in green product development."

"Oh, sorry," I said. Rusty seemed as environmentally correct as the beer cans tumbling like tumbleweeds down Main Street after a busy summer weekend—but what did I know about rich men?

Rusty shrugged. "No worries."

"Anna's being scouted for a spot on the Stella Junior Women's Pro Tour, Rusty. Only the best young female surfers in the world are considered. Isn't that awesome?'"

"Awesome is an understatement," Rusty grinned at me. His perfectly white teeth probably cost more than most mid-sized cars. "You must be totally psyched."

Shrugging, I could feel the muscles in my jaw begin to tighten. My mother sashayed from behind the counter and draped an arm around my shoulder, pulling me close. She smelled of coconut body wash and tobacco. Sara smoked three cigarettes a day, one after every meal; she had great self-control or a controlled addiction, depending on your perspective.

"She is totally psyched, aren't you, Anna?" Sara flashed me a smile, which I interpreted to mean: Get your shit together and make nice to my latest crush or I'll make your life a misery.

I caved. "Totally psyched," I muttered with as much energy as a dead bug.

Rusty barely noticed. "So, Sara. Dinner tonight?"

Sara shook her head. "No can do. Thursday nights are always reserved for dinner at my parents. Anna and me, and the old folks. It's written in stone. But maybe after?"

Rusty grinned. "Meet me at the Castaway at ten?"

Nuzzling up close to Rusty, Sara purred, "You got it, babe."

Yuck, I thought. *Does anyone notice that there is a sixteen-year-old virgin standing in this room?* If a fling with Rusty had officially started, I could count on endless evenings home alone—just me and my microwave ramen. Sara would scramble back at three or four in the morning, if she returned at all. At least she never brought guys home—a minor sign of virtue in her man-crazy life.

The clackety-clack of clam and mussel shells at the shop door announced a customer. *Hallelujah,* I thought. *Saved by the Shell Bell.*

"Can I help you?" I hurried toward the sunburned couple who had entered, fighting my usual flight response, relieved to focus elsewhere, anywhere other than at my mother and her new conquest. "Are you looking for anything in particular? Something made out of shells, maybe?"

Rusty left soon after, but not before whispering something to my mother which set her off in a torrent of sultry sighs. I did my best not to pay attention, talking a lot—at least for me—to the customers about the fabulousity of a deluxe Shelly chalet. As the Shell Bell clattered at Rusty's exit, I mumbled, "Good riddance to bad rubbish."

The young couple looked at me as if I was bonkers. But they bought the Shelly chalet, so maybe my bit of cray-cray hadn't screwed things up. At least not yet.

Chapter Nine

The shop was super busy the whole day, so luckily there wasn't much opportunity for Sara to rag on me. I *did* manage to tell her about the low inventory of tee shirts, which she *did* manage to thank me for; but only after she had phoned our new tee shirt manufacturer and sweet-talked the guy into a rush job—three hundred smalls to extra-larges by Wednesday at no extra cost, free shipping, and a guaranteed discount on our next order. It was obvious, however, that she was pissed at me. I hadn't lived up to her expectations once again. She didn't need to say anything; I knew I had disappointed her just by the way she breathed.

I was pissed, too, though. At least if I knew for sure she was the force behind the Surfing Siren video I could rage against her for something real and substantial. Now she got to play her usual role—the non-supportive mother with her own agenda who made no attempt to help me out of what I saw as a bind, because she saw it as an opportunity.

We kept the shop open every night until 9 p.m. during the summer months, the prime-time for after-dinner tourist shopping. But on Thursdays we closed early because rain or shine, surf or no surf, we were expected at my grandparents' house by quarter past six for dinner. I could tell by Sara's expression as she cashed out the register that it had been a less than stellar day. We closed up and walked to the car in silence. Sara backed out of the parking space like a drag racer leaving the pit, barely giving me time to close the passenger seat door, and swerving inches from a young boy eating a giant ice cream cone. The boy, seven-years-old tops, mouthed the word *asshole* as we pulled away.

"Jesus, Sara!" I cried. "Just because we had a sucky sales day, you don't have to take it out on innocent little kids."

"That's not what's bothering me."

"So you're upset because of me," I said.

"Upset? Me upset?" Sara punched on the radio, and another gangsta grunted about life in the fast lane. Give me back Brad Paisley any day. "*Upset* is not the word for what I am."

"So what is the word?"

"Totally disappointed. Ashamed. Humiliated." She turned left, out of the center of Kendall's, then veered on to Toilsome Lane, a winding road which weaved uphill through pitch pines and shade trees.

"That's four words."

"Stop it," Sara snapped, glaring at me. The speed limit was thirty—perfectly appropriate for a twisty road in a residential neighborhood; Sara was doing at least fifty. "Why are you always so smart-mouthed to me, but you can barely utter a word, polite or otherwise, to anyone else?"

Because I am genetically predisposed to shyness, and since it obviously didn't come from you, it must've come from the guy you had unprotected sex with seventeen years ago, when you were barely older than I am now—is what I wanted to say. But I kept my smart mouth shut. Enough damage had been done for now.

Over the years, when Sara was out, I had scrutinized the photo of my father, looking for clues, hoping I would see something that indicated some kind of social discomfort—was his broad smile a bit too forced? Did he wear that hat and sunglasses to hide from people? Would I ever know?

"Is this about Rusty?" I finally asked. "'Cause I wasn't all nicey-nicey?"

"Oh, gimme a break, Anna. I don't need your approval for who I date." Sara swerved around a curve, brushing the side of the Jeep along the Bennigans' recently planted privet. Sara and I had lived with my grandparents on Toilsome Lane until I was five years old and I knew this road like the back of my hand. I knew everyone who lived in every house, every tree, broken roof, beat-up car, and new pool on Toilsome. I could close my eyes and predict the cracks and bumps in the pavement, know how and when my stomach would lurch when we crested the hills. "This is about your disappearing act at Early's, and your sudden recovery from the mystery ailment."

"I was sick. Really."

"You're a terrible liar."

"So it's about the Stella scout."

"Um, yeah, duh."

"I don't understand what the big deal is," I offered, staring out the window at the blur of green rushing by. "It's a free country. The scout is allowed to watch anyone he wants out there. But it doesn't mean that *I* have stick around to be stared at."

"Well, that's big of you," Sara said sarcastically as she drove up the gravel driveway to a small colonial that I knew better than my own shabby two-bedroom home. I had often returned to my grandparents' house while Sara was off on surf trips, or romantic getaways. Other times I had been fobbed off on them when Sara wanted to hole up alone at home—recovering from yet another broken heart and unable to deal with the demands of motherhood. I thanked every celestial being in the universe on a daily basis for my grandparents.

As Sara pulled to a stop behind Grandpa's pickup, I leapt out of the car and hurried inside. Despite being pissed at me, Sara would never let her parents see the tension between us. Since taking over The Shell Shop, Sara had been trying to prove to them that despite her party-girl rep she had her shit together, that she was both a competent businesswoman and a civil, upstanding citizen.

I swept breathlessly through the door, relieved to have escaped Sara's immediate wrath. Grandpa, cemented to his recliner-throne, was watching TV and didn't bother to turn around. No pleasantries with Grandpa; even compliments were delivered as if they were bad news. While heart surgery had saved his life, Grandpa had to avoid stress so he spent most of his time in front of the TV or barking orders at my downtrodden saint of a grandmother.

Sara slammed the door behind me.

"How much did you take in today?" Grandpa shouted.

"Enough." Sara glared at the back of Grandpa's balding head. Grandpa was tough on Sara; he'd snarl his opinions under his breath, rarely acknowledging her success with the store. You didn't have to be a shrink to wonder if Sara's tendency to look for love in all the wrong places might have something to do with dear old Dad.

I planted a kiss on Grandpa's forehead before plopping down on the adjacent couch. Grandpa loved me in his surly old geezer way—I got hugs and kisses while most everyone else got barks and orders. I adored Grandpa's smell. He smelled of sweat, and something deep and musky, like old tree bark after a rainstorm. Today he smelled different—off and sour. He looked pale, and his skin felt clammy.

"You feeling all right?" I asked.

"As well as can be expected," he grumbled. "Stuck in this goddamn chair for most of the goddamn day."

He was supposed to take it easy, however, his doctors had encouraged him to get regular exercise. His retired friends invited him to take beach walks, play golf, and "boogey down" in aqua-aerobics at the community pool. Grandpa stubbornly chose his chair—outings of the cultural or physical kind were all a big waste of time as far as Tom Dugan was concerned.

"You look pale," I commented.

"I'm fine," Grandpa barked. "I'm just trying to concentrate on my TV show, if you haven't noticed." He squinted at the TV, refusing to wear the glasses that had been prescribed for him.

"What are you watching?" I asked.

"These dumb-ass scientists in Peru are digging around in those ruins. Whaddya call them, Macchu Peanuts or something? Looking for some goddamn necklace belonging to some big Injun who-ha. Everyone getting all excited, getting their knickers in a twist. Waste of time, if you ask me."

Archaeologists in hard hats, with lanterns, picks, and shovels climbed over rocks and slid through tunnels while a low-voiced narrator droned on and on.

"How was the surf today?" Grandpa asked.

I started in surprise. Grandpa *never* asked me about surfing. It wasn't even a commercial break. "Since when are *you* interested in

69

surfing?"

Grandpa shrugged, his large, knobby hands resting on his Santa-sized belly. "Some of the guys mentioned something."

"Some of the guys mentioned something? What exactly is that supposed to mean?"

"Danny said that Jimmy said something about some talent scout coming to watch you surf."

I groaned. Danny Flannigan—Jimmy Flannigan's grandfather—was one of my grandfather's hardware homies; they sat together outside Lundy's Hardware Haven every afternoon with all the other retired geezers, former contractors, fishermen, and firemen, grumbling about the tourists, the world, the weather. Now, it seemed, they also grumbled about *me*.

"Since when is anything one of the Flannigans has to say worth the lint off my butt?" I demanded.

Grandpa grinned. Talking tough and nasty was one of our bonding rituals. "Yeah," he replied. "Those Flannigans are all pieces of—"

"Tom Dugan! Watch your mouth!" Gramma scolded from behind his chair. While Grandpa had gotten larger and softer with age, Gramma had withered like a prune. Years of smoking and lack of exercise had made her bones weak and brittle. Whenever she bent over to kiss me or stooped to sweep stray bits of dust from her spotless floors, I was scared that she might never get upright again. I worried that one day I might find Gramma in a jumble on the kitchen linoleum and Grandpa slumped over in his chair.

"Hi, Gramma." I rose to give her a careful hug as she kissed my cheeks. Her lips were dry and scratchy and she smelled of Salems and sweet liqueur. While cooking, Gramma would swig peach schnapps straight from the bottle; at the dinner table, with company, she would sip it with carefully puckered lips from a crystal glass. She rarely drank anywhere else, but when she was home it was another boozy story.

"Hello, Anna Marie." Gramma was the only person on the planet who called me by my first and middle names. I think it sounded more ladylike and proper to her. Growing up, I had always been considered a tomboy, which from Gramma's perspective meant unmarriageable and, possibly, a lesbian. Unmarriageable? Maybe. But I knew I wasn't gay.

"Where's Mom?" I asked.

"She's helping me in the kitchen."

Yeah, right, I thought. My mother never lifted a finger to help when we came over for dinner, yet Gramma always covered for her.

"You need anything, Tom?" asked Gramma, placing a hand on his forehead as if checking for a fever. So something *was* wrong with Grandpa—I wasn't imagining things.

He pulled his head away. "Nah, I'm fine. Just starved. When's dinner already?"

"Soon, dear, very soon." Gramma, weaving her way back to the kitchen, shot me a wink. "I made your favorite dessert, Anna Marie—peach pie."

"Yum. Thanks, Gramma." Peach pie. Gramma's obvious cover for the peachy smell of her favorite drink.

Once Gramma was safely out of earshot, Grandpa leaned forward, staring right at me. "So, is it true?" he demanded.

"Is what true?"

"Don't be a smart-ass," he muttered. "You know damn well I'm talking about this surf thing."

I shrugged. "It's not such a big deal, Grandpa. I wouldn't get your knickers in a twist over it."

"I don't know," Grandpa shrugged. "You can make a pretty penny on these pro tours. You get to travel all over the world. Go to Tahiti, and Bali, and places like that."

"So?"

"So?" he cried. "Are you kidding me? Let me tell you, for a fat, old guy like me, stuck on a La-Z-Boy chair for the rest of my goddamn life with aching joints and a bum ticker, watching shows about those places; well, for *me* it would be the chance of a lifetime to actually go for real."

"I'm gonna go help Gramma."

"I'm not finished talking, missy—" Grandpa growled.

"Well, I am," I growled over my shoulder as I stormed toward the kitchen. Gramma was struggling to lift a sizzling bird out of the oven, while my mother leaned against the counter, thumbing through a *Woman's Day* magazine. God knows, Gramma would never ask Princess Sara for help. Sara was, after all, Gramma's "miracle." Gramma had been over forty and had given up on ever having children when she became pregnant with Sara. Perhaps Gramma always let Sara off the hook because Grandpa never did. Whatever the case, Gramma let Sara get away with murder.

"Lemme get that." Grabbing a crochet pot holder, I raced toward her—envisioning the fall of chicken, roasting pan, Gramma and all, sprawled out in a mess upon the kitchen floor.

"Thank you, Anna Marie," Gramma smiled as I steadied the pan. "You're a dear."

"Gramma, what's up with Grandpa?" I asked as I rested the chicken on the counter. "He doesn't look so good."

She shook her head. "I'm not sure. He woke up this morning short of breath and with the most terrible cough; but he won't let me near him with a thermometer."

"Probably just a cold," Sara added, without looking up from her magazine. "Something's going around. He probably caught it by sharing a bottle of bourbon with his buddies down in front of Lundy's."

"Oh Sara," Gramma sighed. "You know your father barely ever drinks—much less in the daytime, sitting on a sidewalk bench. That's illegal."

Sara, with an exaggerated sigh, tossed the magazine on the counter and looked pointedly at me. "I seem to be making mistake after mistake these days. I'll be out back. Give a holler when dinner's ready." She was already dialing her phone as the back screen door whacked shut behind her.

Gramma returned to dinner prep without further comment. For the next fifteen minutes I was her little helper. No surf talk at all, just breezy chitchat about other people—so-and-so's such-and-such doing this-and-that for who-knows-why. It was a big relief after the grilling I had been through with Grandpa.

After the food was set out, Sara and Grandpa joined us at the dining table. We passed platters of dried-out chicken, overcooked and over-buttered string beans, and perfect mashed potatoes. With filled plates, we cut and chewed. There was little conversation, which was fine by me—I was biding my time waiting for pie and a speedy exit home.

After dinner, however, Gramma raised her tiny crystal glass of schnapps high. "Let's drink a toast to Anna Marie," she said.

"Why?" I asked.

"From what I hear, you're going to be on TV."

"Excuse me?" Suddenly my appetite—even for peach pie—was gone.

"Your mother told me in the kitchen that you're going to become a professional surfer."

I glared across the table at my mother who was studying the crust of her pie like it was the most fascinating dessert on the planet.

"I told her I wasn't sure how I felt about it all," Gramma continued. "You know how I worry about both of you out there in the ocean. The men are big and strong, but you and your mother are just little wisps—"

"Ma," Sara groaned. "Enough already. Anna and I can take care of ourselves out there, believe me. Maybe if you came and watched us once or twice you would understand."

"Oh Sara," Gramma sighed. "You know I can't tolerate the sun. And the sand is just too difficult for me to maneuver with my arthritis. But I *am* concerned about Anna Marie skipping college. I had always hoped a Dugan would go to college." Gramma shot a glance at my non-college-attending, pie-studying mother. "But I suppose being a professional surfer would be much more fun. You might meet movie stars."

"Can we change the subject?" I muttered. "It's not a done deal. Besides, there are other things in life besides surfing."

But my grandparents wouldn't let it go: "You'll get to be on TV,

Anna," said Grandpa. "I could watch you instead of a bunch of woodchucks building a dam in Oregon, or those CNN talking heads telling me the country's going to hell in a hand basket."

"And best of all, your mom says some of the girls even get to model." Gramma took a sip of schnapps and sighed. "I must admit, all that sounds every bit as exciting as college."

"Enough," I cried. The knot in my stomach had returned, along with the sweaty pits.

"Why do I bother telling you anything, Ma?" Sara snapped. "I *told* you she would freak if you brought this up. You can't keep your mouth shut for a minute."

"Don't you talk to your mother that way, or I'll…" Grandpa sputtered, his eyes bulging and his cheeks on fire.

"Stop it! All of you!" I shoved back my chair. With my head pounding, heart racing, and blood beginning to boil, I shouted. "Do I actually have a say in my own life?" I stormed out the back door, and fumed my way a mile down Toilsome to where the road dead-ended at the bay beach. The parking lot was empty, as I had hoped it would be—bay beaches weren't as popular as ocean beaches for night-time bonfires, drunken hook-ups, and family marshmallow roasting. Infuriated, I kicked off my flip-flops and stomped onto the sand. It was dark out, overcast and starless, so I stumbled along until I got to a spot that, for no good reason, seemed like the spot to sink into.

Everything was still, except for the dull lapping of tiny bay swells—depressing and weak little wavelets, which suited me fine. *A jet-setting, surfing fashion model? Completely and totally not me,* I thought. But what was 'me'? It was like being asked to run for President of the United States when I was the one who sank lower in her chair when student government volunteers were needed. Even Myra's rational idea—'do the surf thing now, and use the money for college later'—seemed impossible. Just the thought of surfing in front of a crowd, knowing there were judges, cameras, and God knows who and what else, made me feel like throwing up, fainting, and only reviving sufficiently to then crawl away and die.

Chapter Ten

I needed Myra. Fortunately, her house wasn't far from my grandparents. I trekked along the beach, cut up at the next bayside parking lot and was at her place in ten minutes.

"Oh my god," Myra gasped as she opened the door. She was wearing a silk kimono her parents had bought her on a recent trip to Japan and had her hair piled up on the top of her head where it poofed out like a giant red mushroom. "What happened to you? You look like the *Walking Dead*."

"I hate my family. *All* of them. I wish a tornado would whisk them all up to Oz where they could whiz around with the evil Flying Monkeys!"

"Whoa. Even good old Tom and Lorraine?"

"They're evil, too. At least for now." I stalked past her into the kitchen.

"Where are your shoes?" Myra asked.

"Back at the beach. I walked over annoying, sharp little bay rocks to get here. My feet are killing me. You should feel honored."

Myra grabbed a bottle of OJ from the fridge and sat at the table, while I collapsed in the chair opposite her. "Here. Drink." She pushed the bottle toward me. "Maybe some antioxidants and Vitamin C will improve your mood."

I took a gulp of the orange juice and felt a little better.

"So, what happened?" Myra asked.

I outlined the basic dinner discussion debacle for her—"Even Gramma! I mean, *hello*? A surfing fashion model? Whose grandmother is this? Since *when* has she wanted me to do anything but go to college, stay a virgin until marriage, and end up teaching Sunday school?"

"She is kind of old-fashioned. But seriously? Compared to some of the other old biddies I work with at the Senior Center, your

75

grandmother is like a Cosmo girl."

"Ha," I laughed. Myra was already making me feel better. "Gramma on the cover of Cosmo in some slinky, sexy dress? Hey, maybe *she's* the one who can be a model."

"Anna, you've gotta give them a break. It all sounds super exciting and adventurous."

"Myra—"

"Okay. Okay. Sorry. They all suck. Even Lorraine."

"Thank you," I sighed.

"So, while we're on the subject of families, can I have a turn?"

"Yeah, for sure. What's going on?"

"At dinner tonight Daniel spills the beans that this upcoming trip to Paris is more than just another magazine assignment," Myra said. "My parents are going to Paris to interview for jobs."

"What?" I sat bolt upright.

"Yeah. Like, to work full time in Paris, running an international travel journal. A big, glossy, French thing. *Une revue elegant.*"

My heart beat faster. "Does that mean you'll have to move too?"

Myra shrugged. "I don't know. When I asked them, they were all vague and cagey. Daniel said something about how Aunt Sheila would be on sabbatical from Columbia so she could stay with me, at least through eleventh grade; but then Judith got so pissed at him for blurting the details that they got into a major argument and stopped talking to me. Once again, I was the ghost child. I probably could've set the table on fire and they wouldn't have noticed."

"Oh God. Please no. I will literally *die* if you move!"

Myra looked away.

"So that's a yes? Like, you might actually move to Paris with them?"

"It's a maybe." Myra leaned across the table and grabbed my hands. "But honestly? I can't imagine living anywhere without you; even if Paris is one of the most romantic and culturally interesting cities on the planet."

"Hey, remember that report you did on France in fifth grade?"

"Oh God, please. Don't remind me." Myra covered her face with

76

her hands.

"The beret, remember?" I laughed. "And the penciled mustache…"

"That terrible French accent," Myra giggled.

"You did the *can-can*, Myra. The actual *can-can*."

"What was I thinking?"

"Probably just fifth-grade-cute-smart-kid kinds of thoughts."

"At least you were paying attention. I have a distinct memory of you sitting there grinning at me while I was kicking."

I shook my head. "You really cemented your nerd status with that one."

"Well, at least Mrs. McMurty loved it," Myra shrugged. "I got an A."

I hung out at Myra's for another hour. We decided to play one of our "Regressive Comfort Games," including *Candyland, Monopoly, 20 Questions* (but only using children's books or TV show characters), and *Go Fish.* We chose *Candyland,* the most babyish game of all. Queen Frostine and Princess Lolly. We felt cleansed afterwards.

By the time I got back to my grandparents' place, the Jeep was gone. Sara had left without me. No surprises there. I limped up the stoop and in through the unlocked front door. The dining table was cleared, polished to Pledge-perfection. The kitchen was dark; the only hint left of Thursday dinner was the hum and rattle of Gramma's old dishwasher. No doubt Gramma herself was upstairs in bed in a schnapps-sodden sleep, dead to the world the minute her head hit the pillow.

The living room TV was still on, the volume lowered to a mumble, one of Grandpa's few concessions to Gramma's needs. Grandpa lounged in his recliner, with his work-booted feet resting on his faux-leather footstool, and his hands palm-up on corduroyed thighs. He looked like he was asleep or meditating—the thought of which made me snicker; Grandpa would no more meditate than he would do the hula. But as I approached, my urge to laugh disappeared. Grandpa wasn't asleep; his eyes were wide open. He wasn't snoring but instead wheezed with a disturbing rattle—as if a bunch of nuts and bolts tumbled around in his chest.

"You sound like shit," I said.

"Shut up," he grumbled. "Oh, and welcome home."

I sat down on the couch and looked at the TV screen. A bunch of tall, skinny girls, not much older than me, stood in an awkward clump. A few smiled as if to crack their faces in half, others looked scared and big-eyed, like feral raccoons.

"What's this?" I asked.

"I dunno," he shrugged. "I think it's called *Top Model*."

I turned to him in awe. "*Top Model*? You're watching *Top Model*?"

He cleared his throat, looked me straight in the eye and growled, "Yes, I am. And if you tell a soul you caught me watching this crap, your ass is grass."

I returned his glare to keep the charade of seriousness afloat, but we both knew it wouldn't last. Grandpa broke first—in a fit of laughter that sounded like a hound-dog with hiccups. I joined in, and momentarily forgot how irritated I was with everyone, including my dear old Grandpa. Eventually, our giggles subsided and we watched the judges lovingly slash each girl to bits, sighing in commiseration when the sweetest, smartest contestant was booted off the show. No mention was made of my surfing or my storming out.

"So, are you staying here tonight or do you wanna lift home?" Grandpa asked.

My grandparents' guest room—which we all still considered my room—hadn't changed much in years. The bedspread was one of those nubby, white jobs with pompoms skimming the floor. Two embroidered accent pillows rested on top—Gramma's handiwork; one featured a fluffy kitten in gray thread, and the other a frisky puppy in brown. I had named them Fluffy and Woof Woof, and they were forever waiting for me at the head of the bed. Gramma had sewn them when I turned six years old. That season Sara had had it bad for an Australian surfer named Damian who had treated me like an annoying pet—one he would prefer to be sent to the nearest animal shelter. I had been thrilled when Sara told me Damian was leaving, and horrified when she told me she was going away with him. Damian had intended to travel down the Eastern Seaboard, and Sara planned to keep him company while he "surfed the States."

The day they drove away in Sara's station wagon—their surfboards leaning up over the back seat—was one of the most awful days of my life. My mother had occasionally left me with my grandparents for a night or two, when she was off doing her party-girl thing. This was different—the packing up of her belongings, the surfboards, the meaningful hug, and the "I love you more than anything, kid. Don't forget it," whisper in my ear before Sara drove off. I was afraid that this surf jaunt with Damian would last a long, long time, if not forever.

I spent that night crying in the guest room, crippled by a really bad stomachache; already, I felt a hole in my heart where my mom had always been. Gramma heard me sobbing into the bedspread and rushed in, carrying the pillows.

"Oh Anna Marie, my poor baby," she sighed. "What's wrong?"

I turned over to look at Gramma, wiping the back of my hand over my snotty nose. "My tummy aches," I blubbered.

Gramma lay down beside me, rubbing my stomach in soothing arcs, and murmuring soothing nothings in my ear. After I had calmed a little, she showed me the pillows. "I made these for you to sleep with at night," she said. "Hug them close because they're little creatures who need lots of love and attention. Can you do that for me?"

I could and I did. Fluffy and Woof Woof. My first and only pets.

Sara returned a week later, with a bruised ego and a broken heart. I went back to the cottage with her, but left Fluffy and Woof Woof at Toilsome Lane. I knew I'd be back soon enough.

Watching the credits for *Top Model* scroll down the screen, I considered Grandpa's offer. The idea of staying was appealing—I could collapse into bed, wake up and be fed hot, delicious food by a slightly hung-over but ever-chipper Gramma, as opposed to back at the cottage where cold granola and nearly expired milk—served by me for me—were my only breakfast options.

I sighed. "I think I'd better go home."

Grandpa drove the ten minutes it took to get me home in silence, but for the croony, fifties music on his radio.

Our cottage was dark, and there was no sign of the Jeep or of Sara. I was disappointed and relieved, flip-flop fashion—like when you slide your hands in front of your face to go happy-up, sad-down. *What would come of seeing her tonight anyway?* I thought. *Probably just more drama.* Still, part of me wanted her around.

"You okay here?" Grandpa asked.

I nodded.

"Suit yourself. Just wave to me from the window once you're in there. Make sure everything is as it should be."

I leaned over and kissed his scratchy cheek. "I love you, you old fart," I said.

"Kiss my butt," he replied.

"Yuck." I slammed the car door. "Not in your dreams."

In the empty house all was as it had been when I had left early that morning—a mess. I waved to Grandpa through the window then gave him the finger. He returned the gesture and drove away.

The dark screen of the computer sat squarely on the desk. The hunk of junk was no longer just another piece of furniture, but had now transformed itself into a taunting, annoying temptation—one I couldn't resist. Sitting down in front of the computer, I pulled up YouTube and clicked on *The Surfing Siren*. The number of views had now reached one thousand and two— five hundred more in less than twenty-four hours! Feeling queasy, I ran to the bathroom where I spent the next ten minutes crouched over the toilet bowl. Fortunately, my belly-cramps eased and, with a few deep breaths, I managed to calm myself down.

I settled into my bed with sketchbook, pens, and pencils, and started a new Wavehouse; the wave-roof, curved in a series of gentle lines that ended in a neat curl. Then, with my pen, I edged the roof with a delicate trim of lacy coral. Under the wavy roof, I sketched an open clamshell with a No. 2 pencil, but I didn't like the open A-frame effect, so I rubbed it out. Next, I tried a more loosey-goosey tiki hut but that didn't do it for me either—I wasn't in the groove. The YouTube and surf scout nonsense were getting in the way, not to mention the most recent bomb—Myra's possible

80

departure for Paris. All the way across the Atlantic Ocean; not exactly an easy paddle. While no Wavehouse emerged that night, a decision did: I would surf exclusively at Secretspot for the rest of the season; and I wouldn't return to Early's until I knew the Stella scout was gone for good, and until I figured out for sure who had posted the YouTube video.

I fell asleep around midnight, hoping to have a nice, watery Wavehouse dream, but as luck would have it, I had a bad surf nightmare instead. I was paddling and paddling, trying to get to a tree-lined shore but the waves were breaking in reverse. All sorts of stuff from The Shell Shop hit me in the face as I paddled—tee shirts, postcards, necklaces, and Shellys. I tried to grab them as they bobbed past, but they fell apart when I touched them, the little families disintegrating, the cottages splintered or turned to pulp.

I was grateful to be woken by the sound of tires on gravel. At the window, I saw, through bleary eyes, my mother get out of a silver SUV with Rusty Meyers behind the wheel. It struck me that this seemed like an odd choice of vehicle for someone into environmental issues, but I wasn't really surprised. Rusty had *major poseur* written all over his smarmy face and buff body. I'd seen many strutting boors of his type drive up to our door. Sara leaned into the driver's window, murmuring something to Rusty before wiggling her way to our front door. It was a purposeful wiggle, a perfectly choreographed sashay executed for maximum impact. Returning to bed, I pulled the covers up around my neck and turned my back to the door. The clock read 4:08 a.m.

Sara cracked my door open, and I heard her sigh. Then something super weird happened. Sara sat on the edge of my bed, near my head—it seemed like she was there for forever. Then she stroked my face, trailing her warm hand down the side of my cheek. I lay still, pretending to be asleep, which was hard, because it felt so good I almost cried. Eventually Sara rose from the bed and I heard the door close behind her.

I imagined Sara kicking off her high-heeled sandals, pouring herself a tall glass of water to purge her alcohol-coated insides, and rummaging in the back of the silverware drawer for the spare pack of cigarettes; maybe she would light one up and take a few drags before burying the wasted cigarette deep in the trash, so as not to be reminded later of her post-date impulsivity. Often she would stay awake all night—sitting zombie-like with that damn photograph of my father in her hand, thinking thoughts she didn't share with anyone, including me.

I tried to stop imagining. I tried not to care.

Trying was as far as I got.

Chapter Eleven

The next day it poured—a relentless kind of rain that beat down on the tin roof like a punishment. There was no surf to speak of, only big, gray washing machine slop without form or reason. Locals stayed home, attending to household chores; tourists stayed indoors too, opting for cable TV in mildewed motel rooms, or quick dips in under-sized but over-heated indoor pools.

The Shell Shop was empty. My mother had given me the morning off, so I stayed home trying to read a book Myra had bought me—*Frank Lloyd Wright: A Life* by Ada Louis Huxtable. As usual, Myra was trying to get me to think beyond my Kendall's Watch existence. But reading about Wright was downright depressing; he seemed like a narcissistic jerk who had come from a really messed-up family. I skipped the story and browsed the photos. The houses he had built were cool, though. Like me, he seemed to like watery stuff, like rivers, waterfalls, and brooks.

Despite my lack of interest in Wright's life, the book inspired me. I drew a Wavehouse of angled driftwood and sharp-edged razor clams on an underwater cliff of coral, covered with succulent, seaweed plants. Schools of bluefish darted in and out of the feathery plants, feasting on plankton and algae.

In the afternoon, I worked at The Shell Shop. When Sara and I were there alone, we circled each other like a couple of territorial cougars with nothing to do but worry about our tails being swiped. That night she went out on the town with Rusty again, and returned late. I waited for her like one of Cinderella's faithful mouse buddies as Sara stepped from Rusty's enchanted SUV carriage and floated back to her humble home.

Saturday morning the sun broke through, and the wind calmed and shifted. At dawn, I heard Sara's door open and her voice: "You want a lift?" Her voice sounded pleasant but forced. "The waves at

83

Early's are decent."

"Nah," I replied, keeping my eyes closed and my back turned. "I'm sleeping in. Maybe I'll bike down later."

"Okay, if you don't make it, I'll see you at the shop. Be there by ten, please. I'll go straight from Early's."

After Sara drove away, I jumped out of bed and checked the week's tide chart in the *Kendall's Kalendar*. The *Kalendar* was our cheap town paper that mostly featured local business ads, church and community events, horoscopes, and TV listings. Occasionally someone wrote a decent article about beach erosion or traffic congestion; the tide chart, however, was a section that both fishermen and surfers depended on. Hitting the ocean at the wrong time or the wrong tide could result in no fish or no waves. In other words, a disaster.

Low tide had peaked at 6 a.m., and it was now half-past. An incoming tide, light offshore winds, and an ocean-born ground-swell would create perfect surfing conditions at Secretspot. Scarfing down a bowl of stale granola, I quickly got my gear together. I didn't bother calling Myra—she was staying home in order to squeeze more information out of her parents before they left for Paris that afternoon. I planned to stay with Myra for the next four nights, even if she claimed she didn't need the caretaking. We would, no doubt, be clinging to each other like barnacles.

I got to Secretspot half an hour later, and the waves looked sweet; four to five feet on the face, and arriving in four-wave sets at a decent three-minute interval. Enough time to catch one, ride it as far as nature intended, and still have time to paddle back out, catch my breath and wait for the next train. After prepping myself with sunscreen and my board with wax, I skidded down the cliff and made my way across the narrow beach to the surf. The bottom dropped away quickly, and I had to paddle from the get-go; there was no time to stand around in the white water waiting for a golden opportunity.

The ocean had a bite; the chill, a residue from two days of rain, rain, and more rain. I paddled like a maniac to prevent my body from freezing and stiffening, duck-diving through the oncoming set, and screaming as my head resurfaced between waves with an ice-cream headache. Once beyond the break, I sat on my board, rubbing my goose-pimpled arms. Sometimes this sport seemed really insane. Then I looked south towards the horizon, where the ocean sparkled like a celebration, and the sky was so perfectly clear that you had to join the party. Surfing, once again, made total sense.

When the next set rolled toward me, I was ready. The first wave looked nice, but the one behind it was the set wave, which meant it was the biggest and the best. I paddled up the crest of the first wave and slid down the back in a stomach-rolling glide. Making my way toward the peak of the set wave, I sat back on my board, spun it around and positioned myself to take off. After a few more easy paddles, I pushed down on the board with my hands so I could lift and hinge my hips, bend my knees, and land my feet in an easy crouch. I carved big loose swoops up and down the face of the wave like I was drawing a series of smiles. My arms did their own dance, billowing at my sides to provide balance; my knees flexed and straightened, maintaining both rhythm and position. A tension-free ride—just what the doctor had ordered.

The next fifteen minutes were pure surf bliss—no thoughts of surf scouts, crowds, or stupid internet sites. I played differently on each wave I took; on some, I flew high up on the top edge, skimming along in a perfect floater, before planting down into the meat of the wave for the rest of the ride. On others, I bee-lined quickly down the face, did a huge bottom turn and shifted back up and over the top before closing out in a big bucket of spray and foam. I played with my feet, walking in a circle on my board. Normally surfers did fancy footwork only on longboards, not shortboard shredders like mine, but I didn't care. I would try anything at least once, and fell off as many waves as I made. I considered it part of my learning curve, and my frequent falls kept me humble.

It was after a particularly spectacular belly flop that I saw him. I was repositioning my body on my board—trying to undo a potentially crotch-rotting wedgie—when I noticed another surfer bobbing a few yards out. He must've been there for a while, sitting on his board like Neptune surveying his ocean domain—and here I was clowning around!

It was the super surfer from Chompers—the mystery man with the bronze skin and lion-like mane who'd paddled off into the horizon. And now here he was on my private turf, in my hidden oasis, and I didn't like it one bit.

I felt paralyzed, and lay on my board like a piece of driftwood—without life or movement.

But he'd seen me, and there was no easy way to smoothly disappear.

"Yo, hey, hello!" he called, waving his arm like a pit stop mechanic trying to flag down a NASCAR gone rogue.

Immediately, I started paddling toward the shore.

"Where are you going?" he hollered as my scared and sorry butt high-tailed it back to the beach.

Where was I going? I was a coward, and paddling away from Secretspot felt like the ultimate self-betrayal. But I couldn't stop myself; I was shaking, and my whole body felt like it had been zapped by electric volts.

With my board slipping out from under one shaky arm, I stumbled to the sand, gasping for breath.

Get it together, Dugan. This is Secretspot. This is your spot. You can't be chased away.

But no one was chasing me away. I was banishing myself—me and my stupid shyness.

Chapter Twelve

I got to The Shell Shop earlier than Sara—nothing like an aborted surf session to make one punctual.

"Wow," Sara exclaimed when she came in the door and found me sitting on the floor, sorting children's Sponge Bob yellow flip-flops into their respective small, medium, and large bins. "You beat me."

I shrugged. "I couldn't get back to sleep. Figured I'd try and do something useful."

Sara came over and sat beside me on the floor. "Do you remember when you were five years old and obsessed with the color yellow?"

"Vaguely," I said.

"All the other little girls wanted pink. You wanted yellow. Yellow shoes, yellow clothes, yellow toys, and yellow food."

That, I remembered. Mac and cheese, eggs, butterscotch, and lemonade.

"You said that yellow was the color of the sun," Sara said.

The 'me' sitting next to her now felt very unsunny. Mr. Intruder, a.k.a. Chompers Lunatic, had totally spoiled my mood; he'd taken my waves as well as my sunny disposition.

"Remember that guy Ivan? The shortboarder from Brazil?"

"Sort of," I sighed. There always seemed to be some guy associated with Sara's nostalgia.

"He bought you that adorable stuffed sunflower."

"Sorry Sara," I said. "But that thing was weird. Who wants to play with giant fake foliage?"

"Well, you're sure in a snitty mood."

"Sorry, but Ivan's goofy, floppy sunflower gift was just a yellow ploy to get on your good side. He didn't give a fig for me."

She stood up. "He *was* on my good side—for a while, anyway. Besides, it was the gesture that counted."

The rest of the day was an uneventful blur of tourists buying things and asking stupid questions. I almost lost it when two little groms arrived with a pile of flyers for the Montauk Junior Surf Tournament.

"Hey, ma'am?" a scruffy-haired blonde pipsqueak asked. "Would it be okay if we put one of these up in your window?"

Sara was in the back room, so I was safe. "Um, no," I said. "We don't put posters in our window. Sorry, kids."

"Really?" The little dude frowned.

"Please?" His buddy, a freckled redhead, still cute in his layer of baby fat, looked as if the world had ended. "All the other shops did it—even the bakery."

I couldn't bring myself to wreck their perfect record. "Oh, all right. Put it over there." I pointed to a spot behind the sun hat display, where it wouldn't constantly remind me of my past, present, and future failures.

Sales were brisk the rest of the day. No little kids had any tantrums or spilled ice cream on the beach towels, and no one tried to return anything they'd broken. Still, I stumbled around The Shell Shop in a dark mood, and couldn't stop thinking about the invasion of Secretspot.

At five, Sara offered to let me leave early.

"You look like someone died, Anna," she said. "Go home, or go surfing. Just do something to change your mood, please."

"Oh, that reminds me, would it be okay if I stayed at Myra's for the next few nights? Her parents are going to Paris and I want to keep her company."

"Paris, eh? Lucky them," Sara said with a bit of snark. "Wish I could take off and go to Paris." She'd never really warmed to the Berkowitzes, even though they'd lived in Kendall's Watch for almost seven years and their daughter was my best friend. Sara was like a lot of born and bred locals who never truly accepted outsiders. It didn't matter if they were from third world countries looking for a better life or from the city looking for a beachier life; unless you went back three generations you were suspect.

"It's for work, Sara. They need to go for their jobs. So, anyway, is it okay if I stay with Myra?"

"Sure. Whatever. See you here tomorrow."

I left the shop and climbed on my bike. Before going to Myra's, however, there was one thing I needed to do first.

I sat on the shore in my rash guard and board shorts, my surfboard waxed and ready, looking out at a Secretspot wave awash in the golden evening light. I knew he'd be out there and on it. And sure enough, so he was—he was a surf addict, after all, just like me.

He was good. Damn good. I wasn't sure if his stellar surfing chops made matters worse, or better. All I knew was this was Secretspot. *My* spot.

Paddling out toward him, I thought about screaming incoherently, like some kind of surf-lunatic—perhaps that would scare him away; but I couldn't muster a sound—my voice was zip-locked deep in my throat, and I was about as scary as a dead leaf. As I approached, he smiled and waved, sitting casually on his surfboard as if he had been born to it.

"Welcome back," he said. "That was a great belly flop you did this morning." He looked vaguely familiar, but he wasn't from Kendall's; perhaps he was from Montauk or further up the island. His smile was even nicer up close—a mouthful of crooked, perfectly white teeth set in skin like melted milk chocolate. Wild hair, like golden seaweed, curled, chaotic, to his shoulders, and green eyes glinted, almond-shaped, on either side of a broad, flat nose.

Pushing myself up to a sitting position, I asked, trying to quell my nervous stammer, "How…ah…did you get here?"

His grin widened. "Nice to meet you too."

"Could you…just"—the zipper jammed, the words pooled in my mouth—"please, answer the question." Zipper opened, *finally*!

"I'm staying up there." He pointed towards the Ramelle house. "I looked down this morning, saw you catch these killers and couldn't resist."

Steady, Anna. Don't let those washboard abs throw you. "Are you related to Ms. Ramelle or something?" I asked.

"Nah. Just a friend of a friend, I guess."

I didn't know where to rest my eyes. His face was too appealing, and his smile seemed genuinely kind. And the body—well, let's just say it was a good thing I was sitting down on my board, or I might have gone all girly and weak in the knees; a stereotype that I wanted nothing to do with. To keep myself steady, I focused on his left ear. A small gold hoop hugged his earlobe.

"Something wrong, Belly Flop?" he asked.

"Um, no. I mean yes…" I stumbled. All over the friggin' map. "I mean, *yes*. *Yes*, something's very wrong. This is my spot, and I don't share it. So you can paddle back in now."

Super Surfer just sat there, smiling at me. It was awesome and totally cringe-worthy at the same time. A hunky guy staring at *me*? Talking to *me*? Once again, I fought the urge to paddle away as fast as I possibly could.

"Stop grinning!" I finally blurted out. "I told you to go! What are you, crazy?"

In four graceful paddles he was at my side. "Yep. That's me, crazy. But you can call me Chris."

Looking straight into his sparkling, green eyes, I told him firmly, "I don't want you here, Chris."

He stared back a moment, his smile gone, before he began: "You really don't know—"

"Actually," I interrupted. "I really *do* know. This is my spot. Mine alone." *Phew. Words were finally coming out smoothly.*

He smiled again and shrugged. "No worries, Belly Flop. Just let me catch one of the next set and I'm out of your life forever."

I caved. "One, but that's it. And please stop calling me that."

"Aw, come on. You know I'm just yankin' your chain. That belly flop was pretty cool, but the waves you made this morning? Even more spectacular."

I was speechless. Was this a compliment? I didn't know how to respond so I just clammed up in my usual shy idiot style.

As we turned our boards to face the horizon, I could feel him staring at me. I felt horribly exposed and full of fatal flaws: monkey arms, eyes too close together, unimpressive chest, the list goes on and on—the basic boringness of me. Thankfully, the next set came on schedule, offering me an escape from his scrutiny. "This one's yours. Go for it," I said. "Nice meeting you. Leave now, please."

Chris turned and popped up effortlessly. He threw a lot of spray and the hump of his wave prevented me from seeing the bulk of his ride, but I had to hand it to him—his take-off had been stellar.

I waited for my turn, letting the next two waves go by and choosing the last wave of the set. Angling my board, I tried to ignore Chris who now stood on shore, watching me. I was self-conscious about everything—the way I looked, the way I surfed, the way I was who I was. I was convinced that his sudden appearance would throw me off. No question, I would make a complete and utter fool of myself.

But as soon as the wave and I connected, all was good—I didn't mess up, I didn't choke. I rode the wave with confidence and connection, added a few tricky moves, some backside slashes, but mostly kept it clean. Then, I cut back up and over the wave before it closed out.

The idea of an audience—no, to be honest, the idea of him— gave me an extra edge. I was showing off for the first time in my life, and it felt kinda good.

But by the time I'd paddled back out and turned toward shore, Chris was gone. The sun was setting, and I had time for only a few more rides. My purpose had been to warn him off and in this I had been successful—he was gone. So why did I still feel grumpy? I should've been glad to have Secretspot back to myself, but I wasn't. *You don't miss him*, I told myself. The first of many lies.

Chapter Thirteen

When I arrived at Myra's house, she was sitting in the kitchen with her laptop. A sketchpad and a set of pens and pencils sat beside her.

"What's this?" I asked, picking up the sketchpad.

"Surprise! You're going to design the flyer for the Kendall's Watch Community Action Group's Beach Clean Up."

"Myra, you know I don't like people to see my drawings."

"Please, please, pretty please? It can be anonymous. Nobody needs to know that you did it. You *have* to help me out! The one Mrs. Kettle did was so horrible that I can't possibly use it. She messed up the time and the meeting place. She drew a picture of a pile of garbage with a seagull standing on top, only it looks like a pile of shit topped with a three-cornered hat."

"Ouch," I said. "That's harsh."

"Here." She thrust a pink flyer at me. "See for yourself."

"Oh wow. That's supposed to be a seagull?"

Myra nodded.

"Okay. I'll do it, but I won't draw a Wavehouse."

"That's cool. Maybe just some killer seashells and other oceany stuff; the creatures and plants we're trying to protect. Something we can scan and email and also print and post. You can lose Mrs. Kettle's garbage theme."

"Don't worry. No trash in my work."

"Yay!" Myra beamed. "I'll order a pizza while you get started."

We kept working even after the pizza arrived, eating while drawing and keyboard clicking. At one point Myra said, "So, the committee is thinking of setting up an information table at the contest."

"What contest?" I asked.

"Oh, you know," Myra tried to sound super casual. "The 7th Annual Montauk Junior Surf Tournament."

I looked down at the mermaid tail I was drawing. "Good for you. Have fun there."

"We were thinking that we might sponsor one of the contestants."

I knew where this was leading. Putting my pizza slice and pen down, I looked directly at Myra. "No way. Sorry. Wish I could, but you know I can't."

"How do you know if you don't even try?"

"*Seriously?*"

"Yeah." Myra snapped the top of her laptop closed and crossed her arms. "*Seriously.*"

"Because entering that tournament when I was ten was the most traumatic experience of my life!"

She rolled her eyes. "Oh come on. You were *ten*! You're almost seventeen now."

"Myra, every time I imagine surfing in front of an audience, I fall to pieces inside. I feel like a combination of Jell-O and ice. On top of that, I start sweating and I want to puke. Does that sound like fun to you?"

"All right, whatever." Myra frowned.

"I'm helping you out with this flyer. Isn't that enough?"

"I guess," Myra shrugged. I was sorry to disappoint her, but there was no way I was going to enter that stupid tournament. No freakin' way.

"Hey, how about you ask Jimmy?" I suggested. "He's a decent surfer, and I'll bet he's gonna compete in the longboard division."

Myra's eyes lit up. "That's a concept!"

"Good excuse for you to contact him."

"Like, call him?"

"Nah. Just go over to the motel and ask him in person."

"Seriously?"

"Come on, Myra. You're always asking people for things. It's your forte."

"No, no, no," she shook her moppy head vigorously. "I never ask dudes for things. I'm fine with old biddies and young mothers. But hot guys my own age? *Brrrr...*"

"Ha! Methinks I detect some Shy-Person-Type-B symptoms…"

"It's my one and only area of shyness. Your aversion to surfing in front of an audience is called performance anxiety, by the way."

"I know what it's called," I said. "Can we change the subject now, please?"

"Sorry."

"No, you're not."

"You're right, I'm not." Myra resumed clicking away on her keyboard, and I returned to my drawing. We sat in stony silence for what seemed an eternity. We didn't always agree, but this sudden surge of surfing challenges—the YouTube video, the Stella scout, *and* the stupid Montauk tournament—was causing way too many snarky exchanges between us. And then there was Paris. Who could forget Paris?

After I couldn't stand it anymore, I broke the deadlock. "Anyway, if you want, I'll go with you to ask Jimmy. Like I said, he's a cool guy."

"Okay," she smiled. "Thanks."

We worked for a few more minutes, before I said, "Speaking of guys, there was a surfer at Secretspot this morning and again tonight."

Myra looked shocked. "And you didn't tell me this news the second you walked in here?"

I hadn't. It was true. "I got distracted by the flyer," I lied. "You know how I get when I'm drawing."

"Wow. So, tell me now."

"He wouldn't leave," I began, "and he was supremely annoying."

Myra raised an eyebrow. "Really? What was his name?"

"Chris."

"Is he hot?"

"Sort of," I mumbled, focusing intently on the seaweed I was drawing.

"Sort of *how*?"

I looked up at her. "Sort of an Adonis-meets-tribal-chief-meets-Buddhist-monk kind of hot."

Myra nodded. "Interesting…"

"Very multiculti-hard-to-place hot," I continued with increasing enthusiasm. "With tattoos *and* a piercing!"

Myra grinned. "Edgy. We like edgy."

"Edgy or not, I hope he doesn't come back. It's my break. Besides, Secretspot is our special place. Yours and mine."

"Well, yeah," Myra said. "But maybe it's okay for us to expand just a little."

I shook my head. "No way."

Myra groaned. "You know, Anna, it's not all up to you. I have a say in how things go at Secretspot too."

"Oh great!" I cried. "So now you want to tell people about Secretspot?"

"Not necessarily," Myra shrugged. "I'm not sure I want anyone else up there either. At least right now. But it's supposed to be a conversation, Anna. You don't get to make *all* the decisions without even asking my opinion."

"You're right," I sighed. "I'm sorry."

There was a moment or two of quiet interrupted only by Myra's tap-tap-tap on the computer and the scratch of my pencil on paper. A knot clenched in my stomach; I hated it when Myra and I were at odds and I wanted to clear the air. "Hey, wanna see what I've drawn so far?" I turned the drawing around so Myra could see.

"Um, okay…" she hesitated. "I love the mermaid and the starfish rocks. But what's this?" She pointed to what was supposed to be seaweed.

"Oh no," I moaned.

"What?"

It was hair—Chris's hair. His wild, edgy, annoying hair. I grabbed the drawing back and worked furiously to erase it. "Sorry. I got a bit distracted."

"I'll say," Myra sighed.

Chapter Fourteen

The next morning at Secretspot, Chris was there—impossible to miss in a yellow rash guard that shone like a beacon in the early morning sun. The waves were killer—six to eight feet high—bright blue beauties with perfect peaks and peeling sides. I watched him catch a gorgeous right-breaking wave, dancing and swaying with unfathomable grace and skill as he carved his way ahead of the lip.

My insides were having a tug of war—one side was pulling me out there, to those stellar waves, to Chris; the other was pulling me back up the cliff to my bicycle, telling me to pedal away.

You can do this. He's just a guy, who used to be a little boy, who used to be a tiny baby, who used to be a little worm in his mother's tummy.

I paddled out at rocket speed making a bee-line right for Chris.

"I told you to leave," I said as my board slid next to his.

Chris's crazy mop of hair was pulled back in a big bushy ponytail. "Well, good morning to you too," he said.

"I'm serious." My heart thumped violently in my chest

"Listen, I'm just here for a few more days. I really don't want to have to surf down with all those other bozos at Eagle's."

"Early's."

"Right. Sorry. Early's. And that other spot with the rocks is a bit too gnarly." Before I knew it, Chris was right next to me. "Look, mind if I stay for just a few more? I promise I won't get in your way."

Looking over at him, I noticed a couple of minor zits around his nose and a gap between his two front teeth. Although relieved that he wasn't completely perfect, my heart was still racing like crazy, but I could tell it wasn't scared crazy, it was happy crazy.

Before I could reply, a set was upon us and I was set up for a six-foot left. Turning my board, I barely had to paddle to catch it, and popped up to my feet and started my own special dance with my own wavy friend. The ride was sweet and smooth, like skating on a lake, only the lake was tipped at a forty-five-degree angle. Paddling back out, I was, for the first time, anxious to hear what another surfer had to say about my ride.

"Nice one," Chris called, giving me a Cheshire cat grin and a big thumbs-up.

"Thanks," I muttered, trying to maintain my outer cool while my insides were singing wildly. I paddled past him, back out to my spot—Miss Chill.

The next one Chris caught took him right by me, and as he passed he was high enough in the wave that his head was visible over the white foamy curl. For a split second he looked back at me, stuck his thumbs in his ears and made googly hands.

When he paddled back out he asked, "Catch my gift?"

"You're really annoying, you know that?" I said. *Annoying? Not really.* He was surprisingly comfortable to be around. It seemed one of my shy pockets was opening up for Chris to nestle within.

"Most people I surf with think I'm pretty cool," Chris shrugged.

"Whatever. You can surf here, today and for the next few days, if you promise on your life, that you don't tell anyone that you came to this place. Or that you saw me here."

"How can I tell anyone I saw you here when I don't even know who you are?"

That's right. He had no clue who I was, and I wanted to keep it that way, at least for the moment. "Belly Flop. That's who I am. Just plain Belly Flop is fine."

"Aha," he nodded. "So the annoying nickname becomes the secret alias. Sweet."

I smiled. "Yeah…sweet."

Between waves that morning, Chris managed to get a little more information out of me, like how old I was, and how long I had been surfing. But I refused to tell him my real name or any of the drama going on with the video and the surf scout. He wasn't much more forthcoming, and we both skirted certain questions. He, by joking— in response to my asking where he was from, he said, "I was born on

Mars and tossed to Earth by negligent Martian parents"—and me, by turning the questions around. When he asked if I had a boyfriend, I replied, "Do I seem like the kind of girl who has a boyfriend?"

He could surf, that was for sure; every move was fluid, liquid—a gift. Chris was a natural. Like me, I suppose. And he was freakishly easy to talk to.

As the morning edged toward noon, Chris took the first big risk. With his eyes averted and nervously tugging on his earring, he stammered, "So, uh, Belly Flop, any chance I could convince you to hang out later? Maybe let me take you out for dinner or something? That is, if there isn't a boyfriend. Or even if there is...I mean, he could come, too." Chris was definitely not as smooth asking a girl out on a date as he was charging up a wave on his potato chip shortboard. And I was even less smooth in my response, having never been asked out on a date before in my life.

"Um, I guess...whatever...sure...why not?" Talk about lame! I was the definition of lame.

Chris brightened, looking up. "Cool. So what is it? Dinner for two...or three?"

I held up two fingers, and Chris gave me a killer smile. Then the best set of the day came through, each wave a winner. Funny thing was we didn't make a single one. We just sat there grinning shyly at each other as the waves passed by, bobbing up and over like two dumbstruck human corks.

Chapter Fifteen

The position of the sun told me it was after 9 a.m. Wicked late, and way past time for me to leave. If I wanted to get to The Shell Shop before Sara—and remain un-surf-detected—I would have to secretly stash my wet stuff and surfboard behind the dumpster in the alley, then quickly wash the saltwater out of my hair in the hopefully not-too-gross public restroom sink around the corner.

"I gotta go," I told Chris. "You should stay if you want. Catch a few more before the wind gets on it."

He smiled a snaggle-toothed grin.

I dawdled. "So, um. I'll see you later."

"Cool," Chris nodded. "Later."

I paddled shoreward picking up a white-water ride to the beach. When I had climbed the cliff, I turned and waved but Chris didn't seem to notice, even though I could swear he was looking my way. Then I realized he wasn't looking at me at all, he was staring at the movie star's house above my head. *Weird*, I thought.

I still wasn't entirely sure this was a date-date; maybe Chris just wanted to return the favor—after all, I had let him surf Secretspot, so perhaps he felt that he should take me out for a meal? I had decided on Brinestellar's Cafe, a popular place that wasn't too blatantly romantic. We planned to meet there at 7 p.m. I decided that I had better spruce up my usual attire, just in case this was a date-date. I was worried that out of the water, in regular clothes, in a public place we'd have nothing to talk about. The local lore that surrounded the Ramelle house would be a good conversational tidbit—although what else we would talk about, I had no idea.

I was so distracted and excited that I nearly forgot to store my gear and almost walked into the shop wearing damp surf clothes with my hair spiked and salted. While I had my head under the not-too-grody restroom spigot, I realized that conversational tidbits were the least of my problems. It was my night to stay late at The Shell Shop, so bye-bye to first potential date with a hot guy ever.

"Dammit!" I yelled, bolting upright and bashing the back of my head against the faucet, the pain of which required four rapid repeats of the *F* word in its pure, unadulterated form.

"Pardon?" A pair of feet encased in pink pom-pom trimmed anklets and ladies boat shoes shuffled in the stall behind me.

"Sorry," I said.

The toilet flushed and out walked a woman about Gramma's age. Her baggy shorts were pale pink and her hair, thin and unnaturally rosy, matched her shorts. I expected a *tsk-tsk'ing*, but instead the woman said, "Gonna be one of those days, huh, sugar?"

I smiled and nodded.

"Well, try not to get too pickled. You're young, you're beautiful. The world is your oyster, and don't you forget it." She reached into her handbag and took out an anti-bacterial towelette, wiped her hands, and tossed it in the trash. "Bye now. You try and have a good one, you hear?"

"Thanks…um…I'll try."

I finished washing the salt out of my hair after she left. Even if I was young, and beautiful—was I really?—even if the world was my oyster, how could I weasel my way out of night-time Shell Shop duty? Lying to Sara would be a waste of time. Kendall's Watch was a smaller than small town and someone was bound to see me and Chris at Brinestellar's and tell my mother.

My only choice was to come clean with Sara, tell her I had "dinner plans," and just ask to switch Shell Shop duty to another night. Cool and casual, no biggie, like this sort of thing happened all the time. The world was my oyster.

I got to the shop at 9:40 a.m. and Sara waltzed in half an hour later.

"Once again, you never made it to Early's," Sara remarked. Her damp hair was up in a top-knot, secured by a glistening oyster shell hair clip (one of The Shell Shop's best sellers). She looked like exotic royalty.

I, on the other hand, probably looked like a wet schnauzer. I fingered through my own shaggy mop. "Nah. I decided to bag it and sleep in; just jumped in the shower quick."

"You can't avoid surfing forever, Anna. I know you. Your gills will close up." Sara was trying to be sweet now, referring to an old game we had played when I was little. Whenever she gave me a bath, Sara would make pretend that I was a mermaid.

"Quick, quick little mermaid," she'd say. "Get your head underwater or your gills will close up." I would gleefully obey, plunging beneath the sudsy surface, and staying underwater till I couldn't hold my breath any longer. Afterwards, I'd shove both my legs into one side of my pajama bottoms and shuffle around the house, pretending I was a landlocked creature of the deep.

"Oh fair lady," I'd lament dramatically. "Please return me to the ocean where I can swim and swim and swim!"

Then Sara would scoop me up and carry me to my bed. "Ah, little mermaid princess," she'd say in a breathy fairy tale voice. "Time for you to go to sleep. I promise you will return to the ocean in your dreams."

And Sara was right. I usually did return to the ocean in my dreams. But now, a lot of time had passed since our days of mermaid play. Time filled with disappointment, conflict, and confusion.

Now I shrugged half-heartedly. "Yeah, right," I grumbled.

"FYI," Sara said, "the Stella scout seems to be history."

"Whatever."

"Although I suppose I could call Stella directly and—"

"Don't you dare, Sara," I snapped. "You've done enough damage with that stupid video."

"I told you I had nothing to do with that, Anna," she groaned. "Get over it already."

"Don't go calling anyone!" I snapped. "Please. Let me make my own decisions."

"You're making a big mistake, Anna. And it is driving me damn crazy."

"Well, too damn bad."

Sara shook her head in disgust and stalked off toward the storeroom.

Get it together, I told myself. *Being bitchy is not going to help with your date night request.* "Which reminds me," I called after her, striving for a nicer tone. "If possible, can I stay late tomorrow night instead of tonight?"

"Why?"

"I have dinner plans."

She turned toward me with a laugh. "Dinner plans?"

"Yeah. Dinner plans."

"What? You and Myra? I'm sorry, Anna, but that doesn't fly."

"No. I'm going with someone else."

"Who?" Sara was suspicious. I couldn't blame her really, as I never did anything with anyone besides Myra.

"This guy I met."

Sara's eyes got wide. "Really?"

"Yeah, really."

"Do I know this guy?" she asked, sounding way too excited.

"I doubt it. He's not from around here."

"I hope this isn't some kind of online hook-up, Anna." Now she sounded mother-to-daughter worried. "All kinds of pervy creeps prey on young girls that way."

"No. I'm not that stupid. He's an old friend of Myra's. From the city." I was such a smooth liar that I frightened even myself.

"Oh." She brightened. "One of Myra's friends."

I knew what she was thinking: If this guy was one of Myra's friends, he was a super nerd and therefore no danger whatsoever. I felt that I was home free, so I milked it. "He's studying meteorology and wants to talk to me about storms, hurricanes, and waves and stuff."

Sara shrugged, nonchalant and no longer concerned. "Sounds really boring, but go ahead. I don't have anything cooking tonight anyhow. Rusty has to take a business client out for dinner. Someone so famous he has to keep it hush hush. Even from me."

"Wow. Cool. That's really exciting." Not really, but since it seemed like Sara and I had reached a peace accord, I feigned enthusiasm.

"I know." Sara smiled, continuing to the storeroom. I heaved a mega-sigh of relief. My heart was pumping as if I had surfed a fifteen-foot face. I just had to get through the next eight hours alive.

Which I barely managed. I was so hyper that I almost broke a vintage Shelly while packing it for a customer, and was so distracted that I ran into the postcard rack about fifteen times. Sara didn't seem to notice. She went about her business, expertly convincing female customers that ugly shell-trimmed sarongs and flip-flops were 'really comfortable and totally sexy,' and flirting with the guys until they bought tee shirts they didn't need.

At 5 p.m. the steady flow of customers had slowed to a snail's pace, and Sara surprised me, saying: "Why don't you just leave now?"

"Okay." I walked toward the door. "I'm going home to get my stuff together and go over to Myra's. See you tomorrow morning."

"You know," Sara started. "If you want to borrow something of mine for this date, go ahead. I mean, if this guy is worth dressing up for at all…"

I smiled at my mother for what felt like the first time in years. "Thanks. I might do that. But he's really just, like, a friend. I'm just doing Myra a favor."

She smiled back. "It's not the end of the world to dress up for friends, Anna."

As I walked out the door she called, "Try the blue halter dress with the low back. It'll look killer on you."

Chapter Sixteen

For once your mother and I are on the same page," Myra said as she tied a blue knot at the nape of my neck. "This dress looks spectacular. You remind me of Audrey Hepburn in *Sabrina*, you know, after she comes home from Paris."

"Ugh. Don't mention that city, please. I hate it. It might steal you from me," I sighed.

"Sorry. It was just a cinematic association I couldn't resist. Now, turn around and look."

Myra spun me toward the full-length mirror on the back of her closet door. *Not bad.* Sara's blue dress gave my meager boobs a bit more lift and the illusion of size; the inward cut of the halter did my shoulders justice, and made my arms seem more like a dancer's and less like a monkey's. And the royal blue did look great with my black hair.

Myra rummaged through her jewelry box and pulled out a pair of dangly pearl earrings. "Overkill?" she asked.

I nodded. "No earrings. This dress is enough of a stretch for me. I can only go so far."

She rummaged a bit more and came up with a tube of coral lipstick. "Please? Just a little?"

"Uh-uh," I shook my head.

"Come on, Anna! One of us—you in fact!—is going on a date. A date! Did you hear me?"

I groaned, but Myra persisted. "This is a life-changing event that requires special attention. And—if for no other reason—you have to wear lipstick for my vicarious pleasure."

I grabbed the lipstick. "Whatever."

Myra stood behind me and watched as I coated my mouth with the stuff, pretending it was SPF 50 zinc oxide lip balm. I had expected to hate the results, but the pinkish lipstick actually looked good on my smashed-tomato mouth.

I smacked my lips together and took a step back from the mirror for one last long view. "Who the bloody heck is this girl?" I cried.

Myra put her hands on my shoulders. "You can do this, Anna. It'll be fun."

I turned around and grabbed both her wrists. "Wanna come along? I'm sure he won't mind."

Myra frowned. "Yeah, right. Fifth wheel—*love* that position; born to play that role. In other words, not on your life." She pulled out of my killer grip to reach up and smooth my hair.

"Hey, how about tomorrow we go to the motel and ask Jimmy to be your contest surfer boy?"

"I don't know. I have to work with the biddies at the church sorting through stuff for Saturday's rummage sale, and I'll want to look good for this, um, Jimmy thing, so I might not have time—"

I held a hand up like a traffic cop. "Like I said the other night, you are *so* worse than me."

Myra shrugged. "Okay. Okay. We'll do it." She turned me toward the door. "Come on, it's time." Myra pushed me out of her room and down the stairs. At the front door, we hugged.

"Wish me luck," I sighed.

"You don't need luck. You're gorgeous and more importantly, you're you. Now go. I'll be waiting for the full report when you get back, just me and my pint of Cookies n' Cream."

Chris was waiting for me in front of Brinestellar's when I got there. He looked as good on land as he did in water, in a sea green button-down shirt and dark skinny jeans. Dry now, his sun-streaked hair was still wild, and ringlet-y, and framed his dark, handsome face like a lion's mane.

"Hey, Belly Flop. You look, um, really nice." He smiled his crooked-tooth smile and reached forward. As I gave him my hand, I hoped mine wasn't sweaty and clammy like Rusty Meyers' had been. Chris's hand felt like a giant warm, friendly paw. A shiver went up my spine, and I tried desperately not to reveal how undone I was by our touching. Chris's hand was shaking a bit too, maybe even more than mine, which made me feel more relaxed.

When we walked inside, everyone—and I mean *everyone*—stared. Even the few people there who hadn't known me since the day I was born. Lots of heads nodded, and a low hum of whispering ensued. Was it really that bizarre that I, freaky Anna Dugan, was out with a guy? Or worse, was this because of the YouTube clip? Maybe these people were some of the new five hundred viewers? Most likely it was my dress. That, in of itself, was an Anna Dugan novelty. No one had *ever* seen me in one of *those* before. As we passed the bar, all the surfers standing around drinking their beers nodded their heads at Chris or gave him a thumbs-up, as if to say "Way to go, Dude." I wasn't sure if I should be flattered or offended. All I knew was in that moment I felt mildly seasick.

I noticed that Chris was also getting his fair share of female attention. Once she got her jaw up from the floor, Clarissa Morrison, the hostess, said, "Wow. Hi. Welcome to Brinestellar's." Clarissa's parents owned Brinestellar's. She was only two years older than me, but dressed for work in a tight black cocktail dress and a whole face of paint.

"Can we sit somewhere out of the way?" I asked.

"Yeah, sure, Anna," Clarissa managed. "Right this way." She led us to a private spot behind a screen covered with old fishing nets and buoys.

We could peek through the nets and see everyone, but nobody could really see us. Clarissa, leering at Chris as she handed him his menu, breathlessly sighed, "Enjoy." While he looked at his menu, Clarissa handed me mine and, with eyes as wide as the Mississippi, she mouthed the words, *Oh. My. God.* Then she winked at me and my seasickness returned.

Once Clarissa tore herself away from our table, Chris put his menu down and smiled nervously. "I thought she would never leave and I would have to pretend to look at this menu forever. I guess I had to take you out to dinner to learn your name, *Anna.*"

"Dugan," I blurted, like I had Tourette's. So far dating was hard work.

Chris looked confused.

I shook my head. "I'm sorry. I'm totally confusing. My name is Anna Dugan. First. Last. In that order."

"But you'll always be Belly Flop to me."

I felt my cheeks get hot. "What's your last name?" I asked.

Chris paused, swallowed and then said, "Kahimbe. Christopher Kahimbe. First. Last. In that order."

Kahimbe. It sounded vaguely familiar. "What kind of name is Kahimbe?"

"It's Kenyan. I've got Kenyan, Hawaiian, and Caucasian blood coursing through my veins. That's why I look like a mutt."

"No, you look like a Wheaten Terrier." What was I saying? I was talking too much. This is a problem for Type B's. We so rarely talk to strangers that once we get comfortable we overdo it, and say *really* stupid shit.

"Excuse me?" He laughed and held his hands up like begging paws. "Woof. Woof."

"Never mind," I croaked. Words were spilling out too fast, as if I had no control. I had to switch gears. "Hey, let's order. I'm starving." I opened my menu and pretended to read. "The fried calamari in this place is sick."

We decided on fried calamari to share, followed by a swordfish burger for him and a salmon steak for me. After Sam, the waiter—luckily not a leering surfer or a gawking local—took our order, Chris cleared his throat and said, "So, Belly Flop. I have to tell you. You're one of the best surfers I have ever seen. And I've seen plenty, believe me."

Blush. Blush. Major blush. At this rate I would be beet red before dinner arrived.

"Are you gonna compete in that tournament down in Montauk?" he asked.

That stupid tournament was like a case of herpes. Erupting at the worst possible times. And truly *never* going away. "No," I said fiddling with my fork, trying to think of another subject to move us away from this toxic one. But I wasn't quick enough.

"Why not?" he persisted. "I'm sure you could win. Not just the girls' division. You could get the overall best surfer prize. To put it in 'dog terms,' I'll bet you'd get Best in Show." He giggled.

I did not giggle. Where was the food already? I wanted to lose myself in a plate of calamari. "Competing just isn't my thing," I whispered.

Chris continued. "I grew up on Kauai, and I've been surfing forever. I've done all the major breaks on the Hawaiian Islands. I've been to Australia, Bali, Fiji, everywhere. And really Belly Flop, you're right up there with the best of them. You could go pro…if you wanted."

I could feel the sweat form on my upper lip.

"Not that pro women make anywhere near as much money as the men," he continued, "which is totally unfair, but there are people trying to change that."

Uh-oh, I thought. *I do not want to go into a panicked state, especially not now. Time to divert with humor.* "Who wants to travel all over the world with a bunch of gnarly brain-dead surfers, in places where you can get malaria, or be bit by a scorpion or maybe even eaten by a shark?"

Chris laughed. "It's not like that. Believe me."

"How would you know?" I managed to stay calm by sitting on my hands and digging my fingernails into the backs of my thighs.

Chris shrugged. "I've done a few competitions."

"What's a few?"

"I dunno. I've sort of lost count."

While Chris fumbled with his napkin, the busboy arrived with our bread basket. I shuddered inwardly when I saw it was Kyle Yeager, an over-eager fifteen-year-old surfer who was way too energetic for his own good.

"Dude!" Kyle exclaimed, grinning foolishly at Chris. "I am, like, so stoked that you are here. I just started shredding with my new Ceekay five-seven and I am so ripping on that board, it's insane."

Ceekay five-seven. Sudden realization clicked on like a spotlight. It wasn't me, or my sexy dress that had caused the commotion.

It was *him*. Chris Kahimbe. *The* Chris Kahimbe. Better known as Ceekay, current Men's Junior World Surf Champion and god to all gromettes—known for his signature, radical moves. Even I, in all my surf-culture ignorance, knew the nickname, even if I hadn't recognized the face. Or the body.

"Holy shit!" I gasped. "You're Ceekay."

"Surprise, surprise," Mr. Christopher Kahimbe—a.k.a. Chris, a.k.a. Ceekay—said weakly, and I swear he looked a wee bit scared.

Chapter Seventeen

Surprise, surprise. The understatement of the friggin' century. Kyle Yeager hovered like a buzzing insect, while Ceekay stared at me with a freaked expression I hadn't yet seen on his face.

"Dude. You totally kicked ass at the Billabong Invitational at J-Bay this year," Kyle blabbered. "Like, my cousin has this satellite dish that gets so many channels it's insane. Like four hundred, or something. We got to see the whole competition, man, in like real time, ya know? It was four in the morning, a whole bunch of us, totally wasted—"

"Later, bro," said Ceekay.

Kyle wagged his head.

"Like, leave. Now." Ceekay's hands formed fists, and his expression got tight and aggressive. For a split second, he looked like a different person altogether.

Luckily, the dim bulb that resided in Kyle Yeager's brain seemed to flicker on. "Oh. Yeah. Later. Right. No worries."

Ceekay's expression softened as he hiked his thumb in the direction of the kitchen.

After Kyle left, Ceekay looked at me and shrugged. "I'm sorry," he said.

I wasn't sure if he was apologizing for almost whaling on poor Kyle, or for not telling me who he really was.

"I should have told you sooner," he continued. "But when I met you and you obviously didn't know who I was, it was sort of cool. You know, to just be..."

"Chris?"

"Yeah, just Chris. I like that guy, Chris."

I liked him, too. It was Ceekay I wasn't so sure of.

"Well, what are you thinking?" he asked, after a moment of tense silence.

What could I say? *Hey there, super surfer. I'm a bashful loser who's never been on a date before. I've worn a dress, like, twice before, and one of those times was to my great-aunt's funeral so it doesn't even count. I make weird drawings and have only one friend. I was nervous enough before about this date and now I think I might faint.* I swallowed and took a deep breath.

"Okay. It was a big deal to come here with you. And now I learn you're a celebrity. From someone else, I might add."

"Just forget all that celebrity BS," he said. "I'm still the same guy."

"You probably have groupies. Girls swarming all over you."

"Not exactly."

"But some. Right?"

"Some girls like to hang out." He was fiddling with his earring. "That doesn't mean anything happens."

I didn't know what else to say. I had begun feeling comfortable with Chris and now Shy-Person-Type-B-ness was threatening to come back with a vengeance.

"I swear I'm not some asshole surf jerk," he said. "I've got more going on than that." Chris's hand rested near the breadbasket. It was shaking, in a nervous, vulnerable way; the way my hand shook sometimes. Maybe he did have more going on than that.

"Okay. Maybe you're not some asshole surf jerk," I mumbled.

We sat in silence for a moment and then he spoke. "Can we start over?"

"I guess." I reached for a dinner roll. It was still warm. Maybe I had an appetite. Just maybe.

"Okay. So, what do you want to talk about?" he asked.

I didn't really know what I wanted to talk about, but I did know I no longer wanted to talk about myself or surfing. I took a bite of bread. It might be a good time for my tidbit. "So, wanna know what locals say about that house you're staying at?"

"Sure," he nodded.

"Well…um…one story is that it isn't really owned by Ms. Ramelle. That it really belongs to some Colombian drug lord who stashes major shipments of weed in it." There. I got it out. Easy, if not breezy.

Chris shook his head. "No weed. I would know."

"Okay, then… This one's my favorite. A coven of witches—hundreds of years old—that live in the house and only come out at night."

"I think I would have heard them by now."

"Dead bodies?" I squeaked. "Buried in the basement?"

"Okay, that one creeps me out. I'm sleeping in the basement."

"Sorry. It's just, you know, a local rumor."

Chris laughed. He grabbed a roll of his own and took a big bite. His hand was still shaking a little but I could tell we were back on track.

Look at me, I thought. *I'm actually having fun. Having fun with a guy. A guy who's a world-famous surfer. But I'm not supposed to think about that part.*

Sam came with the calamari. While we dug in, I asked, "So besides surfing, are you into anything else?"

"Well, I'm totally into music," Chris replied, popping a crusty calamari ring into his mouth.

"What kind of music?"

"Classical, mostly," he acknowledged, a little self-consciously.

"Classical? You?"

"Yeah, me," he replied with a slight wince. "Why is that so hard to believe?"

"Sorry. You just don't look like the kind of person who listens to classical music, that's all."

"Well, I am. Classical music reminds me of nature, the ocean in particular. Take Wagner's *Ring Cycle*; totally reminds me of a hurricane swell with all that clash and clamor. All that danger and anticipation. And then there's melancholy music that reminds me of gray, murky water. The calm before the storm. It's also like the stuff people feel, but don't express. The deep, dark secrets we hide from each other. Schubert's *Sonnambula* is one of my favorites. And then Beethoven—that dude's string quartets slay me."

"Sounds like you know a lot about it. The music, I mean."

Chris shrugged. "I guess. I used to be into other kinds of music. I was in a rock band when I was younger, but it kind of went bad and soured me on the whole scene." His expression got dark for a moment and then he looked up, back to bright. "Besides, what does someone who's into classical music look like?"

I thought for a minute. "You got me. I don't have a clue."

"And so what about you? Any other hidden talents, besides that smoking take-off and world class bottom turn?"

Am I ready to tell Chris about my Wavehouses? Not just my stupid stories about the movie star's house, but my own wacky, watery homes? I took the last rubber band of calamari and dipped. "Not really," I said. "But, it's cool that you're into classical music. Really, I totally get it."

The calamari basket was swept away by Kyle, as Sam delivered the entrees. Between bites, I gabbed for fifteen minutes straight about Myra, about Gramma and Grandpa, and The Shell Shop. I avoided talking too much about Sara, and the Wavehouses were completely locked away.

"What's the deal with your family?" I asked. "Where are they while you're traveling the world?"

Chris dropped his eyes to his nearly empty plate. "Oh, they're all back in Kauai. Scattered around the island. At least, last time I checked."

Then, Chris looked up, his eyes bright. "Hey, why are surfers generally more cheerful and relaxed than other people?"

"I don't know," I said.

Chris smiled. "Because they're the only grownups who get to pee in their clothes on a regular basis."

"That is the lamest joke I've ever heard," I giggled.

"Yeah, it may be but you're laughing."

As the evening wore on, we talked about less personal stuff—more jokes from him, local lore from me (jokes were not my *forte*), some tour-related gossip from him. It got easier to ignore all the people staring at us. Clarissa went up in my book when I saw her stop slobbering surf fans from storming our table, napkins and pens at the ready for a Ceekay autograph. To surf-ignorant Sam, we were just a couple of relatively well-behaved kids. By the time we finished our entrees, I had almost forgotten that Chris was anybody other than Chris—a funny, sweet guy who seemed to like me, maybe, as much as I was starting to like him.

And then the fun ended. Not because of the adoring crowds, or a Kyle *faux pas*, or a Clarissa oversight. No, the fun ended because of my mother, as usual—Sara Dugan, my own personal party-pooper. Always there to burst my bubble, take the wind out of my sails, gum up my works, put a wrench in my wheel, wreak all-around havoc, disaster, and doom.

Okay. Blaming Sara isn't *entirely* fair. She wasn't directly pooping on any parties. What messed me up was glancing over toward the bar and seeing Rusty with his arm draped around a blonde with major curves. Rusty leaned toward her, whispering in her ear. Whatever he said must've been totally hilarious because the blonde laughed hysterically, before giving Rusty a big, fat smooch. I swear I heard her lips smack from across the restaurant. *Some business client*, I thought. "Two-timing turd," I muttered.

"Excuse me?" Chris said, startled.

I looked back at him. "I wasn't talking about you."

"But I'm the only one sitting here."

"Sorry. No. He's over there." I tipped my head towards the bar. "Someone evil." Rusty and the blonde were snuggling on barstools with their foreheads together. They couldn't get cozier.

Chris peered through our fishing net privacy screen. "Shit. Is that guy with the blonde woman your two-timer?"

"Not mine. Someone else's." I didn't want to say "my mother's." Telling the truth was too painful; although Sara was undoubtedly immature and maternally challenged she was still my mom. I wanted to protect her and kill her at the same time.

Chris looked at me seriously. "I think we should leave."

I turned back to my half-eaten salmon and forced myself to shovel in a few more bites. My eyes were glued to my plate but I could sense Chris wasn't eating. I glanced up at him. "It's okay," I lied. "I'm fine."

"No, it's not okay," Chris shook his head. "Hey, dude," he called Kyle over.

Kyle scampered eagerly over. "Yeah, Ceekay? What can I do for you?"

"Is there a back way out of here?"

"Really, Kyle," I said, "it's not necessary."

But Kyle only had ears for Chris. "Sure, man. Through the kitchen."

At the bar, Rusty and the blonde were now full-on making out. No coming up for air. In another minute he might have his hand up her shirt.

"Unbelievable," I said, shaking my head in disgust.

"That's it." Chris stood. "Come on, we're going." He grabbed my hand and together we followed Kyle through the double doors, dashing past a kitchen crew—who were so busy frying, stirring, dicing, and slicing that they barely noticed us. Kyle pushed open the rear exit for us.

"Thanks, dude," said Chris. "You rock."

"Anytime," sighed starstruck Kyle. "Oh Anna. So tell me, everyone's dying to know, are you or are you not the awesome *Surfing Siren*?"

I froze.

"What's the surfing siren?" Chris asked me.

"It's nothing. Come on, let's go already." I pushed past him and out the door.

Chris and I might have escaped an awkward encounter with Rusty Meyers, but the price of freedom landed us in a back alley next to the Brinestellar's dumpster.

"Well, this is lovely," I said. "*Eau de* rotten fish."

"I still owe you dessert, you know," Chris said. He gave my hand a slight squeeze, and it struck me—I hadn't held hands with a male person since Gramma and Grandpa had taken me to Disney World when I was seven and Grandpa wouldn't let go of my hand for the entire day.

"How about we get some now?" I said.

Chapter Eighteen

We walked down Main Street to The Seaside Ice Cream Parlor, where customers were offered twenty homemade flavors, each with a beachy cornball name. I ordered "Coral Reef Chocolate Chip," and Chris went for the "Sea Foam Strawberry." We took our ice cream cones down to the beach and ate as we walked along the shoreline.

I was having a really good time. Chris was funny and smart. He asked more questions but didn't push. Silent pauses were okay, for both of us.

"You may find this hard to believe," I said. "But I'm, like, pathologically shy."

"Really?"

"I used to be a lot worse. Now, I'm fine around family and all the people I've known growing up. And I can handle customers at the store, if I have to; though I prefer not to. I'm more of a back-room sort of girl."

"You seem fine around me," Chris smiled.

"Yeah, well, it took some work, believe me. Performing, though, is impossible. Even on a surfboard. It's torture."

"That sucks," he said.

"I'm just so not the surf tour type," I sighed. "Don't take this the wrong way but besides my performance anxiety, I'm just not interested in all the hype. Other surfers know the names, the places. They read all the magazines. When I watch surf movies of professional competitions, I get nauseous."

He was quiet.

"And now you tell me I wouldn't even get paid as much as a bunch of brainless guys? I mean, why would I even bother? For fame? Free travel? A few surfboards? That's so totally not my thing."

"Some of us need the money," Chris shrugged. "Those of us who come from nothing."

"I'm sorry," I said. "I'm being an asshole. I can get way too critical."

"That's okay," he said. "So, what was the deal with that guy at the bar? If it wasn't you he was stepping out on, who was it?"

"It's my mother he's two-timing. They've been hooking up for the last week or so. And Sara's sort of dramatic, so I'm worried she will blow some major fuses over this one."

"I know all about dramatic mothers," he looked at his feet.

I waited for him to say more. Give advice—something. But he didn't. Finally, I spoke. "Rusty Meyers. What a sleaze bucket."

"Well, he sure seems to be." It was dark so I couldn't see his expression clearly, but something seemed off. *I screwed up*, I thought, *and now he thinks I'm an emotional basket case daughter of a skanky mom. Plus, I probably hurt his feelings when I was mouthing off about 'brainless' surfers.*

"You must think I'm some kind of reverse-snob bitch when it comes to surfing," I sighed.

"No, not at all. I was just thinking of something else. I was off in la-la land for a minute. But I'm back."

Wherever he had been in that rapid-fire mood shift, he was again back at the beach with me and his rapidly melting Sea Foam Strawberry cone. The way he looked at me told me so; that, and the way his non-cone-holding hand let go of mine so he could put his entire arm around me. That was it, I decided. No more discussing my neurotic professional surf aversion or my mother for the rest of the evening.

Myra opened her front door before I even had a chance to knock. "So?" she asked loudly.

"Can I at least get inside?" I whispered, looking back at the empty street. Five minutes and ten seconds earlier Chris had been there. 12:35 a.m. on the corner of Fairview and Emerson. I mentally marked the time and spot where we had kissed goodnight.

"Yes, m'lady." Myra stepped aside, sweeping a deep bow.

"Very funny," I said, poking her in the ribs as I passed. In the living room, I collapsed on the Berkowitzes' mammoth pillowfest of a couch. My butt hit something hard, and I reached behind and picked up two books, *Study Abroad: Paris* and *The Sorbonne: An American's Perspective.*

"What are these?" I asked.

Myra plopped down next to me and offered me her Cookies n' Cream container, which still had a few slurp-able spoonfuls left.

"Don't try and distract with ice cream. That's not fair."

Myra shrugged. "If I do have to move to Paris, I should be prepared."

"Do you want to go?"

"No. I don't think so…"

"*I don't think so?* You don't sound very convincing, Myra."

"Come on, Anna, you know me. I'm an information junkie. My parents could be moving to Cleveland and I'd read books about that not-terribly-exciting city."

"I guess," I sighed. "Just promise you'll keep me in the loop, okay?"

"I swear on this stack of potentially irrelevant Parisian guidebooks," Myra proclaimed with mock grandiosity. "So, some ice cream for your thoughts?"

I shook my head and gently pushed the ice cream away. "No thanks. Already had some." It was probably the first time I had ever said no to more ice cream. I looked down at the slip of paper Chris had given me with his cell phone number and a sweet little note:

For Anna,
The most beautiful girl in the world.
I am so glad our surfboards collided.
Keep this number safe. 917.555.9531
XXXXX-Chris

What a night of firsts! A date, a kiss, a love note, and no appetite for Cookies n' Cream. A day for the history books.

Myra stared at me as if I were a frog she was eager to dissect for extra credit in bio. "Please," she pleaded. "This is painful. Put me out of my misery. Speak!"

"Um…" I stared up at the ceiling. "I had the salmon. It was

delicious. It was covered with crumbly stuff and—"

Myra swatted my arm. "Big whoop. No more food facts, please. Human details only. Date details."

"Clarissa Morrison was wearing a dress that I swear she will have to cut herself out of when she gets home."

"Anna. I couldn't care less about Clarissa's dress. Boy details, *please*."

"Okay, okay…he's famous."

"Yeah, right."

"No. Seriously. He is. He's a professional surfer. His real name is Christopher Kahimbe but he's known as Ceekay."

Myra eyes widened. "No joke?"

"No joke."

"*The* Ceekay? The surfer? With the wild blond, sexy hair? The one from Hawaii who does the deodorant commercial on TV?"

"Deodorant?"

Myra nodded. "It's actually a very tasteful ad. Ceekay's first personal hygiene product endorsement. Filmed in Fiji, I think. Artistic. Sort of film noir…or surf noir, I guess."

"How is it that you know more about Ceekay than me?"

"I watch more TV than you."

"True." Myra had a real appetite for pop culture. "And I have been known to peruse certain youth-oriented websites to keep abreast of the inane trends and vapid celebs our fellow teenagers follow."

I was quiet. The idea that I had just kissed someone who did TV commercials—for deodorant no less—was bugging me out.

But Myra was chatty as ever. "Which is why I also know who your dreamboat used to date."

"He's not my dreamboat. He's my, my…I don't know what he is. Well, who did he use to date?"

"Inga Ward."

"Who the frig is Inga Ward?"

"Hello? Who's Inga Ward? Geez, Anna, sometimes you're the most clueless person n the universe."

I stared Myra down as if I was the school principal, and she, a juvenile delinquent sent to my office on a regular basis. "Inga Ward. Details. *Now!*"

"Okay, okay," Myra rolled her eyes. "Inga Ward is an actress who won almost every single film award last year for her role in *Hop, Jump, and Skip*. She played Candace, a white-trash kid from the South who cons her way into Harvard without ever having graduated high school."

"You're kidding."

"I kid you not. It gets worse. Or better, depending on your perspective. You want more?"

I nodded, but my stomach felt queasy.

"Before acting, she modeled. She was, like, every major designer's muse. She's older than us, but not much. Home schooled. And really smart. I just read at yewawtono.com she's deferring enrollment to Yale, where she got early admission, so she can do a film in Tibet with Jess McMaster."

"Jess McMaster?"

"The next Leonardo DiCaprio."

I groaned.

"Personally, it's the Yale thing that gets under *my* skin," Myra continued. "I'll give Inga her natural beauty and talent. But brains, too? I mean, *hello*? That's just depressing."

I grabbed a pillow from the corner of the couch and covered my face. "So what's Chris doing with me?" I mumbled into the fabric.

"First of all, I think Ceekay and Inga are history." Myra tossed their names around as if she had known them for years. "I mean, they've been back and forth for a really long time. But now rumor has it that Inga's on to some other hottie."

"Rumors aren't truth, Myra," I sighed. "What if he's still with her?"

Myra frowned. "I seriously doubt it. I saw tons of photos of her on a yacht off the Riviera with an English lord who plays polo."

"Where did you see these photos?"

"In the totally reliable *People Magazine*."

I looked at her doubtfully.

"Anna, it's the most respected tabloid around."

"For now I'll pray you're right." I peered over the pillow at Myra. "You said 'first of all.' So what's the second reason Chris is with *me*?"

Myra grabbed the pillow out of my hand and tossed it across the room. It hit a stone Buddha, which wobbled then steadied, smiling its impenetrable, sturdy Buddha smile. "Secondly," Myra proclaimed, "you are infinitely likable, smart, cute, and all sorts of other things. Plus, you and Ceekay have the whole surf connection going. And I think surfing is one thing Inga *doesn't* do. So don't be such an insecure weenie."

"Easier said than done." I sat upright, grabbed the Cookies n' Cream, now completely liquid, and slurped it in one big gulp.

"So now give me the blow-by-blow of the date. Without food facts."

I told Myra pretty much everything. How the date began; the stuff he told me, and the stuff I told him; how we bolted through the Brinestellar's kitchen like a couple of secret agents; how we discovered we could both wiggle our ears and touch our noses with the tips of our tongues; how I thought the date was over when I brought up the pro surf stuff, but how Chris put us back on track; how we had agreed to surf together at Secretspot for the next few days until he had to leave to do a promotional event in Manhattan. And, then there was the kiss. My first ever. Right there on Myra's corner. The kiss that washed away any lingering doubts I had as to whether it was a real date or not. After the kiss, I knew; this zany, wonderful night had been the real deal.

I hadn't known what kissing was supposed to be like, where lips and tongues were supposed to land, if eyes were supposed to remain open or closed, or where you put your hands. All I knew was that I liked what had happened at the corner of Fairview and Emerson. The secret crushes I had had on guys before had caused minor tingles and tame fantasies in my body and mind. The kiss with Chris was something else—it left me jazzed up and jittery. Not that it had started out all that smoothly. When I realized he was about to kiss me, I puckered my lips the way I did when I kissed

Grandpa's forehead. I must've looked like a blowfish. Then Chris's warm, smooth mouth met my own and I realized I was supposed to relax my lips, so I went all slack, like a dead flounder. Chris's lips felt like pillows, pressing tentatively at first, and then with more urgency.

Just relax, I told myself, *and do what he does.* Finally, I found my kissing stride. Like a swell gathering momentum, my lips parted and soon we were riding the kissing wave full on, both our tongues doing a crazy dance around each other, our bodies pressed together, our arms like thick ropes keeping us entwined.

Myra, of course, wanted all sorts of details about the kiss. Usually I could tell Myra everything, but I couldn't tell her about the kiss. I wanted to keep the actual mechanics all to myself. Plus, at some point Myra would have her own first kiss and whenever that happened, I wanted it to be without expectation or comparison—as new and fresh as a first real kiss could possibly be. So I told her the bad news: there would be no kiss news.

"You suck," she said without any real malice.

"I know. But you'll get over it."

Myra shifted her seat, assuming a faux casual position. "So, has he changed your mind at least a teensy tiny bit?"

"Changed my mind about what?"

"About the whole professional surf thing. I mean, if he's such a nice guy maybe that's a good sign. Maybe it means there are other nice people in the professional surf world."

"He's probably the exception to the rule."

Myra blew a puff of frustrated air. "I don't know, Anna," she shook her head. "Not to get all psycho-babbly or anything, but you really need to sort out your issues on this professional career stuff."

"Issues?"

"You've got to get over this. I mean, look at you!"

I looked at me. My body had gone from a comfortable couch sprawl to a tense, tight ball. My arms locked around my knees, bound tight like the straps of a medieval torture device.

"Studies show that one of the best ways to get over performance anxiety is to do the thing you're most anxious about over and over again until it's a no-brainer."

"Yeah, right," I said.

"Like surfing in front of an audience, competing, winning money," Myra persisted.

"Not happening. Sorry. We need to talk about something else that's freaking me out. My mother. Remember Rusty Meyers?"

"The advertising guy. Huge, potentially compensating Yupmobile. What about him?"

"He has just gone from sleazy to total slime." I told her about Rusty and the blonde, and their Siamese twin, lip-locking behavior at Brinestellar's Bar. "We were sitting off in a corner so he didn't see me," I said. "So here's the dilemma: do I tell Sara, or what?"

Myra frowned. "If it were anyone else besides your mother I would say tell. But Sara is so, um, unpredictable."

"Exactly. I'm really scared she'll do something embarrassing. Go banging on doors in the middle of the night. Screaming bloody murder in the center of town. Throw things. None of those would be firsts. I hate it when she makes a fool of herself. Why does she always spoil things even when she doesn't know she's spoiling things?"

"Because that's what our mothers do. Both of them. One way or the other, even when they don't mean to, they spoil things."

I had lost count of the many times Sara had unintentionally made my life worse. There was the time she volunteered to work at the fourth grade bake sale, and proceeded to donate a case of beer. When the principal told her that alcohol couldn't be sold at a school event, Sara shrugged and said, "That's lame. It's made with yeast." Or the time she chaperoned the sixth-grade Halloween Hop and came dressed—or rather un-dressed—in a form-fitting nude bodysuit and a pink beret, and kept yelling, "No, I'm not a penis. I'm a manicured finger, for Christ's sake!" I cringed in the corner while everyone, kids and grown-ups alike, stared at her and snickered.

But other times Sara had been my savior. Once as I was building an elaborate sandcastle, a bunch of older boys came over and destroyed it. Sara raced over and chased them away, yelling that they were "little shits who deserved to rot in hell." Okay, so maybe that wasn't the way to talk to eight-year-old boys, but it was the gesture that counted. Or the time I had been assigned to play an elf in the Kendall's Watch Elementary School Holiday Pageant; I was so freaked out that Sara marched me into the principal's office, pointed to my quaking little-kid body, and said, "See? See what you're doing to her? I will sue your ass if you make her appear in your silly show." Again, not the most polite way to get things done, but thanks to Sara I got to hand out programs instead.

Myra got off the couch. "Don't stress about Sara now. You'll figure something out. I'm going to bed. And I think you should, too. Sleep on it." Myra seized my arms and pulled me off the couch. I was all limbs and loose joints without muscles. I hadn't realized how tired I was. I let Myra drag me down the hall and up the stairs to her room. The air mattress was already inflated, with sheets and blankets arranged; Myra had even turned the covers down and placed a stuffed bunny on the pillow.

"You are the hostess with the mostest." I hugged her, then lay down on my perfect guest bed. "Have I mentioned that if you move to Paris, I'll kill you?" I mumbled.

"Numerous times. But, please don't. Like they say in 'Bye-Bye-Birdie,' I've got a lot of living to do."

"Yeah, yeah..." I didn't even take my dress off. Sleep came on like a Mack truck. No worries—at least till morning.

Chapter Nineteen

I left Myra's at 6 a.m. in a foggy, groggy stupor, fueled by jitters of excitement and panic. I was meeting Chris for an early morning surf session that could be disastrous or blissful, now that I knew who he was, now that we had kissed. I had to find out for sure what the deal was with Inga Ward.

When I got to Secretspot, I found him on the beach, waxing his board in neat little circles. The muscles in his back undulated like sheaths of wheat and I could've stood there for hours, just staring at him from behind.

"Hey, Belly Flop." He turned and saw me staring, mouth agape. "You okay?"

Closing my mouth, I said weakly, "I'm fine. You?"

He looked at me with a sparkle in his eye and that snaggle-toothed smile. "I'm just hunky dory."

"I've always wondered," I said, too loudly. "What or who is 'hunky dory' anyway?"

"I don't know. Is it like a buff boat, or a chick named Dory who's built like a dude?"

I laughed, but it was forced. My anxiety was starting to get the best of me. *I have to ask him about Inga*, I thought.

He stood up and I almost fainted. I hadn't yet been on land with a basically naked Chris. In the water, moving around was one thing; dressed up for a dinner date was another. This was something else entirely. He walked over to me and grasped my shoulders gently. "You're shaking. Are you cold?"

"Something like that," I gasped.

"Well, then…" His arms slipped down my arms and made their way around my waist. *Oh my god. He's gonna kiss me again.*

I pushed away from him and blurted, "Are you still with her?"

He looked confused. "With who?"

"Inga Ward."

"Who told you that?"

"No one. Besides, why would it matter who?"

A dark cloud passed over his face. "Listen," he said, as he grasped my shoulders a bit too tightly. "Inga and I are history. You have to believe me. We haven't been together for six months."

"Okay, okay," I said. "I believe you. So chill with the Iron Man routine, please."

Chris looked at his hands and instantly softened his grip. "I'm so sorry. Did I hurt you?"

"No, not really," I said.

"Sometimes I get a bit carried away." His hands stroked my arms, then pulled me into a hug, warm and welcoming. "But I'm working on it."

"I'm kinda nervous," I murmured into the center of his smooth, warm, and wicked hard chest.

"Me too," he said.

I popped my head up to look at him. "Really?"

He nodded. "Scared shitless."

"Good," I said. "That makes me feel better."

I tucked my head down into the warmth of his chest, and let my arms find their way around his waist. Chris smelled like almonds and seaweed. We stood there for a moment longer, my shivers melting, our breathing in sync. "Let's just surf," he said. And so we did.

We paddled out side by side, which was totally strange for me—I had never paddled out, on purpose, companionably, with anyone before. The waves were sizable, but breaking unpredictably across the front of our boards like a choppy meringue.

"Is that as fast as you can go?" he grinned. "I mean, really. You are the lamest paddler I've ever met."

"Oh yeah?" I said, pouring on some extra steam. "I'll race you through this slop to the outside."

"You're on," he panted.

"I'll bet you don't make it," I called over my shoulder as I sped forward. "You'll be lucky not to have one of these rogue suckers crash on your beautiful head."

I made it with yards to spare.

Chris, arriving next to me a moment later, moaned, "Ouch! My lungs are about to explode."

I mussed his curly head—my first spontaneous gesture of affection. "Sorry."

"Yeah, right," he chuckled. "You're a paddling hell-raiser."

Chris took the first wave and rode it like a wild man genius. Not many surfers could've done what he did on such an unforgiving mess of a wave. I waited for the third wave of the set, hoping it wouldn't be quite so testy a beast. I managed to stay on and carve a few times before my wave decided to wall up and spit me out.

The following hour of surfing was the most fun I had ever had in the water, which had me wondering about all my years of self-imposed exile. Despite this twinge of regret, I still couldn't imagine surfing with anyone other than Chris.

There were a series of not-quite-as-fabulous-as-expected waves, not-being-in-exactly-the-right-spot-but-okay-you-made-it-so-stop-whining waves, time-to-bail waves, and a bunch of should-I-shouldn't-I-oops-too-late waves. One wave threw me for a major loop. I took off on it, feeling all cocky and cool, but before I knew it the sucker walled up, closed out, and sent me careening over the falls. I tumbled like a lost sock in a dryer, but fortunately my churn-fest only lasted a few seconds, and I emerged with both head and board attached and intact.

Chris had his own share of close calls and dork moves, and I think in the end, we laughed more than we surfed. I wished that it didn't ever have to end, but I had to get to work.

"I gotta go," I sighed. "The next one is my ride in."

Chris paddled up next to me and jumped off his board.

"What are you doing—" I started but couldn't finish because he came up and tipped me over.

"Now I'm the one who's cold," he said, sculling water next to me.

What happened next would've been beyond my comprehension twenty-four hours before—we made out in the ocean; above and below the waves. When we finally came up for air, Chris said one word: "Wow."

"I hope that was okay?" I garbled.

"Are you joking? That was more than okay." He leaned in for more. This time his hands traveled. Nothing too advanced. No private parts explored. But I wasn't sure I was ready for where this would take us next.

I had to get going before I did something I regretted. "Bye." Climbing back on my board, I started paddling away.

"Wait! When am I gonna see you again?" Chris called.

"When do you want to see me again?" I hollered back.

"As soon as possible?"

"Tonight?"

"Where?"

I wasn't sure how much public exposure I could tolerate. Brine-stellar's had been quite a challenge. And even though being alone with him might lead to places I wasn't sure I was quite ready to go, it still felt like the safer option. "Here. We can hang on the beach. I have to stay at work till nine. How about nine-thirty?"

He smiled. "That sounds perfect. And you—you're perfect, too."

Oh my god, I thought. *He really likes me.* "Look who's talking. Right back at ya." I gave him a thumbs-up and instantly regretted the nerdy gesture. Inga Ward probably would've done something sexier—at the very least, blown him a kiss.

Chapter Twenty

As a little kid, I loved going grocery shopping with my grandmother. Buying food with Gramma was like being on a slow but fun train ride. I got to sit in the kiddie seat up front as she strolled up and down the aisles, examining prices and asking my opinion.

"What do you think, Anna Marie? Should we get the Green Giant peas or the Shop-rite brand?"

The answer was obvious. "The Giant, of course!"

Food was much more fun when it had a fictional buddy smiling at you from the label, so my choices had more to do with the character than the price. The Giant, the Chicken of the Sea Mermaid, Uncle Ben, Aunt Jemima, Little Debbie. Even if it was going to cost her more, Gramma always got me what I wanted.

Shopping with Sara, on the other hand, was inevitably a harried, last-minute ordeal. She could never plan ahead so we were always buying for that day, or maybe the next. She'd grab a handbasket and expect me to scurry along behind as she pulled things off the shelves without checking prices.

One afternoon, when I was about four, Gramma and I had been wheeling a cart full of supplies through the parking lot to the station wagon, when I saw Matt, the guy my mother had been dating that summer. I had liked Matt. He'd stuck around longer than some of the others; he'd even helped me learn to surf, holding my board steady as he pushed me onto super small waves, cheering when I stood up with my legs wide and my arms out like propellers.

"Hey Gramma," I'd cried. "There's Matt!"

Matt was emerging from behind the dumpster, zipping up his jeans, a woman behind him buttoning her blouse. I waved and called, while Gramma yanked me out of my seat and plopped me in the back seat of the station wagon.

"That's enough now, Anna Marie. You hush up, you hear?" She'd belted me in, scrambling to get the last bag of groceries out of the cart before shoving it away from the car. Then, gunning the engine, she tore out of the parking lot as if she were an ambulance driver.

When Sara came to pick me up later that day, Gramma told me to stay upstairs while she delivered the bad news to Sara. Hugging Woof Woof to my chest, I listened at the door.

"It probably wasn't him," Sara had said defensively. "Your eyes aren't great, Ma. And Anna's just a kid."

"Oh, it was him all right. They'd been, been…having relations!"

"Gimme a break. You don't know that for sure."

"Fornicating!" Gramma cried.

"Fornicating? What century are you from? Don't be silly, Ma."

"I'm not being silly," Gramma huffed. "And I know more than you give me credit for, young lady."

"I'm sure he's got an explanation." Sara's voice got high-pitched and trembly, which meant she would either break out in sobs or start yelling. Hugging Woof Woof tighter, I wasn't sure which alternative would be worse.

"Don't kid yourself, Sara," Gramma warned. She had only ever used that particular tone of voice with me when I was about to do something dangerous or stupid, like trying to roller skate down the stairs, or stick my finger in a fan to see if I could stop it. I'd never heard her use that tone of voice with Sara.

The front door slammed and I could hear Sara's Jeep speed away.

Now here I was, twelve years later, with a Slimy Rusty situation that was a Dumpster Matt redux. The only difference was that Gramma didn't need to be the bearer of bad news, which was a minor blessing, as I don't know if my frail little grandmother could handle the fallout. The onerous task of telling my poor unsuspecting mother that she'd been betrayed again was mine. Whether I could survive the Sara storm that would follow was another question.

"This is a large. Do you have it in a medium?"

I smiled tightly at the woman as she brandished a Kendall's Watch tee shirt in my face, but I really wanted to punch her. She was a bully and had shoved her way to the front of the queue. *Pushy bitch*, I thought. But I managed to say, "I'm sorry. That's the last one."

Pushy Bitch rolled her eyes, as if I had insulted her, dumped the shirt on top of the counter and walked away. *Darn*, I thought. *We needed that sale*. It took every ounce of retail cool I had to bite my tongue when I really wanted to scream curses at her. This was the fifth time that day that I had been tested by rude or stupid customers. And it wasn't even noon.

My mother, of course, was MIA. I had left Chris and Secretspot to open the shop at nine forty-five, expecting Sara to arrive by ten. Now, she was two hours late. She hadn't answered the home line, and voicemail picked up immediately when I tried her cell.

As flaky as my mother could be, she never, *ever* bailed on the shop. Had she found out about Rusty's blonde? Gone down to Easton and made a scene? Found them in Rusty's hideaway, going at it on 500 thread count sheets, then wandered off in a drunken, heartbroken stupor to who knew where? Managing a busy morning at The Shell Shop on my own was challenge enough, but imagining my mother dead in a ditch somewhere made me want to jump out of my skin. I considered calling my grandparents, but they would only panic and call Joe Logan, Chief of Police, and Gramma's second cousin. Joe and his half-baked police squad usually had nothing better to do than write parking tickets or break up bar fights. I imagined them—all excited by the prospect of an actual missing person—driving with sirens blasting, interrogating every person and pet dog within a ten-mile radius.

At quarter past twelve, I was helping an indecisive woman choose from a variety of equally unflattering sun hats when Sara waltzed in, smiling and laughing, easy breezy. And who should waltz in right beside her? Rusty slime-bucket, two-timing, how-dare-you-show-your-face Meyers.

"Hey babe," Sara said as she gave the shop a quick once over. "Looks like the troops have been through. Busy morning?" She bent down to pick up a discarded sarong.

I was speechless. Both Sara and Rusty looked squeaky clean, like they had just stepped out of the shower—wild sex clean-up, no doubt. I shot an evil dart glare right between Rusty's bushy eyebrows. I wanted to shout, "Where's your blonde friend?" but I restrained myself. No scenes in the shop—bad for business. Instead, I turned to Sara: "Where the hell have you been?" I demanded.

"Didn't you see the note?" she asked.

"What note?"

Sara pulled a piece of paper from where it had been tacked, to the left of the light switch. "This note." She read it out loud: "'I'm going down to Easton for brunch. I'll be back by noon.'"

I imagined her and Rusty sitting at some overpriced restaurant sipping mimosas and playing post-coital footsie under the table. "I never look at the light switch when I open the shop. I always just reach sideways and flick it on."

"Well, how am I supposed to know that?" Sara asked, defensively.

"You could have called."

"No, I couldn't."

Rusty cleared his throat and said, "Hey, guys. What's done is done. No worries, right?"

Sara smiled at Rusty and patted his arm. "No worries." She turned to me and her smile took on a saccharine sheen. "Right, Anna?"

"Whatever." I turned to re-fold a stack of folded beach towels.

"Anna," said Sara. "You look beat. Why don't you grab some lunch?"

"Hey, my treat," offered Rusty. "Whatever you want, it's on me."

Rusty was quickly becoming the sixth person I wanted to punch that morning. "No thanks. I'm not hungry," I said tightly.

"Well, maybe some other time," Rusty said brightly. "Nice to see you anyway, Anna. Maybe I'll get to watch you in the water sometime soon. Sounds like the surf's gonna pick up in the next few days. At least that's what your mom tells me."

Fold, fold, re-fold. That was all he got from me.

I heard a bit of whispering and shuffling, then, "See you, Sare." *Sare*, not Sara. One syllable. Shortened. Rusty's special pet name for my mother. The Shell Bell jingled as he yanked the door closed. *Sare* walked past me to the storeroom without saying a word, nasty or otherwise. I wondered what the hell they had whispered about.

Chapter Twenty-One

The post-lunch crowd began to descend at 1 p.m. The shop filled with whiny kids drawn to the most breakable and expensive Shellys. I wanted to tell everyone to go back to their hotel rooms, turn on their AC's and take nice, long family naps. I was fried and starving, and felt now that it had been stupid not to have taken Sara's offer of a lunch break. Now a break was impossible because Shellys, towels, and sweatshirts were flying off the shelves. We were raking it in—it seemed like people couldn't buy enough. With Sara manning the over-active cash register, I had to pick up discarded sunglasses, re-fold towels, re-stack flip-flops in size order and, most importantly, catch kid-handled Shellys before they crashed to the floor.

At two, Myra arrived—or at least it looked vaguely like Myra.

"Um…hi," I said slowly. "What exactly are you wearing?"

It wasn't that Myra was wearing anything particularly outlandish, but her outfit, which was so normal for Kendall's Watch, was so abnormal for Myra. Instead of her usual flouncy skirt and pedal pushers, Myra now boasted a pair of super tiny, tight red board shorts. Gone were the quasi-old lady orthopedic sandals with the bows that she loved to wear in summer, and instead she wore a pair of flip-flops—footwear she was continually telling me led to fallen arches and back problems. It was her tee shirt, however, that really caught my eye—a cropped pink number featuring a goofy cartoon surfer on the front with a word bubble coming out of his mouth that said, "Surf's up, Dude!"

Myra frowned. "I thought I would try and tone it down for our talk with Jimmy." There was something odd about the way she was standing—all tight, with shoulders hunched and knees locked. "Dress like the natives."

"But you look so, um, uncomfortable." *And totally doofus-y*, I wanted to say, but didn't.

133

"You're right," she sighed. "These stupid shorts are about to cut off my circulation."

"It's just so totally not you."

"What do you mean?" Myra asked, tugging at the bottom of her tee shirt.

"You look better in your own clothes," I said. "Myra-type clothes."

"Argh. What was I thinking?" she cried. "I'm gonna go home right now and forget the whole thing."

"Well, let's not forget the whole thing; let's just postpone it, okay? Besides, it's a madhouse in here and I probably shouldn't leave, even just to go across the street."

"Okay. Tomorrow then?"

Word on the street must have been that we were giving stuff away for free—the shop was so packed. "I might be stuck here if it's like this tomorrow. Can we play it by ear?"

"Sure," Myra said brightly, the tiny furrow in her brow betraying her disappointment.

"I'll really try. I promise. I'll call you either way. Just don't come dressed like that."

"Don't worry," Myra sighed. "Momentary insanity. Won't happen again. See you later."

"Yeah, see you later. And Myra, that comb you have stuck in your hair?"

"What about it?"

"It's a comb for scraping old, dirty surf wax off a surfboard. It's not a hair ornament."

Rusty, surfing, late-night dates, crazy best friends—none of it could matter in frantic Shell-Shop times like these. It was all business and no pleasure. Thankfully, Sara had a bag of pretzels and a few granola bars stashed under the cash register. When I wasn't on Shelly rescue alert, I rolled my eyes at Sara in a they're-driving-me-loco kind of way; she nodded back and snuck her finger up to her temple, miming a shot through the skull. In this way we connected, acknowledging our love-hate relationship with the summer crowd. It was not as if a busy store made everything okay between us, but somehow our other problems took time off while we made sale after sale, and answered stupid question after stupid question. In times like these we were united, and I loved the feeling. I dreaded telling her about Rusty. I figured it would be best to wait until after closing, after adding up the sales of this *ca-chink ca-chink* day. Hopefully making megabucks would soften the blow of bad news. Fingers crossed.

At four the phone rang. Sara picked it up. "Dugan's Shell Shop. How can we help you?" Sara chirped.

I was barely paying attention, focused instead on untangling a mess of slipper shell necklaces. But when Sara's tone of voice suddenly changed, I stopped and listened.

"No way…this never would've happened with our old guys… this is totally unacceptable." Her tone was no longer bird-like, it was strident and bossy. "I'll be there tomorrow night… You bet you'll pay for this. You owe me big time."

Sara hung up the phone, looking angrier than I'd seen her in a long time.

"What's the matter?" I asked.

"Goddamn new manufacturer printed three hundred tee shirts that say, 'Kendall's Witch.' This is what I get for trying to save a buck," she snapped. Then she noticed the quiet, that all customer eyes were upon her, and she changed her tone. "Sorry, everyone. Just a little business snafu."

The customers resumed their browsing.

"So what are you gonna do?" I asked her. With Labor Day around the corner, this was one wicked disaster.

"The only thing to do is to drive down to New Jersey tonight and supervise the re-printing tomorrow myself. Make sure those a-holes get it right this time. I'll haul an initial load of tee shirts back in the Jeep to tide us over. Hopefully, it won't take more than a few days, but with these bozos, who knows? We can't afford to waste any more time."

"No need—"

"—to get my knickers in a twist," she smiled. "Yeah, yeah. I know."

I smiled back. "Well, if anyone can get it done, it's you," I said.

"Damn straight it's me. Go see if Meghan can help you cover

while I'm gone. Tomorrow shouldn't be too busy. But later in the week will be a bitch, once the next crop of vacationers arrive." Sara paced behind the counter. "I can't friggin' believe I'm gonna miss surfing Early's on the big swell. Maybe I'll bring my board with me and stop off in Manasquan on the way to the factory. Surf the inlet with those *Joisey* boys." Her lips curved in a smile. "You remember Joe Pirella, right? Joe lives in Manasquan."

Fireman Joe. Sara's main squeeze the summer after fifth grade. How could I forget? Joe had been a real honest-to-goodness firefighter and a bulldog of a surfer. Joe seemed head over heels for Sara that first week, and great fun with little-kid me. When Sara remarked on how natural and dad-like he was, Fireman Joe would shrug with a goofy "aw shucks" grin.

Thing was, Joe really was a dad. Someone else's dad. Three someone elses', in fact. And someone else's husband, too. We learned this the second week when Joe finally revealed he was married with kids. Wife Beth had kicked him out; they'd been going through a rough patch, so technically he wasn't exactly cheating. But now he and Beth needed to work things out, *blah, blah, blah*. Surprise, surprise. So back to Jersey, bye-bye Joe.

"Joe lives in Manasquan," I repeated. "And so does Beth, and all the Pirella juniors."

"Oh Anna," she sighed. "Don't worry. I'm way over Joe. It would just be a hoot to surf with him again, you know? Like friends. For old times. You know I'm totally into Rusty."

Rusty. I had to tell her. "Sara?"

She looked at me. "What?" Her eyes were wide, she was stressed. The knickers were a tad twisted.

If I told her about Rusty now she would explode; the customers would flee, and it would be as if Godzilla had entered The Shell Shop. "Do you, um, want anything from the bakery? I'm starved. I'm gonna grab a cheese Danish."

"No. I have no appetite whatsoever. And hurry back. I think that brat over there just pulled a bird off the roof of a Shelly and stuck it in his pocket."

Chapter Twenty-Two

I locked the door at nine after the last customer left with enough stuff to open their own Shell Shop Outlet. I was dying to get to Secretspot and Chris, but it had been a crazy day and I wanted a moment with Sara. The strip of printout paper—I couldn't remember it ever having been so long—spewed from the top of the cash register. Sara tore it off and read the final tally. "Oh my god…"

"How much?"

"We took in $1,789.50."

I did some crude calculations in my head. "So we cleared almost a thousand bucks?"

"Right." Sara took the tally ribbon and draped it over my shoulders like a special medal.

"Sweet," I nodded.

"Maybe our luck is changing for the better. In more ways than one." Sara absentmindedly caressed her right ring finger with her left hand. I had been so distracted all day I hadn't even noticed there was an actual ring there. It was brand new, expensive looking, and not from the Dugan Shell Shop jewelry display.

"Nice ring. Where'd you get it?" I asked, already knowing and dreading the answer.

"Rusty bought it for me." Sara held her hand out for my inspection. "Is it beautiful, or what?"

"Um, Sara? I need to tell you something."

"What?"

She looked tired and wired, but happy.

"Are you gonna see Rusty before you leave tonight?"

"No, the only date I have tonight is with the Westbound Long Island Expressway. Hey, speaking of dates, how was your dinner with the weather nerd?"

"Oh fine. He was a nice guy. Went right back to Manhattan on the nine o'clock train."

I couldn't tell Sara about Chris. She would get way too excited, spin all sorts of surf-centric romantic drivel, and take it as a sign that I had changed my mind about the pro stuff. Sara was bound to find out soon enough, since the gossip mill in Kendall's ran twenty-four-seven. "So, um, when will you see Rusty again?"

"Probably not till I get back from Jersey. Why?"

"Just curious." I stalled. Better to wait until she returned with the new improved tee shirts. Then I would tell her about Rusty. Let her fix one problem before hitting her with another. "Sara, you did great today."

She smiled at me. "You too, kid. Hey, you'll be staying at Myra's while I'm gone, right? I want you to have company while I'm away."

If only she knew how much company I had these days. "Yeah. I'll be at Myra's," I smiled. "G'bye Sara. See you when you get back. Hopefully sooner rather than later." I started to leave. Before unlocking the door, I glanced back. Sara leaned over the display case fiddling with her ring, looking exhausted and devastatingly beautiful.

My mother, what a piece of work.

That night, Chris and I spent hours lying together on a blanket on the beach—and not doing much in the way of talking. When we did come up for air, Chris shared more of himself, information that wasn't always easy to hear.

"So you remember while we were eating our ice cream the other night, and I told you that some of us have to surf professionally because of the money?" he asked.

"Yeah."

"Well, for me, surfing has also kept me out of trouble. Big trouble."

"What do you mean?"

"I grew up in a really messed-up family. My mom's sort of a waste case. She means well, but she's been with tons of dudes and had kids with a bunch of them. I have eight half-siblings."

"Wow," I said. At least Sara hadn't been reckless like that after having me. "That's a lot."

"No kidding. And some of my brothers are into seriously bad

shit. Like dealing drugs and stealing. When I was really young, my oldest brother, Max, got me to help him rob a bunch of rich people's summer houses. I was so tiny I could squeeze through security gates and scoot under cameras and stuff. Then, one time, I got caught, and the whole thing exploded. I got sent to a series of foster homes for a while, because the courts thought part of the problem was that my mom wasn't paying close enough attention. Which was kinda true." The dark cloud came back over his face. "That was bad. Like, *really* bad."

I put my hand on his arm. "I'm so sorry."

Chris shrugged. "Yeah, well. Thanks. Anyhow, my mom got a little better at taking care of me. Once I was back living with her, the surf community saved me from spending too much time with the wrong crowd, which in my case, was my own family. Honestly, surfing kept me out of jail. People think surfers are a bunch of losers, but the folks who I hung out with in the waters of Kauai are my heroes and heroines. Those dudes and wahines took me in when my own mother was MIA, or just too drunk to get up off the couch. They kept me from following in my brothers' footsteps. Kept me clean and relatively sober. They steered me in the right direction. I owe them my life."

We were quiet for a while. It was time for me to share something, but I wasn't sure what I was ready to tell. I looked at his face, so open and vulnerable, and imagined him as a little kid who had never been cherished by his family—by the people who were supposed to care the most. I had to offer him something. "You know," I started. "I was conceived in Hawaii."

Chris smiled. "Really?"

"Yeah, I'm the proud product of a one-night stand in Oahu." It felt as if nasty, trapped fumes had just been released from my body and wafted away forever. Maybe sharing wasn't so hard after all, at least with the right person.

"Whoa. Is your dad still there?"

"No one knows where my dad is," I sighed. "It's weird to refer to him as 'Dad.' I don't even know who he really is. He could be dead for all I know."

Chris nodded. "Mine, too. Haven't seen him since I was ten."

"You know what I call my father? Clueless Sperm Donor."

"That's harsh," he giggled. "But also kinda funny."

I smiled. "It's true. He has no idea I exist."

Chris pulled me back down to the blanket. "Okay. Enough talk about deadbeat dads. And for the record, *I'm* very glad you exist."

Things definitely progressed, but only so far. For one, I was totally inexperienced and scared I would make a sexual fool out of myself. Plus, I couldn't stop thinking about Sara and all the guys she'd fallen for, and how her heart had been broken over and over again. I wanted no part of that. Chris was different, or so I thought, but I had no relationships to compare him to. My brief hand-holding stint with Benji Shaw in kindergarten didn't really count. I could feel Chris's goodness in my bones; still, were bones trustworthy sources?

And then, as if Chris were a mind reader, he sat up after one really long and powerful kiss and said, "Hey. We don't have to be in such a rush. We've got time. I'm not going anywhere."

"You're not?" I squeaked. *Didn't all guys end up leaving?*

"I've got that one publicity gig in the city in three days, but after that I plan on sticking around Kendall's Watch for a while."

"Thank you, bones," I murmured, as I leaned my head on his shoulder and stared out at the dark ocean, waiting for the next wave to rally and crash. Good as it all felt now, I couldn't help but feel—in another set of bones—that I was in big trouble.

Was I falling in love? I wasn't sure—I had never been in love before. If Sara was anything to go by, I was genetically predisposed to fall hard and fast. I barely knew Chris, but still I was a goner. Going, going…gone. I couldn't help myself.

I floated through the next two days like a delirious fool. Chris and I surfed together in the mornings, mixing it up with kisses way out in the ocean where no one could see us. Then I went to work in the shop where I was uncharacteristically nice to just about everyone, even Meghan De'Errico, who was a compulsive talker and usually got on my nerves in about ten seconds. It was a good thing she was helping out in the shop, because I was so lovesick that I rang up items incorrectly on the cash register and stocked beach umbrellas in the body lotion section.

I also avoided Myra. But just temporarily. I was relieved to find her asleep when I got back to her house after my nights with Chris. I wasn't sure I was ready to talk to her about all this intimacy stuff. Talking about sex with Myra was easy. We'd done plenty of that. But it felt like a betrayal of Chris to tell her how our two bodies connected, how he was becoming important—maybe too important. Things were shifting faster than I expected. On the third night, I stumbled into Myra's house after yet another romantic evening surf, and found her sitting at the table eating a leftover semi-stale bagel from the most recent Sheila shipment.

"Any more of those around?" I asked. I was starving. Food hadn't even entered my Chris-smitten state of mind.

"Nope. This is the last one," Myra said coldly, as she smeared cream cheese on her sesame. She was pretending to read the *Kendall's Kalendar*—in which there was absolutely nothing of interest for someone like Myra.

"Hey, are you okay? You seem sort of out of it."

"I'm fine." She didn't look up.

I grabbed the newspaper out of her hands.

"Hey! I was reading that!"

"No you weren't. You were pretending to read it."

"Whatever," Myra sighed.

"So, what is it?"

"Nothing," she said unconvincingly.

"You're lying."

Myra looked at me with that little furrow in her brow. "Well, for one, you never called to reschedule our Jimmy Flannigan event."

"Oh damn," I groaned. "I'm sorry. I've been really busy." Now I was the one who was lying. I hadn't been busy. I'd just been really self- and Chris-absorbed.

"Well, it doesn't even matter. I found out two days ago that they're charging vendors a fee to exhibit at the tournament now that it's a money-prize event. The Kendall's Community Action Group doesn't have enough to cover the cost of real brochures or a decent website, much less a rental fee."

"That blows, Myra," I said. "I'm really sorry."

She shrugged. "Yeah, well, I was really upset two days ago, but I'm over it now."

Two days ago I'd been MIA. Now my best friend looked like there was a black cloud pouring little cold pellets of rain on her head.

"Hey," I tried. "We could still go over to the motel so you can meet Jimmy."

"Never mind. I'm not really interested in him anymore." Myra took a passionless bite out of her bagel.

"Are you sure?"

"I'm sure." She rolled her eyes. "Who cares about some lame Kendall's local."

"Um, I'm a lame Kendall's local," I muttered. "And by now, you qualify as a lame Kendall's local too."

"Oh, you know what I mean." Myra got up from the table. "Anyway, I'm tired. You can finish the bagel. I've lost my appetite." She left the kitchen without saying goodnight.

We've had our spats in the past, I reminded myself, as I devoured the half-eaten bagel. We'd gotten through those; we'd get through this.

Before going to bed, I took out my sketchbook and drew a special Wavehouse with a peaked coral roof that resembled the Eiffel Tower. I drew stone-walled turrets that looked like Notre Dame, in and out of which fish swam wearing berets and accompanied by mer-people carrying baguettes in fishnet satchels. Underneath I wrote: *For Myra. Sorry about Jimmy. Here's your own underwater Parisian home. Note the hot merman floating behind the south turret. Now you don't have to go anywhere. Love always, Anna.*

Chapter Twenty-Three

On our fourth night together, I told Chris about the Wavehouses. We were lying side by side looking up at the stars. Chris knew his astrology.

"And that one there is Cassiopeia." He pointed to a jumble of stars. "She was this super-hot Greek queen, but she was also a wicked bitch. Thought she was hotter than everyone, including the Nereids, which is near to impossible."

"Who were the Nereids?"

"The sea nymphs." He took my hand and kissed it. "The ocean dwellers. The real beauties. The ones like you."

"You know, I do sometimes fantasize about living in the ocean. In a Wavehouse."

"Wavehouse," he mused. "Sounds kinda cool."

"They're super weird, and I can't stop drawing them. It started when I was a little kid. A Wavehouse is a home made out of all sorts of ocean-y stuff; shells, rocks, fish bones, sea grass, coral. You name it. I'm sort of obsessed. Probably a little insane."

"It doesn't sound insane. Your Wavehouses sound awesome. Can I see them?"

"Maybe. Sometime. If you stay nice."

"I'm trying." He pulled me on top of him, and I could feel the rapid beat of his heart against my chest. He gently coaxed his fingers under the waistband of my shorts and pressed me hard against him. "Oh man," he sighed, "I am really, really trying."

A week went by, and reports from Jersey were still not good. Sara was running into all sorts of snafus at the factory. She would call to check in and jabber away about everything that was going wrong, but I barely paid attention. All I cared about was when she was coming back, which I hoped would coincide with Chris attending his publicity gig. I couldn't imagine being around my mother while

143

he was here and I in such a state. Guaranteed she would know I was lost the second she saw me. It takes one boy-crazy girl to know another.

The night before Chris left for New York, I left Meghan in charge of the shop and ducked out early. I stopped at the bakery for a baguette, then at Ronnie's Gourmet Market—which was really just a deli with a few stinky cheeses and fancy nut mixes—where I bought the fanciest, most expensive, and least stinky cheese in the store. I shoved the food into my backpack along with a pilfered bottle of wine from the Berkowitzes' liquor cabinet.

"They'll never notice," Myra told me that morning as she handed me the bottle—a peace offering in exchange for the Parisian Wavehouse. We hadn't talked much, and while she still seemed a little distant, we were more or less back on track. "They only drink Scotch. Wine is for parties, and they're never here long enough to make friends and have one of those."

Halfway to Secretspot, I stopped to change into Sara's blue dress. When I appeared at the edge of the cliff, Chris was waiting for me below on the beach. He whistled. "Belly Flop, you are a sight for sore eyes."

I made my way down to the beach and pecked him quickly on the cheek. I pulled out my sketchbook and thrust it toward him, scared that if I didn't show him the Wavehouses immediately I would lose my nerve and never do it. "Show and tell."

Chris surveyed me from head to toe and said, "Well, now I certainly can't be held responsible for my actions." He took the sketchbook from my hand and bowed graciously. "But right now, these may interest me more." He opened to the first page where I had drawn a wave shaped like a house with walls curled and leaning, and windows extruding like taffy.

"Pretty weird, huh?" I chuckled nervously, my heart beating like a trapped bird in my chest.

Chris didn't say anything. He turned the page and looked at the next Wavehouse, and the next, and the next. Finally, he spoke. "Where do these come from? Like, how do you think these things up?"

I pointed to my head. "Up here. Some from dreams, some just from, I dunno, my imagination?"

Chris nodded slowly and kept turning the pages, studying each Wavehouse. *Uh-oh,* I thought, *now he really thinks I'm bonkers.* He finally got to the last sketch, closed the book, and looked up at me.

"So?" I whispered.

"These are incredible. I totally want to live in them. Especially this one." He thumbed back through the book, stopping at one of my personal favorites—a modest little cottage shaped like a conch shell, held aloft and nestled in the crux of four waves curled in toward each other.

"I really like that one, too." I sighed in relief and leaned against him.

"Maybe we can live in one of your Wavehouses one day," he said. "Together."

"In your dreams," I said.

"No," he pointed to my head, "in yours."

I had had wine only once before, with Myra—another stolen Berkowitz bottle in tenth grade. We both got shit-faced, nauseated, and horribly hung over and decided never to drink ever again. With Chris, I was determined to sip in a ladylike fashion.

The rest of the night we talked between bites of bread and cheese and sips of wine. I learned that Chris had left regular school at the age of ten to travel around the world on the Junior Pro Circuit—with a number of tutors in tow.

"No school?" I asked wistfully. "Sounds like fun."

"It still sucked. Book-based learning of any kind has never been fun for me. I'm majorly dyslexic."

"Really?"

"Any letter or number that can be twisted around and turned upside down, I'll spin so it looks like nonsense," he said. "Getting through a dumb kid's book is still work, takes me forever. When I was in foster care I would lose my shit if I couldn't understand something. I felt really stupid. I'd throw stuff, hit other kids. I was a mess. Major anger management issues." He twisted his earring, clearly agitated. "But I'm much better in that department these days. I do my deep breathing, practice yoga. It helps."

I leaned forward and kissed his forehead. "Well, you are far from stupid."

"If you say so," he sighed.

I took a big swig of wine. My head was starting to feel like it was floating slightly—but not unpleasantly—off my neck. "Hey, you want to hear something school-relatedly stupid about me?"

"Sure."

"In fourth grade we had a substitute teacher who was really mean. And as a shy kid, mean people terrified me the most. It was after lunch and I had to pee really, really badly."

"*Uh-oh.* I think I know where this is going."

"Yeah, exactly. Well, I was too shy to raise my hand and ask to go to the bathroom, so I peed myself. But I was wearing sweatpants so there was minimal, um, leakage."

"That's intense, Anna." My real name. He understood how deeply humiliating this incident had been for me. He grabbed my hand and squeezed. "I'm so sorry."

I downed the rest of the wine. "I sat in my own pee for two hours. When it was time to leave, the other kids got up and I stayed in my seat. The substitute yelled at me to get out. I had no choice. I got up, and there was a puddle of pee in the seat. She saw it."

"What did she do?"

"She laughed. Harder and louder than any of the kids would have if they had seen the pee puddle. I still remember the way she sounded—like a goddamn circus clown."

"Bitch. She should've been fired."

I poured myself a third—or was it a fourth?—glass, and took another hefty gulp. "You would think. But who knew? I never told anyone, not even Myra. You're the only one who knows."

Chris stroked my hair, and I started crying—maybe out of relief, having let him know something so brutally embarrassing about my past; or from reliving that horrible day in fourth grade; or maybe because the entire evening had been so intense, wonderful, and sad. I started to drink more wine, but Chris took the plastic cup out of my hand.

"Slow down, Belly Flop. I think you've had enough."

I lay down and pulled Chris down with me. Chris's hands ran all over my body and it felt like I was being caressed by something or someone magical. I melted into the blanket, touching him all over in return. Messing around with Chris felt as glorious and natural as surfing. With the stars sparkling overhead I let my instincts and desires guide me, riding the most generous, intense, and fantastic wave ever born.

Chapter Twenty-Four

I am not sure whether it was Chris who took his clothes off first, or me. I felt like a tipsy nymphomaniac Nereid. We almost went all the way, but Chris stopped just in time.

"This isn't right," he gasped. "Not without protection. Not here. Not now." He got up and started to get dressed.

Without Chris's body next to mine, I started to shiver. Unsteadily, I reached out for my clothes and got dressed, feeling like an idiot.

"We could go up to your house," I suggested. "Just hang out more." *Please say yes,* I prayed. *Show me that you still like me.*

He shook his head. "Not a good idea. My friend is up there. It would be too weird." He sat down again next to me and kissed my forehead. "I really want to. But we'll just have to wait. It's late, and you should get home. I'll see you in the morning. We'll surf together before I leave for the city. Deal?"

He was being a gentleman. I let myself relax. Maybe I wasn't such an idiot after all. "Deal," I agreed.

Chris walked me to the end of the path, and made sure I was sober enough to ride my bicycle back to Myra's. I was, but still, I barely slept that night. Luckily, Myra had to get up at dawn to join the blue-rinse ladies at the Community Center, so she made sure I was up as well. I'd arranged for Meghan to open the shop, so I had time for a last surf with Chris.

Our breakfast choices were limited to Peanut Butter Captain Crunch—which we usually ate with guilty pleasure knowing full well it had zero nutritional value—or plain yogurt with mushy brown bananas. I opted for the Captain, while Myra went for the more sensible choice of yogurt and fruit.

"So, how was last night?" Myra asked, staring at her phone while spooning healthy glop into her mouth. Her tone reeked of disinterest.

"Do you really want to know?"

"Yeah, sorry." She shook her head as if trying to clear it of cobwebs. "I'm distracted."

I wanted my best friend back. So even if she really didn't want to know, *I* wanted her to know. What happened, and what *almost* happened, with Chris had been overwhelming. I felt frazzled and confused. I wanted Myra's levelheaded advice, so I told her all about my night. She stared at me from across the table, eyes wide open, mouth agape.

"You did it?" She was interested after all.

"No, we almost did it.'"

"Almost is, well, almost as good as *it*," Myra said. "No, actually almost is better. It shows restraint and commitment."

"The restraint part was all him. It's a good thing he stopped me. I was being really stupid. I am so totally ashamed of myself."

"Anna?"

"Yeah?"

Myra looked upset. "Thanks for telling me."

"Okay. So why do you look like someone died?"

"Just forget it."

"I can't forget it. What's wrong with you? Are you jealous?"

Myra stood up. She looked like she might cry. "I'm not jealous, okay?"

"So what is it about then? Paris?"

"No."

"Then it is about me and Chris."

"Okay. Sure. Believe whatever you want." Myra stood up. "I gotta go get ready."

She left me at the table with my hangover and my soggy cereal. I never expected Myra to be any kind of mystery to me. I felt like a snail without a shell, but I needed to rally. She had her old biddies and I had my waves.

I got to Secretspot twenty minutes later. The waves were mad, good, humungous machines that would be challenging but exciting to ride. I could see them form, first just a hump, then a hill, then a mountain topped by white water spray. This wouldn't be a session for trying new tricks. I'd be lucky to stay on a wave without getting snuffed and boiled underwater in the impact zone, hell-munched, and forced to hold my breath for dear life until I finally popped up for air, thanking my lucky stars.

There was no sign of Chris. Maybe he was waiting for the surf to clean up. I glanced up at the Ramelle house, but the sun bounced off the big glass windows and prevented me from seeing anything.

I was bummed that Chris hadn't been waiting for me on the beach, and that he still hadn't arrived. I had spent much of the night fantasizing about Chris and me as a grown-up couple, living happily ever after as professional surfers with little surfing kidlets. It was the first time I'd let myself really consider the possibility of a pro career. I'd tossed and turned for hours. I would somehow have to get over my performance anxiety before anything resembling a surf-centric life—with or without Chris and kidlets—could ever happen.

I decided to paddle out, hoping that he would soon join me. The waves were brutal, which provided a good distraction. Facing the reality of challenging waves, I tried to focus on preparing myself for a dicey surf session. I waited for a lull, which would give me thirty clean seconds to paddle out before getting pummeled. Between sets the ocean turned deceptively flat, the kind of calm that fooled beginners into thinking, *Gee, this doesn't look so bad.* I'd often seen novices paddle out leisurely in a lull, only to get creamed seconds later and have to turn back to shore exhausted and ashamed. Even ace surfers didn't always figure the timing out—luck played a big part. Mentally crossing my fingers, I dove in and paddled like a steamboat, a turbine engine, a windmill. A super gnarly current pulled me westward, messing up my intended entry spot, and increasing the odds I would get completely mashed by a breaking monster. I was forced to "duck dive" under one chaotic wave, pushing the nose of my board down with my arms rod-straight before the mess broke over my head. I wedged my knee in the middle of the board for extra leverage, and channeled myself deep under the wave. When I felt the current was right, I angled back up and shot out of the water like a rubber ducky, leaving the frothy mess behind me.

The first wave I chose was a bomb. It had so much power and such a steep face that I didn't even have to paddle to catch it. It swelled underneath my board and propelled me downward. I hunkered in a low crouch, shoulders forward, back curved, joints fluid, and feet riveted to the board.

I iced it, found the sweet spot, and rode that killer for a blissful fifteen seconds, boosting it back over the horizon at the end. In surf time it was a long trip, like a transatlantic flight, a journey to the bottom of the sea, or a shot to the moon. The next hour would've been a total blast, except that Chris had still not arrived. *Maybe I got the time confused*, I tried to tell myself. *Maybe he'll show up soon.*

At 8 a.m., it started to cloud over, another minor weather system coming through that would make the waves bigger and better, but wouldn't be great for business. The morning would be slow at The Shell Shop and Meghan would be fine on her own, which bought me a little extra time in the water. Once noon hit, however, vacationers would exhaust all the cloudy-non-beach day activities that Kendall's Watch had to offer—miniature golf, the lighthouse tour, the petting zoo, the whaling museum—and there would be nothing left but retail recreation. Then it would be all hands on deck at Dugan's Shell Shop.

But Chris never showed. In between sets, I peered up at the house and thought I saw someone looking out the window, but it was hard to tell for sure. Maybe he overslept, or maybe he was just… gone. By 9 a.m., I had given up hope. I took one last wave—a brutal steep right with so much power that I had to knock my knees together to stop my legs from shaking as I careened down the face. Instead of cutting back up and over when the wave was about to close out, I pointed my board toward the shore, lay on my stomach, and rode the foaming white water boogie-board style all the way to the beach.

I stumbled onto the sand and started packing to leave. Once my heart calmed after ninety minutes of exertion, I expected the physical pain to stop. But all it did was shift, lodging lower in my stomach. I recognized this feeling from childhood, from the many times I had wanted Sara for something, and she was nowhere to be

151

found. This time, it was Chris who had left me hollow.

"Screw this," I said aloud. Dropping my backpack, I trudged farther up the cliff, following a narrow path that wound its way toward the house on the hill. I scrambled over rocks and ducked past branches that slapped my legs and face—but I barely felt a thing. Fury fueled me, even though I'd surfed like a madwoman for over an hour and should've been exhausted.

The path ended at the lower section of the house. The sliding glass door wasn't locked, so I walked right in. Funny how feeling jilted makes a person do things entirely out of character. This was so not a 'me' I was familiar with; I seemed disturbingly Sara-esque.

I entered a finished basement that was dark and funky. A few slouchy couches surrounded an old coffee table; an outdated TV and sound system were stacked in one corner, and a guitar leaned against the wall. A bed in the corner of the room was perfectly made—for a split second I thought, *Chris sure is neat for a guy*, but then I realized it hadn't been slept in at all. There was no sign of Chris here—no clothes, no suitcase, and no surfboard. I stared at the hotel-neat bed, while my dripping board shorts made a wicked puddle on the shag carpet.

Then I heard a voice from upstairs, muffled by the intervening ceiling and floorboards. Bounding up the basement stairs, I paused at the top as it suddenly occurred to me that I was trespassing. Quietly, I made my way slowly down a long hallway lined with photos; casual family portraits that featured—in the middle of every shot—Rusty's blonde friend from Brinestellar's. At first I couldn't quite believe it. I thought, *Why was that boozy chick in these classy photos hung in the hallway of this expensive house?* I recognized her immediately. In some of these photos, she stood next to a skinnier, face-lifted version of herself, an older woman who wore glittery gowns and held little trophies and statuettes. *Mother and daughter Ramelle*, I thought.

I heard the voice again, down the hallway—a man's voice, low and nondescript. The hallway opened to a vast living room filled with tan leather couches, a glass coffee table covered with fancy art books, and pristine walls covered with abstract art. It was the camcorder, however, that drew my attention. It was set up on a tripod pointing down at the beach below. Another camera, with a telephoto lens, had been left on the side table—beside which, I saw two manila envelopes—both addressed to the Stella Surf Company, San Diego, California. At the bottom were scrawled the words: *Attention: Publicity Department: Anna Dugan, a.k.a The Surfing Siren.* And on the other: *Ceekay and the Siren.*

Chapter Twenty-Five

Inside one envelope, I found twenty close-up shots of me surfing, and in the other were as many shots of Chris and me kissing. One, I was horrified to see, showed Chris with his hand super close to my boob.

When I heard Rusty Meyers' he-man chuckles coming from beyond a set of double doors, my suspicions were confirmed. I gathered all the photos and stomped over just in time to hear him say, "Babe. I miss you, too. But we'll make up for lost time when you get back in two weeks." He was probably talking to the blonde, the Ramelle. Or maybe it was some other woman altogether. Who knew? This guy was out of control. I busted through the doors, desperately wanting to shout, "You asshole! Who the hell do you think you are?" But I couldn't. I just stood there trembling.

Rusty was leaning against a stainless steel refrigerator peeling an orange, with his iPhone wedged between his shoulder and ear. I noticed he had shaved off his hipster beard, and a Band-Aid decorated the tip of his pointy-evil chin. His jaw dropped—along with the orange—when he saw me. He recovered the jaw quickly and said to the person on the other end of the phone, "It's nobody, Amelia. Just one of Ceekay's little friends."

One of Ceekay's little friends? Implying there was more than one. If I hadn't been so angry, I might have crumbled in a heap on the beautifully tiled floor.

"Gotta go. Love ya." Rusty ended his call and stared at me with a smile as fake and sickeningly sweet as Redi-Whip. He started walking toward me and I bolted in the other direction, back toward the basement door.

Rusty followed. That slimy dude was quick, grabbing me just as I got to the hallway. I shoved him off and felt rage boil up from within.

I shook the photos at him. "So you *are* the Stella scout after all!" I said bitterly. "I had you pegged the first time I met you, you liar." I ripped the photos to shreds and threw them at him in a cascade of confetti. "Don't you ever, *ever* take my picture again. And don't you ever, ever come anywhere near me or my mother again or I swear I will kill you." I hoped my sudden surge of bravery lasted, at least until I was out of that house.

"Anna, let me explain—"

"Don't bother. I don't want to hear it!" Then I turned and raced down the stairs, through the basement and back along the wooded path. I managed to get to my bicycle but left both surfboard and backpack behind, scared that Rusty would be on my tail. At the main road, I pedaled furiously—barefoot, in board shorts and bathing suit—toward town. It was raining steadily now, which suited me fine. I wanted to lose myself in the raindrops and gray sky.

There was only one person who would know how to help me, if she was still interested.

I found Myra in the musty basement of the Kendall's Watch Community Center. She and the biddies were sorting through donated clothes for the weekly Saturday rummage sale.

"Jesus Christ, Anna!" Myra cried when she saw me. One of the biddies *tsk-tsked* her immediately. "Sorry, Mrs. Dougherty. I mean, uh…oy vey, Anna! You look like an orphaned baby seal. You're sopping wet. Come on, let's dry you off."

Myra pit-stopped at 'Linens' and grabbed an old beach towel, then pulled me into the women's bathroom. "Take off your clothes before you freeze to death," she instructed.

"I can't believe this. It's like a bad dream," I stuttered, shivering with cold as I rubbed myself with the towel as if it were sandpaper and I was a piece of burly wood. Then I told Myra everything.

"Maybe there's an explanation?" she tried.

"Myra—"

"Okay, okay. You're right. This sucks. Rusty sucks. And Ceekay may suck also."

"Thank you," I sniffled.

"Anna, I really wish I could talk about this, and other stuff also, but I've gotta go supervise before one of the biddies has a coronary."

Other stuff. The stuff between us. "Okay. Later then?"

"Yeah. Later. When do you need to be at the shop?"

"Not until noon. I got Meghan to open."

"Okay, hold on. Stay here." Myra left me in the bathroom. I looked at my woebegone expression in the filmy mirror over the sink and thought, *Look at you. Look at the mess you're in.*

When the bathroom door swung open five minutes later, I expected to see Myra. But instead, Gramma came waltzing in with a pile of pastel colored clothes in her arms.

"Anna Marie!" she exclaimed with a big grin on her face. "Charlotte Dougherty said you were here and Myra tells me you've come to beat the Saturday crowds."

"Huh?" I said.

Myra came up behind Gramma and shrugged, mouthing the word *sorry*.

"I'm so happy you're thinking of expanding your wardrobe," Gramma declared, then added conspiratorially: "You know, as volunteers, we get first dibs on the treasures in the women's department." Gramma deposited a pile of pink and turquoise clothes on the counter. "I chose these just for you. They'll look fantastic with your complexion."

I forced myself to smile. "Thanks, Gramma."

Gramma patted my arm. "I've got to head back to 'Bric-a-Brac' and make sure Edna McNully keeps on track with the price tags, and doesn't run off with some of the better pieces. Myra, you make sure she comes and shows me how she looks before she leaves, okay?"

"For sure, Mrs. Dugan," Myra said.

I reluctantly dressed in the cotton candy button-down blouse and light blue capris.

"You look like a clown who performs at children's birthday parties in that outfit," Myra giggled.

"If you're trying to lighten the mood, it's not working," I sighed.

"Okay, I'm sorry. This whole Rusty-Meyers-Chris-photograph

thing is really a bummer," she said. "But right now I suggest you go back to my house. You need to have a good cry before going to the shop. Maybe get a bit of this out of your system. Plus you can change out of your clown costume."

"Okay. Good idea."

Myra gave me a set of instructions on how to have my very own pity party. "Call me if you need any other suggestions, or if you're still totally bummed and wanna talk. I'll see you back at my house tonight. Gotta get back to the biddies."

Chapter Twenty-Six

According to Myra, the first step to a successful pity party was a bubble bath. I took a nice long one in the Berkowitzes' double-sized tub. To intensify the mood and encourage tears, I set Myra's ancient boom box on top of the toilet and blasted her recommended old-school collection of mopey love songs as I soaked. No crying, though. Not even a dribble. But the long soak gave me plenty of time to think about the cast of characters messing me up over the last few days.

Was there any chance that Sara knew what Rusty had been up to? If she had any knowledge of his creepy maneuvers, I swore I would legally emancipate myself, move in permanently with my grand-parents, and leave her to fend for herself. But it seemed more likely that Sara had just been blinded by desire. Rusty had been conning us both.

The worst part was that I could tell Sara had fallen hard for Rusty. I knew I had to tell her about all of this; I also knew it was going to suck big time.

After the bath, I put on Myra's ratty old bathrobe and scuffed bunny slippers—because Myra believed that one should never have a good cry in good clothes. Shuffling into the kitchen, I made myself a hot chocolate, and reheated a slice of pizza from the night before. Next pity party assignment was to watch a cheesy tearjerker while devouring cheesy pizza and drinking hot chocolate. Myra had recommended a movie featuring a jilted lover or a kid dying of an incurable, rare disease, but at 10 a.m. my choices were limited to home improvement makeovers, cooking shows, celebrity interviews, infomercials, Sponge Bob reruns, and Law and Orders from every possible city.

And then—as luck would have it—I settled on exactly the wrong channel.

A bald guy, leaning across his desk, smiled at the camera. "Hey there, and welcome to my world. Coming to you live from New York, it's me, Larry Romanoff and this is *Live with Larry*!"

The off-camera audience clapped and hooted, and the camera drew back to reveal Larry's guest—Chris! Startled, I almost fell off the couch. Chris's blond hair had been combed but it still sprang up rebelliously around his perfect ears. The gold hoop glistened under the TV studio lights. He was wearing the same clothes that he had worn on our first date.

"So, Ceekay, you leave soon for Fiji, eh?" the bald guy asked.

"Yeah, can't wait. They say the waves are going to be really sweet this season."

Fiji, I thought. *The other side of the earth. As far away from me as possible.*

"'Sweet' for you means what? Like the height of a two-story building?"

Chris shrugged. "A little bigger would be okay."

The audience chuckled.

"And after that?" the bald guy asked.

"Indo, probably," Chris shrugged. "For as long as the waves are good. I dunno. You'll have to ask my manager, Rusty, for the itinerary. I just go where the waves are."

Rusty—his manager.

"And what about you, Inga?"

The camera swiveled over and there Inga sat—cross-legged and gorgeous in a green dress that had the same emerald sparkle as Inga's saucer-big eyes. The dress was the size of a postage stamp. Inga's waist-length red hair shimmered as she whipped it to one side. "Are you kidding?" Inga said breathlessly, as she reached over and put her hand on Chris's thigh. I had touched that same thigh less than a day before. "I'm going with him. I can't let this one out of my sight for a minute!"

I stumbled out of my seat, shaking like a leaf.

The show host turned to the studio audience and said, "Well, here they are, folks. America's favorite young couple. Aren't they adorable?"

Chris and Inga sat holding hands; Chris looked a little uncomfortable, but Inga, smug and self-satisfied, looked like the cat who'd eaten the canary.

"You can keep him!" I yelled at the TV. My heart pounded in my chest as if I'd just paddled across the Atlantic Ocean and back. I was so angry, I couldn't cry. All I really wanted to do was go to bed, pull the covers up over my head, and pretend the last few days had never happened. But that was impossible. And I was too damn responsible to leave Meghan in the store by herself all day.

Zombie-like, I trudged upstairs, found Myra's surfer girl clothes and put them on. As I got ready to leave, I saw Chris's love note on the dresser where I had left it. My heart sank further from its already low position in my gut to a spot somewhere south of my toes. This love stuff really hurt.

I picked up the note, intending to rip it to shreds, but something stopped me. I folded the note into the pocket of Myra's board shorts. If and when the time was right—and if I was brave enough—maybe I would call Chris and let him have it.

The bike ride from Myra's to The Shell Shop was usually a snap, a total downhill coast along Emerson to Main Street. Today, the wind was so intense that I had to pedal hard against it all the way to town. A bank of gray clouds loomed like a giant, moving mountain to the southeast. A storm was coming. If we were lucky it might take a northward curve before hitting land and heading out to sea; lucky, because "Slide along Storms"—as we surfers liked to call them—left bright sunshine and great waves in their wake. But feeling jilted, I glumly hoped the waves would suck for the rest of my life so that I would never have to make the decision to surf or not surf again.

By the time I got to The Shell Shop, I felt as if I had just finished the Tour de France. Meghan, behind the cash register, was way too chipper. "Hey, Anna. It's fun working together, huh?" she squeaked.

"Yeah," I grunted. The last thing I needed was a motor-mouth day with Meghan De'Errico. I was out of patience, and no longer a lovesick fool floating in a mirage of fake romantic bliss.

"We haven't worked together since we did that volcano project in sixth-grade science, remember?"

How could I forget? Meghan had talked the entire time, and done next to nothing on the project. When it was our turn to present our project to the class, she dropped the volcano model, and baking soda and papier-mâché exploded in a riot all over the floor.

"This shop is so cool," Meghan babbled on. "Your grandfather started it, right? How are your grandparents, anyway? I haven't seen them since I was, like, seven years old. Do they still live on Toilsome? I remember that birthday party you had at their house when we were in second grade. I thought it was so cool that your grandfather got dressed up like Santa—"

"Meghan." I interrupted her to save her life—if I allowed her to ramble on any longer, I would lose my mind and become homicidal. "Would you mind going through all the towels in the storeroom and making separate piles according to color?"

"Sure! Cool! I can do that." Meghan happily pranced to the back room. As long as I could drum up enough useless tasks for her to do, I might survive the day, and she might, too.

The afternoon dragged on. Focusing on work proved impossible. An entire gang could have come in and stolen every item in the store and I wouldn't have noticed. When I wasn't stressing about how to break the Rusty news to Sara, I couldn't stop wondering whether I should call Chris. My heart just wasn't into selling lighthouse key chains and dangly shell earrings, so I let Meghan run the show. I moped behind the jewelry display, thinking about the photos I had ripped to shreds and how fitting it was that my life now felt the same way—torn up and wrecked. Then I really lost it when I realized that even though I had destroyed the prints in the envelopes, Rusty probably still had copies on his computer.

I had to call Myra; she would know what to do. But the only phone in the shop was right next to the cash register, and in just about as public a spot as you could get. I didn't want Meghan to catch any whiff, drift, or hint of what was going on in my private life, so unless I found a way to get rid of her, I wouldn't be able to call Myra.

A lull just after three brought the perfect opportunity "Hey

Meghan." I took a ten from the cash register. "Can you go grab a copy of the *Kendall's Kalendar* from Ronnie's? I wanna check our ad placement this week." Stacks of *Kendall's Kalendars* were piled at Ronnie's next to the register. Nabbing a spot in the first ten pages was the goal of every local business, but it was luck of the draw; no one could ever figure out how the editors decided on layout. "And I'm famished." Not quite true—even though I had not had lunch, the thought of eating made me sicker than sick. "Get me a banana strawberry smoothie and something for yourself too."

Meghan stopped untangling a mess of abalone encrusted eyeglass chains. "Are you sure that's all you want? That's not really enough, Anna. You should eat more than that. You know, you're kind of on the skinny side—"

I pulled an extra five out of the cash register and literally threw it at Meghan. "And a cheese and avocado wrap, okay? A smoothie and a wrap."

Meghan skipped out of the store. For real. *Skip, skip, skip*—like Goldilocks on her way to the Bears' cottage in the woods. I had about fifteen minutes till she came back, maybe twenty if the to-go line at Ronnie's was long. I dialed Myra and waited. It picked up after seven rings.

"So, did it work? Did you cry? Are you feeling any better?" Myra asked. I could just imagine her rushing away from the chirpy seniors to some private corner of the mothballed basement of the Community Center.

"No tears, but Myra, he's still with Inga. I know it for sure now." I told her about the show. "That's why he had to leave. *That* was his promotional appearance."

"Oh shit," Myra moaned.

"Yeah, so your *People Magazine* isn't so reliable after all. There's more, and this is even worse. I just realized those photos Rusty took are probably digital, right? Who cares if I ripped up those prints? Rusty probably already sent them through the little internet fairies!"

"Anna, relax."

"Relax?" I started pacing. "This is a potential disaster. I mean, *The*

Surfing Siren YouTube thing is bad enough. I will die, I mean literally *die,* if there are photos posted on the internet of me doing…well, you know, with Chris."

She was quiet.

"Myra? Hello?"

"Okay, yeah. It could be bad."

"Arrrggggghhhh! I knew that was what you would say."

"Anna, I've got to get back to the biddies. We can talk about this more later. Bye."

Myra hung up and I felt as if she'd just slammed a door in my face. Something was still bothering her. I just wished that she—of all people—would be straight with me.

Meanwhile, I needed to set something else straight. I would call Chris and tell him I never wanted to see or hear from him ever again. I took his note out of my pocket and smoothed it on the counter. *To the most beautiful girl in the world. Glad our surfboards collided.* The paper was getting wrinkly because I had folded and unfolded it so many times. Tears welled up in my eyes and one dropped on *surfboards,* blurring and breaking the letters as if they were individual surfboards shattered against the rocks. Finally, I was crying, just when I really didn't want to.

The shell-bell jingle jangled on cue and Meghan came waltzing into the shop. "Here I am," she sang as she two-stepped toward me. "Did ya miss me?"

"Ah, yeah, sure." I quickly wiped the remaining tears away from my eyes.

Meghan executed a last, dramatic whirl toward me; then, suddenly she slipped, slamming the take-out food bag against the counter. The bag exploded—plastic utensils and napkins went flying, and the pages of the *Kalendar* scattered across the shop like sheets in the wind. My avocado and cheese wrap torpedoed the postcard display and Meghan's Cobb Salad rained corn kernels and ham cubes all over the floor.

But worst of all, my smoothie and her Diet Coke spilled across the countertop oozing over Chris's note, ending in a gloppy mess on the front of my shorts.

Chapter Twenty-Seven

When Meghan regained her balance and saw the liquid disaster, she shrieked, "Oh my god, you're a mess!" She slipped her way toward the storeroom and came racing back with a wad of paper towels and pawed at my crotch like an attention-seeking dog.

I held the note overhead, out of reach of her swiping hands. "Get off, De'Errico! Just go away!" I frantically wiped my note, trying to save it from total glop destruction but the numbers were now a blurred line of black regret; they looked like an inkblot test used on psych patients, which was fitting because at that moment I felt like a person with big-time mental health issues.

Meghan backed off, looking wounded. "Just trying to help," she sniffed.

"I'm sorry," I sighed, trying to muster up a smile. "Please just clean up the floor. I can take care of myself." I wadded up the useless piece of paper and lobbed it into the garbage pail.

In the back room, I changed out of my sticky board shorts, which I left soaking in a sudsy froth of Sea Goddess All-Purpose Cleanser and pulled on a pair of Kendall's Watch sweats. Sara would be irritated that I was pilfering valuable merchandise. Sea Goddess—at twenty bucks a bottle—claimed to include "only the finest, purest, sea-worthiest ingredients"— ingredients like pulverized Japanese eel bones and sea salt from the Dead Sea. If *that* couldn't clean shorts, I had no idea what could.

Meghan didn't bug me much for the rest of the afternoon. When she did ask a few store-related questions I shot her a look that kept her brief and on point. I had to admit, Meghan was better suited to The Shell Shop than I had expected. The customers loved her. Kids especially. And she stayed on top of shelving, stocking and other chores—when not spazzing out and spilling food. Sara would be pleased with how well we had managed while she was away.

Thinking of Sara got me thinking of Rusty, and thinking of Rusty got my blood boiling. It was time to warn her; I couldn't put it off any longer. At four, I tried my mother's cell. When it immediately went to voicemail, I left a message. "Hey, Sara, I really want to talk to you before you see Rusty. There's something we need to discuss. So if you ever get around to picking up your messages, you better call me back ASAP. Oh, and I hope things are moving along with the tee shirts. I just sold our last large."

The next hour inched along, and finally at five, the phone rang.

"Dugan's Shell Shop."

"You're supposed to add 'How can we help you?' How many times do I have to tell you that, Anna?" It was Sara. The sound of her voice had me tearful again.

"When are you coming home?" I sniffled, carrying the phone into the storeroom.

"Anna, are you okay?"

"Yeah, sure. I may be coming down with a cold." I wished.

"You and your mystery illnesses…"

"Whatever, Sara," I muttered, feeling a growing irritation with my mother, which at least served to dry up my tears. "When are you back?"

"I'm not sure. Hopefully tomorrow night. Things are a mess here. First, they screwed up the words; then today, they printed the whole Kendall's Watch image on the *front* of the tees instead of the back. I tried one on to see if it would work, but it looks terrible. Unless you're a double *D* or have a major gut, the whole design gets lost. So, lucky me. I have to stay and make sure they do it right tomorrow."

"Oh no," I moaned.

"Oh yes. Only plus is that I can surf Manasquan Inlet again tomorrow morning before these cretins get in to work. Anna, you should see the way the wave bowls up and wedges down here. It sets you flying. Totally insane. I'm so glad I brought my board. At least something good has come out of this fuck-up. Oh, and Joe says hi. We surfed together this morning. Geez, that guy can still ride it clean, I tell you," Sara sighed.

Big whoop, I thought. "So what do I do about tomorrow?"

165

"Can Meghan come in again?" Sara asked.

"I don't know. Probably. I think they're happy at the bakery without her. She's got pretty cool retail chops, by the way."

"Excellent. Good to know. So, what did you so desperately need to tell me before I see Rusty?"

I paused. Maybe this wasn't over-the-phone material after all.

"Anna, come on. I have to get back to supervise those bozos in the factory. What is it?"

I swallowed hard. I tried to tell her, but I chickened out—again. "It's no big deal. It can wait till tomorrow."

"Good, because I am so overwhelmed here. I can't deal with any more drama."

Just wait, Sara, I thought. *It's only gonna get more tragic.*

"Also, I spoke to Gramma earlier. She wants you for dinner tonight. I don't know why, but she worries about you. You should probably stay overnight, too. They like it if you do that when I'm away."

I was relieved to go to Toilsome that night, particularly since things with Myra seemed so off. At least at my grandparents' house I could sit around and watch dumb shows with Grandpa, help Gramma not burn food, and squeeze Fluffy and Woof Woof against my aching heart all night long.

"Fine," I said. "I'll be there. When exactly will you get back tomorrow?"

"Um…I'm not exactly sure."

"Just promise me we'll talk before you see Rusty."

Sara sighed. "Sure. Okay, gotta go." She hung up, leaving me a whole extra day to wait and worry.

When I walked out of the storeroom, Meghan almost mowed me down.

"Anna," she said excitedly. "There's someone here to see you."

He had picked up the cottage Shelly, the one with a thatched roof of painted matchbook covers and a film canister chimney with cotton ball smoke.

"These are really cool." Chris smiled nervously. "Did you make them?"

Chapter Twenty-Eight

What are you doing here?" I demanded.

"I had to find you," Chris said. "We need to talk."

Yes, we did. But now that he was actually standing in front of me, I didn't know if I'd be capable of saying what I really wanted to say.

"I've been trying to reach you," he continued. "I called here earlier and left a message."

I turned to Meghan, who looked as if she had just swallowed a slug.

"I'm sorry, Anna," she croaked. "It was, like, so super busy I forgot to tell you. If I had known it was…him, I would've probably remembered but—"

"No worries, Meghan," I interrupted. "It doesn't really matter."

"Whoa," Chris said. "It matters to me, Belly Flop."

I cringed at the sound of my nickname.

"Why didn't you call?" he asked. "You have my number."

"I lost it," I managed. *Never thought I'd see you again anyway*, I thought to myself.

The Shell Bell went off, and in walked a "double load"—Shell Shop lingo for two families on vacation together, with a minimum of six hyper kids and four frazzled parents at the ends of their ropes. "Hi, can I help you?" Meghan asked eagerly. Then, turning to me, she added, "I've got this covered, Anna. Why don't you show your friend our storeroom?"

Chris followed me to the back where I sat on the stack of beach towels, arms folded defensively across my chest—hoping to hold my heart in. Chris paced, still absently holding the Shelly in one hand. He looked like he was ramping up to deliver bad news.

"Well, you sure got back to Kendall's Watch quickly," I grumbled.

"Huh? I haven't gone anywhere," he said.

"Yeah, right," I managed to whisper.

167

Chris's shoulders hunched and his hand clenched the Shelly. "I'm. Not. Lying," he said slowly, through clenched teeth.

Ignoring him, I started folding a pile of sarongs that were headed for the sale bin.

"Anna."

I wanted to ask about Rusty and the photos; *Live with Larry*, Inga, and Fiji. But I couldn't—all I could manage—with those damned tears welling up in my eyes again—was to pretend to care about the stupid mess of sarongs.

"Can you make this quick?" I mumbled. "I'm really busy."

"Anna, please," he pleaded. "Would you just look at me?"

So I did; I raised my eyes to his face, and, to my surprise, he looked like a scared little boy—like one of the brats I routinely chased out of the shop when they got too close to the Shelly display. Somehow his vulnerability gave me a smidge of courage.

"Can you please put the merchandise down?" I said in a shaky but determined voice.

Chris looked at the Shelly in his hands as if he had forgotten he was holding it. He placed it carefully on a shelf next to a mermaid figurine.

"So get to the point already," I said.

"I need to apologize."

"Go on then."

"Rusty—those photos he took. I had no idea he was doing that."

"Okay, so you apologized about Rusty. Your fabulous dirtbag of a manager. Duly noted. Anyone else you want to apologize about?" I asked.

"Who else would I need to apologize about?"

Her name is Inga, I thought. *Inga friggin' Ward*. I turned back to the sarongs. Chris was a liar, and I was damned if I was going to let him see me crushed. "Nobody. Never mind. Can you please leave now and never come back?"

"Belly Flop—"

"What's the point?" I cried, unable to contain my emotion any longer.

"You. You're the point," Chris pleaded. He was almost convincing.

"Just go!" Tears flowed like rivers down my cheeks. "Please."

"But—"

"Go!" I shouted. "This is my store and I need you to leave. Now!"

"This is so unfair, I can't believe it," he muttered; then, shooting me a glance of bewildered anger, he stalked from the room.

I sent Meghan home early and closed the shop on my own. The long bike ride to my grandparents' house calmed my nerves a little, and I could smell the roast chicken even before I skidded my way up their driveway.

"Hello," I called, trying hard to sound chipper. "I'm here!"

Gramma called from the kitchen. "Hello, Anna Marie. I'm in here." Grandpa's La-Z-Boy was empty, I noticed, as I made my way through the living room.

"Hey Gramma." I kissed her forehead. She smelled like fermented fruit and I noticed her bottle of schnapps was uncapped. Usually, for decorum's sake, she kept the cap on in between swigs. "Where's your Tommy-kins?" Sometimes, when chatting with Gramma, I called Grandpa cutesy names, names I imagined she might have called him back in the day. Gramma would smile, blush, and swat my arm— but not today. Instead, turning back to the stove, Gramma said, "He had to run a quick errand. He'll be home soon."

"What kind of errand?" I asked.

"Nothing important." Gramma seemed nervous somehow. "Nothing at all." Then, noticing my clothes, she frowned. "What happened to that attractive outfit I picked out for you this morning?"

Oh yeah. That. "Too fancy for the grunt work I needed to do in the storeroom today. I wanna save it for a nicer occasion."

She smiled. "Good thinking."

"So where's Grandpa?" I persisted.

"I sent him to the supermarket to get some fat-free heavy cream. Now be an angel and drain these potatoes for me."

"Fat-free heavy cream? Isn't that some sort of oxymoron?" I asked as I lifted the heavy boiling pot over to the sink.

169

"Anna Marie, that's not nice," Gramma *tsk-tsked*. "We don't call anything or anyone an ox or a moron in this house, do you hear me?"

"Gramma, 'oxymoron' is a term for combining two contradictory ideas. Fat-free. Heavy cream. Get it?"

"No, I don't," Gramma frowned. Sure, she was toasted on peach schnapps, but she seemed preoccupied and distracted—something was wrong.

Grandpa's pickup rumbled outside, and a few minutes later he walked in with a pint of cream. I could see Gramma visibly relax when she saw him. Maybe that was really all it was—Grandpa on a quest for a precious dairy product.

"There she is," Grandpa said when he saw me. He kissed me, handing the cream to Gramma. "I don't know why you need to use this stuff, Lorraine. It's gonna taste like piss. It's bad enough that now I have to take these horse pills."

That's when I noticed the bag from Whitaker's Pharmacy he held in his other hand. Grandpa took out a vial of pills and read the instructions: "May cause constipation, headaches, nausea, and dry mouth. Hell, like I need any of those things."

"Oh please, Tom," Gramma protested. "You know what the doctor said. Now shoo. Both of you."

Grandpa and I did as we were told, taking our standard spots in the living room—he on his La-Z-Boy, and me horizontal on the couch. As usual, Grandpa reached for the remote and began channel surfing.

"So Grandpa," I said. "What's with the pills? What did the doctor say?"

"Not much. Did you talk to your mother? What's going on down there with those idiot printers? I can't believe the shirts aren't done yet. If I were down there at that cockamamie excuse for a factory, I'd be whipping their butts. You can sure bet—"

"Give it a rest, Grandpa. I'm sure Sara's doing as good a job as anyone could do. Even you, tough guy."

"Yeah, yeah," he harrumphed, clicking the remote.

"So answer my questions."

"What questions?"

"What's with the pills and what did the doctor say?"

"He thinks I need to go in for another operation on the old heart. A valve replacement. Can you believe that? Like I'm a car or something. But I wouldn't jump to any conclusions. The pills are gonna keep me fine till then."

I bolted upright. The fat-free cream suddenly made sense. "What the hell, Grandpa! Why didn't you tell me sooner?"

Grandpa stopped on an infomercial, watching an automatic carrot grater pulverize carrots over and over again. Grandpa hated infomercials. And he hated carrots. Finally, he cleared his throat. "The doctor ran some tests yesterday. We're still waiting for the results."

"Jesus, Grandpa."

He shrugged. "It's nothing to get your knickers in a twist about. Those medical clowns probably just want to make a buck. I probably don't even need the damn heart operation. God knows I don't do a hell of a lot to tax my ticker, why should it need a whole new car part?"

"Maybe that's the problem, Grandpa. You're supposed to walk thirty minutes every day and use those hand weights we got you last Christmas, but you don't. You sit around like a tub of lard, maybe drive to town to hang with your hardware homies, but that's about it."

"Tub of lard?" he cried.

"Okay. That was harsh. Tub of Jell-O. Better?"

He nodded. "Better. I like Jell-O. I don't want to talk about this anymore. Go to the kitchen and help your grandmother. And don't talk about this heart stuff with her, you hear me? She gets way too emotional about it all. If we're not careful, *she'll* have a heart attack before I do."

"Oh, that's great. Just great. What positive thinking." I got up and arrived in the kitchen just in time to save the green beans from overcooking.

Here's what I learned at dinner: First, that Edna McNully had been found rummaging in the garbage can outside Corbin's Automotive Repairs. The mayor claimed his mother had been hunting for Shelly accessories, but word among the retired set was that Edna had now officially gone off the deep end. Second, that the department of highway maintenance had still not repaired the giant pothole on the corner of Breezy Way and Main. Third, that the price of eggs at the supermarket had gone up seven cents; milk, a whopping five. And lastly, that some rowdy teenagers, looking like vampires, had visited the post office the day before, and that one of them was Brian Steinkamp's grandson visiting from Michigan—definitely a bad seed.

Nothing about Grandpa's medical condition; *zip* about Grandpa's impending surgery; *silence* about Grandpa's actual broken heart. And absolutely zero shared about my own aching one.

I kept quiet, ate my food, and nodded at the appropriate times. After a "heart-healthy" dessert of low-fat frozen yogurt and strawberries—odd for Gramma not to bake, but then again the whole evening was odd—Grandpa and I settled silently in front of the TV for a quick peek at the Weather Channel. Storms were raging up and down the East Coast, but most were blowing out to sea. A cautionary advisory was in effect for the next forty-eight hours, especially in coastal communities. The surfer in me was momentarily stoked—the waves would be epic. Then I remembered the state of my life, and I was instantly back on dry land, glumly landlocked.

"G'night, Tommykins," I sighed as I got up to go to bed.

"You leavin'?" Grandpa asked. "A funny comedy show with this big, fat Australian guy and his dumbo Kiwi kids is about to come on."

"I'm exhausted," I croaked. "I'm going to sleep."

I leaned over for a comforting last whiff of Grandpa's scalp before trudging upstairs.

Chapter Twenty-Nine

Sixteen-year-old me usually slept like a baby when I stayed at Toilsome Lane, but that night was different—that night I was a grown-up with way too many woes. I clutched Woof Woof to my stomach, and positioned Fluffy under my head, hoping my pet pillows would soothe me as they had done so many times before. But pillows couldn't do anything for this kind of pain. Chris had played me as cunningly as Rusty had played my mother, and I had never, in my whole life, felt uglier, stupider, or more used up.

On top of that, I had Grandpa's faulty heart valve to add to my worry-pile. After his first surgery, he had needed to recuperate for a long time. I had helped take care of him while Sara worked the shop. A second operation now, years later, would be even harder for everyone to manage. I couldn't leave Kendall's Watch on a surf tour, even if I had wanted to. So bye-bye almost-boyfriend, and almost-had-but-really-never-wanted professional career. Good-bye any kind of bright and happy future.

I couldn't sleep, so I got a stash of paper and pens from the dresser drawer. I started on a new Wavehouse, letting my mood dictate my drawing. A curled and awkward cave with a pitch black entrance emerged—a barnacle-encrusted tomblike place with fish scales scattered around like brittle and treacherous confetti. A dark and dismal Wavehouse to match my dark and dismal life. I was in a state all the next day at the shop. Sad, mad, and totally had. Not at all glad. Thankfully Meghan took up the slack. At half-past two, Sara called and said she was going to be held up by tee shirt issues for another day. Part of me had hoped she was staying in Jersey because she had rekindled her affair with Fireman Joe, which would make the Rusty news easier to bear. It was just as well—one doomed love affair at a time was quite enough.

By three, I was almost functioning normally. Then something

happened outside the shop that yanked me back under the gnarly current.

"What's going on out there?" I asked Meghan, who was looking out the window.

"Wow," she said. "I saw that awesome van earlier, but didn't realize it belonged to *him*."

Chris sat in the driver's seat of a retro-cool VW van across the street. It was a classic old 60s model—probably worth a mint—with surfboards piled on the roof, and vintage stickers of smiley faces and peace signs plastered all over the bumpers. A shiny SUV had pulled up behind the van and sat with its engine idling, which made my blood boil. I hated it when people didn't shut off their engines, when they operated as if the atmosphere was their own personal emissions dumping ground. But that was the least of my worries. Chris was parked across the street from my shop. What was he doing there? I took a deep breath and walked outside.

A large, sunburned man rapped sharply on the van's window while Chris stared straight ahead, pretending not to hear the guy.

"Hey buddy," the man yelled, in a threatening kind of way. "Move it along!"

Chris was still as stone.

"Can't you read, you idiot?" the man persisted.

Finally, Chris reacted. Rolling down the window, he scowled at the man. "I can read just fine," he said.

"Um, no you can't." The man laughed condescendingly, as he pointed to a parking sign partially obstructed by the branches of a maple tree. "It says *Parking by Permit Only*. This junk heap of yours has no permit. I paid a fortune to get my summer parking permit and I'm not gonna let some young punk come and take a spot that belongs to someone who's paid."

Chris looked up at the sign, his face tightening in anger. Had he been unable to read the sign? Or had he not even noticed it?

"Please get away from my car, dude," Chris said, through gritted teeth.

"Move your car, *dude*," the man said mockingly.

With lightning speed, Chris whipped his door open almost knocking the man down. Then Chris was standing on the sidewalk face-to-face with the man or rather face-to-chest—the man was huge.

"Stop it!" I yelled, from the other end of the street. Crowds stopped to stare at me. Usually, this kind of scrutiny would've been enough to make me run back inside the shop. Chris, with a hopeful smile at me, started across the street. The man yelled after him, "Unbelievable! I'm calling the cops, buddy. Get this stupid van of yours towed away!"

Chris, without even turning around, raised his middle finger to the guy sputtering in the street behind him. I thought the bully was going to run across the street and tackle Chris, but fortunately he got back in his SUV and drove away. As he sped by, I could see a woman in the passenger seat with an embarrassed expression. *Not your fault, lady*, I thought. *Not yours, or mine.*

"I was working my nerve up to come back into the shop and try to talk to you again," Chris said once he stood next to me.

"What were you going to do to that guy?" I asked.

Chris shrugged, his expression dark and unsettled. "Nothing. But that asshole deserves to have his butt kicked."

The look on his face unnerved me for a moment—a look of barely controlled rage as if with one push he would be over the edge. It reminded me of a creep named Stanley who had given Sara a black eye the morning of my ninth birthday.

"You were about to punch him!"

"I didn't do anything, Anna," Chris laughed nervously. "That dick wad was all over me and all I did was give him the finger, so what?"

"I don't want you anywhere near me or this store," I said calmly.

"You're totally overreacting! I didn't even call him any names, goddammit!"

"Please, Chris. I'm asking nicely."

"Great," he threw his hands up. "Just great. I give up. I can't win with you. You don't seem to believe anything I say or do."

I turned to go back into the store.

175

"Anna," he reached for my arm gently. "Please."

It felt good to be touched by him again. So good, I could barely stand it, until I thought of *her*. I slipped my arm away, like a shell pulled out to the sea with an outgoing tide. "Go back to Inga."

"Wait a minute, please!" Chris ran his hands through his hair, his fingers caught in his curls. "Did Inga talk to you?"

"Fly off to Fiji. Go have fun in the sun. The waves are really sweet this time of year."

He reached for me again. "Anna—"

"Leave, now," I cried, pulling my arm away, much rougher with him than he had ever been with me.

At last, closing time arrived. I gave Meghan one hundred and fifty bucks, which was more than she had expected, but she deserved every bit of it. She could sweet-talk customers into purchases better than I ever could. And she could make change without needing the cash register to tell her the amount. I decided to let her close up and asked her to open the shop on her own the following morning, which thrilled her to no end. I was exhausted and useless—if there was any chance of sleeping in the next morning, I was determined to take it. After trying to appear interested as Meghan told me a really boring story about her mother's bunions, I showed her how to turn off the display lights and lock up, and left.

I kept thinking of Chris and Inga about to fly off to Fiji. What would Chris's other 'little friend' think of the photos of Chris and me when she saw them? Maybe Fiji didn't have internet, tabloids, or trashy news feeds. Maybe Inga would never know, and Chris could play her just like he had so brilliantly played me.

I got on my bike and high-tailed it to Myra's, arriving before she did—no doubt she had gotten coerced into some act of do-gooding. I wasn't sure what the tension between us was about, but we had to deal with it. The idea of Myra in Paris made me want to weep. There were so many unanswered questions, I felt like an unraveled spool of thread.

And then there was Sara. That was the one thread I could try to wind back up. I decided to call Sara from Myra's and give her the bad news. When my call went directly to voicemail, I started and couldn't stop: "Sara. I hate to tell you this without seeing you, but I have to. Rusty is a total creep. A scumbag. He's been seeing another woman—I've seen them together myself. He's staying at her house, the Ramelle house. I think she's the daughter of the movie star. Also, he tried to get this…this…guy…"—talking about Chris unhinged me but I kept going—"this famous surfer to convince me to join the Stella tour. Well, not just convince me but seduce me. That's the thing, Sara. Rusty is the Stella scout. He's not a venture capitalist. Screw his bogus environmental correctness. He's been secretly taking pictures of me and he's using you to get to me. I'm sorry. Please. When you get this message call me at Myra's."

I hung up, hoping to feel better, or at least somewhat relieved, but only felt worse than before. Myra was still not home, so I decided to take another stab at her bubble bath approach to self-pity. I brought the phone into the bathroom hoping Sara would call. I used an extra cap of bath bubbles, but it didn't do much good. I was a shy, incompetent human being. Chris didn't really care about me. My grandfather needed a life-saving operation. My mother was screwing Evil Incarnate. I stayed in the bath and let the water get colder and colder. I didn't move. I didn't see the point. Then, I heard a voice call, "Okay, you super freak. Where are you hiding?"

My heart lightened. Myra was finally home and she was calling me a freak, which was a positive sign. "I'm up here," I called back. "In the tub!"

Myra clomped up the stairs Clydesdale style and into the bathroom. She stuck a hand in the cool water. "Geez, Anna. Are you trying to poach yourself or something? You're looking sort of wrinkly."

"It feels good."

Myra reached in and pulled the plug. "For you maybe, water-girl. For mere mortals it's unbearable. Get out now." She handed me a towel and sat down on the closed toilet seat while I stood and dried myself. "You hungry?"

"Not really."

"Well, you need to eat, and I'm starving. Meet me downstairs when you're ready."

I did as I was told. Myra was in the kitchen, boiling water for pasta. She had an apron on over her daisy printed skirt. "You look like my old pal Betty Crocker," I said.

"Minus the preservatives, thank you very much," Myra said as she dumped linguine in the pot.

"I have it figured out now," I told her, as I sliced tomatoes for a salad. "Rusty must've been the one who filmed me and posted it on YouTube. To start some kind of buzz, or whatever they call it. Now he's gonna up the *ante* with those photographs."

"Anna." Myra started twisting a curl of her Brillo pad hair— something she did only when she was nervous, and Myra was almost never nervous. Not even for the SATs.

"What?"

"I have something to tell you." Myra looked down. "You're gonna kill me. It's the reason—well, one of the reasons—I've been acting so weird."

"What already? Jesus, Myra. You've been acting weird for days."

"It was me," she whispered.

"It was you *what*?"

"I posted the YouTube video." Her shoulders hunched up to her ears, and she shut her eyes tight.

"Excuse me?"

"I filmed you at Secretspot with that tiny camcorder I bought myself last year. The one you said was a waste of money because I never used it—until now."

I was trembling. "How *could* you?"

"How could I not?"

"But you know how I am about performing!" I was breaking into a cold sweat. "I've explained Shy-Person-Type-B-hood to you a gazillion times."

"I'm sorry. But I couldn't take it anymore. I took a risk. I even thought you might secretly be happy."

"Happy? Me?" I shrieked. "Are you kidding? Do you even know me anymore?"

"Of course I know you," Myra said and then added with an edge, "Well, at least I knew you before all this Ceekay stuff."

"What's that supposed to mean?"

"Oh come on. You know you've been, like, totally focused on him."

"But you said you weren't jealous," I cried.

"I'm not. It's just that it changed you."

"No, *you're* the one who's changed. I don't know the Myra who would secretly film me and post it on the goddamn internet. That's devious."

"Okay, so I lied," Myra shrugged—like it was no biggie. "But it's done, and now you have to deal with it."

"Easy for you to say." I stormed out of the room.

Myra followed. "Come on, Anna. What's so bad about it? So people see you surf. So you hooked up with a total hunk of a guy, so what? So you might actually have a career? Make money?"

"You probably just did this so you could be part of all the hype," I snapped.

"That is completely and totally unfair." She was yelling now.

"You need to get a life, Myra," I said.

"I have a life, thank you very much. In fact, my going-somewhere life is taking me to Paris."

My heart stopped. "Paris? You're going?" I was angrier at her than I'd ever been at anyone, but the thought of her moving to Paris threw me as if I'd been tossed off a cliff.

"Hell, yeah, I'm going. Judith called two days ago to tell me we're all moving, but you were so preoccupied with Mr. Dreamboat that I never got to tell you."

"Don't put that on me," I said. "I kept asking you about friggin' Paris."

"Maybe you gave it lip service, but only after we'd talked about you and Ceekay ad nauseam."

"That's low," I grumbled. "Besides, we talked about Jimmy, too."

"For, like, one second."

"That's not true," I said. But I knew she was right.

"In any case, I'm blowing this popsicle stand. Leaving this one-horse town. I've put an application in to study at the Sorbonne in a special high school program."

"Another thing you forgot to mention?"

She shrugged. "Why do you care? You seem to hate my guts right now. Maybe you'll be better off without me."

"Maybe so," I muttered.

"Just think of me drinking espressos in a cool little Left Bank café, while you're stuck at the safe old Shell Shop tagging Shellys."

"That's even lower!" I yelled.

"Well, sorry, Anna. It's the truth. It's *your* life that's going down the drain."

"I'm leaving," I snapped, shoving my belongings in a shopping bag. My beloved backpack was still up at Secretspot. I felt like I had body parts scattered all over town.

"You're like a scared little mouse who has all this ridiculous potential," Myra snapped back. "Wasted potential."

"Well, this scared little mouse is leaving now, so you can stop setting your traps!" I stormed out of the room like a raging bull. Nothing mouse-like about me—at least not on the outside.

Chapter Thirty

I ran the mile or so home, the shopping bag swinging from my hand, knocking my leg like a scolding. I hadn't been to my own shabby house for days, and it came as no surprise that Sara had left it a mess before she headed to Jersey. Scared to see how truly filthy the place was, I sat in the dark for a while—feeling cruddy enough without seeing the dirty dishes piled in the sink and the clothes scattered across the floor. I had no idea who was on my side anymore. Even in my own house, I felt like a vagabond without my backpack, sketchbook, and surfboard. I needed those things to feel whole. I called a cab and fifteen minutes later was on my way to collect some of the missing parts of me.

The Secretspot path would be impossible to navigate in the dark and my flashlight was busted. I decided to sneak around the side of the Ramelle house to the path that led to the cliff's edge, where I had left my backpack and surfboard. Plus Joe Shore, sole proprietor and cabby of Shore's Taxi Service, would definitely get suspicious if I asked him to drop me on the side of the road by a bunch of brush. As it was, I hoped he wouldn't ask any questions about the Ramelles. Mr. Shore knew that under normal circumstances I didn't hang out with movie stars.

The homemade sign posted on the back of the driver's seat of Shore's Taxi Service read *Be Sure with Shore*. Joe was known for driving slowly and carefully, which I appreciated. I was in no rush. "Hey, Mr. Shore," I said when I got in the back of the rattling, old mini-van. "Can you take me up to the Ramelle house, please?"

"Of course, Anna," he said. "You can be sure with Shore."

Thankfully that was all he said. I stared out the window, listening to the static buzz of the radio—the same station Grandpa liked to play in his truck. When we got to the Ramelle place, the gate at the end of the driveway was open.

181

"If you don't mind, Mr. Shore, can you just wait here? I'll be back in a flash."

"Whatever you want, Anna," he said. "But I could go up to the house."

I doubted Chris or Rusty was still around, but I couldn't take any chances. If they heard or saw the cab, I wasn't sure what they'd do. Or what I'd do.

"Nah, that's okay," I said. "It's good exercise for me."

I edged along the side of the driveway, trying to stay out of view. Trees grew together over my head like a canopy.

There weren't any guard dogs, and I didn't see any hidden cameras. It was just a stupid driveway like any other. A minute later, when the house came into view, I stopped short. Just when I thought my life couldn't get any more complicated, it turned into a Rubik's Cube. Sara's Jeep was parked out front, but Rusty's slime-mobile and Chris's VW van were nowhere to be seen. *What the hell was she doing there?* I had to know. Striding up to the door, I rang the bell. A moment later the door opened—

"Babe, why'd you buzz? You have the—"

"Hey, Sara," I said. "Fancy meeting you here."

"Anna?" cried my totally confused-looking mother. "What are you doing here?"

"What am *I* doing here?" I asked. "What are *you* doing here? You're supposed to still be in Jersey."

She smiled sheepishly. "I thought I could sneak back into town and see Rusty tonight without having to let you or the old folks know. His old college buddy is gone for a while and gave him use of this gorgeous place. When I found out he was at the Ramelle house, the house of a thousand rumors, and I had the chance to see the inside, I couldn't say no, could I? I mean, a whole overnight here? Pretty romantic, huh?"

"Old college buddy?" I cried, walking past her into the foyer. "Amelia Ramelle?"

"Yes, 'Amelia Ramelle.' What are you getting at, Anna?"

The Ramelle family portraits lined the walls around us. It felt like we were being spied on by a tribe of rich, blonde cannibals. "You didn't listen to my last message, did you?"

"No. My phone died and I left my charger in Jersey. I'm juicing it now, on Rusty's charger."

"Where is it?"

"In the living room, why?"

I ran down the hall into the living room. Rusty's spy camera was gone, but Sara's phone rested on the coffee table next to a bottle of champagne on ice and two long, skinny glasses. I held her phone out to her. "Listen to my message, Sara. Please."

"Jesus," Sara grimaced. "You can be so annoying sometimes, you know that?" She grabbed her phone, punched in her code, and raised it to her ear. Her expression darkened as she listened, then her knees buckled and she sank onto the couch. Any lingering suspicions I had had about Sara's involvement with all this Stella nonsense were gone.

"Sara, are you okay?" I asked.

Sara was quiet for a moment then she murmured, "I'm sure there's some kind of explanation."

"Are you kidding me?" I cried.

She looked up at me. Her eyes were pathetic, worse than a sick puppy's. I had seen sick puppy eyes on Sara before. These were more like terminally ill, full-grown dog eyes. "Rusty will have an answer for this."

I heard the front door open. "Sare?" Rusty called from the foyer, as if he had arrived on cue. "Babe? You here? There's this funky old minivan cab parked at the end of the—"

He got to the living room, and found more than he had expected. "Anna. Shit. You came back," he gasped.

Surprise, surprise, asshole, I thought.

His expression shifted chameleon-style from shocked to stoked. "Geez. Wow, um. This is great!"

"This is not great," I snapped, fury coursing through my veins. I'd never been like this before. This guy got me going like no one else ever had. "This is terrible. Tell my mother the truth!"

Rusty stumbled. "Truth? The truth is that Sara and I are hanging out. We're cool, right, Sare?"

My mother smiled weakly.

"Tell her you're the Stella scout," I demanded. "Tell her about the cameras. The pictures you took of me. Tell her about Ceekay."

"Ceekay?" Sara asked. Of course she recognized the name. "What does Ceekay have to do with this?"

"He's the guy I mentioned in my message," I explained. "Rusty is his manager; he used Ceekay to get to me while he worked on you himself."

"Well, I don't know about Mr. Kahimbe, but I certainly wasn't using your mother." Rusty crossed his arms across his chest defensively.

"So who are you cheating on, then, my mother or Amelia Ramelle?" I challenged.

"Rusty?" Sara's voice cracked. "Is there something I should know about you and Amelia?"

"He and Amelia Ramelle were kissing nonstop at Brine-stellar's last Tuesday night," I said.

Sara turned her dog eyes on Rusty. "Is this true?"

Rusty sat down next to her on the couch and took her hand. "Babe, it's a lie. Amelia and I went out for a drink. We talked about the old days. Maybe she kissed me on the cheek; maybe I hugged her—nothing more. And I'm so sorry I didn't tell you about this Stella stuff earlier, but I wanted us to establish a solid relationship first. It was a total coincidence that you happened to be the mother of the girl I was searching for, I couldn't believe it myself. I planned on telling you my own way tonight." He glared at me and added, "Anna is misleading you, babe. She's totally off-base."

"Sara." I tried to keep my cool. "You're not buying this, are you?"

Sara put her face in her hands.

"Mom?" I tried again. "Don't you see what's going on?"

Finally she spoke, but without lifting her head. "Anna, maybe you should just leave."

"You're gonna stay here?" I shouted. "With *him*?"

She nodded, cracking my already weakened heart into a million pieces.

I ran from the house toward the cliffs, jumping over rocks and twigs in the dark, tears streaming down my cheeks. I found my surfboard by Pee Pee Rock, stumbled and slid down the cliff path with it wedged under my arm, and catapulted myself into an ocean of howling surf—waves so out of control, and so massive that no sane person would ever, ever consider going in, even in the full light of day. My life sucked and I needed to go out to sea. I wanted to get beyond the break, where the ocean was calm, where I could think. I needed to be where I felt most at home.

Salty white water slammed against me, knocking me repeatedly off my board. My clothes plastered and bunched uncomfortably against my skin, weighing me down. But the sea would soon settle, I knew, and I might settle with it. I managed to make it past the break, and, in the bright moonlight, I could see a figure on the cliff waving their arms at me. I sat on my board, trying to calm down, but I was a quaking mess—my heart a pounding hammer in my chest, and my body shaking violently from inner turmoil mixed with wind and cold. The only warmth came from the hot tears that ran like rivers down my cheeks. My disappointing mother, my failed romantic life, my ailing grandfather, my best friend's betrayal: these were things that even the ocean couldn't wash away.

The moon dropped behind a dark mass of clouds, and the night fell dark. I needed to get back to shore and, with little to no depth perception in the black night, it would be a difficult paddle. I decided instead to catch a wave and ride it to shore.

I felt a wave coming, and turned my board, waiting for the water to rise beneath me, to take care of me. It was a perfect wave; it was an insane wave. I took off and rode it like I was a teardrop running down a monster's cheek. The wind picked up, whipping my face. The ocean's surface was a frothy mess and I was a mess too, bobbing on my board, crying like a baby. I blubbered and the wave howled—I swear the wave called my name out loud, more than once.

And then things fell apart. A small bump in the wave tripped me up. It was a bump easily maneuvered in daylight, but not in the dark. I wobbled, trying to regain my footing, but couldn't. I lost it and wiped out.

I was stuck underwater, churned and mashed, tumbled like a piece of trash. Disoriented, I couldn't find the surface and my lungs were bursting. I was in deep, way too deep. I felt a sudden pain in my arm and leg as I was thrashed against the rocks; then, right before everything went dark, I thought: *This is it, you stupid idiot. This is how it ends.* And in that second, what bothered me more than dying was that everyone would think I had done this on purpose—that I had wanted to die. And I didn't want to die. Not at all.

Chapter Thirty-One

Hush now," a voice murmured. "You're having a bad dream."

Opening my eyes, I stared up at acoustic tiles. Clicks and beeps sounded around me.

"Well, hello there, Anna Marie. Welcome back."

I stiffly turned my head toward the voice. Gramma sat next to my bed, her hand in mine.

"Where am I?" I asked.

"Easton Medical, dear."

"Am I okay?" I asked.

"You're fine. Just a bit bruised. No concussion, thank goodness, but that ankle of yours has some nasty cuts. They gave you a sedative last night to keep you comfortable. When you first came in, you were in quite a tizzy. You don't remember that?"

I shook my head. The last thing I remembered was running away from the Ramelle house.

"The doctor said that you might have some amnesia, but it's nothing to worry about. The nurse said when you woke up you could walk around a bit and see how you felt."

"So what happened exactly?"

"You almost drowned, Anna Marie."

And then it all came back in a rush—my stupid surf, the wave, the wipeout. "I didn't plan on killing myself. I just needed to get away."

Gramma patted my arm and sighed. "Well, next time do us all a favor and take a long walk on the beach instead."

"I'm sorry, Gramma." I squeezed her hand and tried not to cry.

"It's okay, dear. Come on. I think it's time for you to take that walk."

I stumbled down the hallway with my frail little grandmother holding my elbow. I hadn't been to a hospital since Grandpa's heart surgery. Amid all the hushed hallway conversations and PA announcements, I thought I heard Grandpa's voice coming from another room.

"I could've sworn I just heard Grandpa."

"You did," Gramma said. "He's right in there." She pointed to a room opposite.

"Oh God, no!" My idiocy had caused him to have that second heart attack. I pulled away from Gramma and half-stumbled and half-ran to the door.

I heard his booming voice, loud and clear. "You're being ridiculous. I can run the shop. If it makes you happy I'll get a goddamn stool and sit behind the cash register all day."

I shrieked as I entered. Sara was trussed up in the hospital bed, with her right arm and left leg in casts, jacked up on pulleys; her beautiful face swollen with bruises.

"Shh, Anna," hushed Grandpa. "It's gonna be fine. No need to get your knickers in a twist."

I took Sara's hand. "Mom, you look like shit," I cried.

Sara mumbled, with a pitiful attempt at a smile, "And that's what I get for trying to save your sorry ass."

"Ma, Dad, could you give us a few minutes alone?" Sara asked. After my grandparents left, she said, "You look really hot in your blue sack, Anna. Much sexier than me."

Leave it to Sara to make a lame joke while lying in a hospital bed with multiple limbs in a cast, a black eye, and a swollen face.

"What the hell did you do to yourself?" I asked.

"What any mother would do. I went into that gnarly mess after you."

I shivered as the realization hit me—it was not the ocean that had called my name, but my mother. Sara had found me, grabbed me, and saved my life. But it looked like she had almost lost her own in the process.

"Just so you know. I wasn't trying to kill myself," I said.

"Well, that's a relief," she sighed.

"I just needed to get away and go somewhere safe."

"You call that spot safe? Twelve-foot surges in the dark? Wicked undertow? And those dicey rocks on the inside?"

I shrugged. "Obviously not the best choice."

"Obviously." Sara's eyes got all misty and tears started to dribble down her swollen cheeks. "I don't know what I would have done if..." She squeezed my hand tighter and I thought it was a good sign that she still had a killer grip. Then she *really* started crying, like I had never seen her cry before—more intense than after any romantic breakup, fight with her parents, or work-related meltdown. Seeing her cry got me started again, too, until it was both of us sobbing our hearts out.

"Sara, chill," I managed in a quavering voice. I couldn't remember Sara ever crying over *me* before. Or maybe I had been so busy rejecting her these past few years that I hadn't given her a chance. Either way, it felt weird. But maybe, also, kind of nice.

"You were right about Rusty. He was a real scumbag. What kind of guy sits there and doesn't even lift a finger to help when you're trying to save your daughter?"

"Sara," I sighed. "I get it now."

"Get what?"

"You know, the whole guy thing—how you want to believe whatever they tell you; how it feels good when they like you, or you think they like you. It's a super amp. A major stoke. At least at first."

Sara sighed. "The beginning is always the best part of the ride."

"And then, when things go south, you keep telling yourself that if this or that were different, if you could rewrite the whole thing, or make him a different person it could all work out. But it doesn't. It just sucks, and feels like it will suck forever."

Sara took my hand again. "That little fucker Ceekay really got under your skin, huh?"

"I guess," I shrugged. "Falling in love blows."

"Yeah. It's totally overrated," she sighed sadly. "And hard to avoid."

I sat quietly with my hand resting in her non-injured one. Rusty's ring was gone, a pale strip of flesh below her knuckle marked its short-lived stint. Knowing Sara, she had probably had a nurse flush it down the toilet or had tossed it out the back door of the ambulance herself. After a few minutes, Gramma came in and said, "Sorry, Anna Marie, but the doctor told us she wants you back in your own room."

"See you later, Sara," I said as I stood.

"Later, 'gator," she whispered, eyes closed.

Grandpa waited for me on one of the orange plastic chairs in the hall.

"The doctor's in your room," he said. "She wants to give you a quick look over. If everything is okay, she says you can go home this afternoon, but your mom's gonna need to stay for a few more days. I'm gonna go down to the business office and pay the damn bill."

I imagined dollar bills flying out of Grandpa's pockets, all because of me. "What's wrong with Sara exactly?" I asked.

"Her lower leg is broken in two places and she fractured her wrist. The bruises on her face will go away, but probably not as quickly as your beauty queen of a mother would like. One thing's for sure: She won't be doing any surfing, or much of anything else for some time."

"How come she's so messed up but I'm not?"

"She smashed into the rocks while using all her strength to get you out of the water," said Grandpa. "At least that's what Joe Shore says it looked like from the beach. He heard Sara screaming and ran around to the cliffs just as she raced into the water. He's the one who called the Volunteer Ambulance Service."

"I guess you really can be sure with Shore," I said.

"Joe said your mother swam out to you—supposedly a helluva distance. Your leash must've snapped off. After she grabbed you, Sara hauled your sorry ass all the way in like a real lifeguard. Got even more banged up herself on those rocks, keeping you above water."

My mother, Sara Dugan. She might have broken bones, but she was more whole than ever to me.

Chapter Thirty-Two

The doctor gave me a green light to leave the hospital. Gramma stayed with Sara while Grandpa took me home. Grandpa took the usual left off Emerson to Main, but instead of turning on to Toilsome he took a right on Early's Point Road.

"Where the hell are you headed?" I asked.

"I wanna see the big swell that everyone's jabbering about," he shrugged. "You got a problem with that?"

"Actually, yes. I don't want to see waves at the moment. In fact, I don't know if I *ever* want to see waves again in my entire life."

He snorted. "Well, well. If you aren't the little Miss Gloria Swanson. I can imagine your mother saying something dramatic like that, but not you."

"Well, maybe I have more in common with my mother than you think."

He nodded. "Well, maybe you do. Maybe you do."

"Anyway, can we just skip it, Grandpa? Really, let's just go home."

"Anna, one rotten apple doesn't spoil the whole bunch. Just because that Rusty character turned out to be a crook doesn't mean you have to give up on the whole surfing thing."

I crossed my arms and stared out the window. I wanted to mention the second rotten apple—Chris was moldy at the core too. But I really didn't want to have a conversation with Grandpa about Chris. And then, as luck would have it, he decided to have it all on his own.

"Maybe we'll see your young man there," he said.

"My what?"

"Myra told me about your professional surfer friend."

"You talked to Myra?" My heart lurched.

"Of course," Grandpa said. "I called her last night. She's your best friend. I figured you would want her to know what had happened to you last night."

191

"Not really," I said. Man, how I missed Myra.

"Trouble between you two?"

"Something like that."

"I was wondering why she didn't come to the hospital. She did ask me to keep her posted, though, told me to call again this morning to let her know everything was okay with you."

"Whatever," I huffed.

"You wanna talk about it? This stuff between you and Myra?"

"No."

Grandpa sighed. "Well, I won't pretend to understand what goes on between two females. But if that surfer boy is at the beach, I can shake his hand or give him a piece of my mind. Whichever you choose."

"Leave it, Grandpa, will you?" I cried.

"Geez. Okay. Forget it," he muttered.

"Besides, he's on his way to Fiji." *With Inga Ward*, I thought. *Ms. Perfection.*

"Oh. Well, then."

We drove the rest of the way in tense silence. When we got to the parking lot, I was glad to see it was packed.

"See? There's nowhere to park," I said. "Just do a U-turn and leave."

"Hold your horses. I think I see someone pulling out ahead." Grandpa inched his pickup forward. A spot was open—left by a SUV with three stacked boards strapped to the roof. The surf-mobile careened past us, causing a minor dust storm.

"Hey, Bub, watch it!" Grandpa yelled out his window. "I don't get it," he muttered. "What's his hurry? He got his waves already, right?"

"There's nothing to get, Grandpa," I sighed. "Some surfers always have something to prove. Even on land."

Grandpa parked the car and turned off the engine. "What are you waiting for, Grumpy?" he asked, opening his door. "You're not gonna let me go down to the beach and make an asshole of myself without you, are you?"

"Oh great," I exclaimed. "I just can't win with you." Hauling

myself out of the car, I walked through the crowded parking lot with
Grandpa. "You have to promise—no mention of what happened
last night. They'll all learn soon enough, but I can't deal with it right
now, okay?"

"Okay," he agreed. "Hey, there's Bob Tellings. Hey Bobby, over
here!" Grandpa waved his arms at Bob, who was making his way over
the slippery low-tide rocks.

Bob had spent the summer between college and law school
working for Grandpa's construction company. Now, Bob walked
toward us looking demented and deliriously happy. I knew that look.
He had died and gone to heaven at least twenty times on at least
twenty waves.

He shook Grandpa's hand. "Mr. Tom Dugan. To what do we owe
the pleasure?"

"Anna here needed a ride, so I gave her one," Grandpa lied
through his teeth.

I narrowed my eyes at Grandpa.

"Super Surfer, where the hell have you been?" Bob asked.

I shrugged. "I haven't felt too well."

"And where's Sara? Her admirers have all been looking for her."

"She's been sick, too," I told him. Kendall's Watch was a small
town that fed on gossip. Word would be out by the end of the day
as to what had happened last night, but I didn't have to rush the
onslaught of embarrassing chatter.

"Well, girl, I hope you're on the mend. It is pumping out there.
Get on it. Where's your board?"

Where *was* my board? Probably floating in broken pieces and
halfway to Europe, or scattered in shards of fiberglass and foam on
Secretspot beach. "I didn't bring it."

"Well, that's a mighty shame. Hey, if you want, you could take out
my seven-six. It's in the back of my truck."

"Go ahead, Anna," said Grandpa. "The doc said it would be
okay."

"You talked to the doctor about my surfing?"

"Yeah, so what if I did?" Grandpa shrugged. "Come on. I'll stay and watch."

"I don't have my surf clothes," I said through gritted teeth.

"Yeah, you do. I tossed the ones you stash at our house in the back seat." Grandpa smiled.

I glared at him.

"Hey, it's a free country. I'm allowed to toss whatever I want into my own car."

"Fine."

I turned back to Bob and shook my head. "No thanks, Bob. I think I'm just gonna watch for now."

"Suit yourself, Anna. But if you want the board, you know where to find it." He shook hands with Grandpa again. "Great to see you, Tom. Give my love to Lorraine." Bob stumbled up the beach to sit with a bunch of his cronies. Once he was out of earshot, I poked Grandpa gently in his soft side.

"I can't friggin' believe you, Grandpa."

"I had to at least give it a try," he explained.

"Well, now you can give it a rest."

We sat together on an old park bench, stolen years ago from the Town Green and dragged onto the Early's beach for surf viewing.

"Who's that guy out there with the purple shirt on?" Grandpa pointed toward the waves.

"That's Nick Fleming. And it's called a rash guard, Grandpa. Not a shirt."

"Little Nicholas Fleming? Dorothy's boy?"

"Nick Fleming is no boy, Grandpa. He's a beast. He rips really hard."

We watched Nick paddle for a huge wave. He was a power surfer, pure gritty muscular strength, but not a whole lot of grace. He took risks and made them work, popping up clumsily before the wave had really formed, but when it started to crank he timed his moves to easily slide across the face. Nick squatted, knees bent so deep that his butt almost hit the back of his board; a posture which made him go super-fast like an arrow parallel to the crest of the wave. Then he slowed down ever so slightly and the wave covered him.

"Jesus Christ," Grandpa cried. "Is he gonna be okay?"

"Don't worry, he's just getting barreled. A little driving through the cavern. He'll pop out the other side in a second. You'll see."

Nick appeared as I had predicted. When he emerged, he whipped over the top of the wave, beating his chest and screaming.

"Can you do that?" Grandpa asked.

"Yeah. But without the Tarzan bull."

"Impressive. That move, I mean. The driving thing. Not the macho shit. That's just embarrassing."

"Welcome to my world," I sighed.

"Maybe I should take up this sport," Grandpa said. "Maybe then I wouldn't need that other surgery."

I looked at him closely. His color was off, and he kept clearing his throat as if he had a mothball stuck in his gullet. He didn't look good. "Grandpa. You don't have a choice, do you?"

He shrugged, defeated for once. "Seems like I don't, according to the doctor."

"So, when are you gonna do it?"

"Not until your mother and you are back on your feet, and I know everything at the shop is running smoothly. Until I've paid the goddamn co-insurance on your hospital bill. Then I'll save up my pennies and fork them over for mine."

"But Grandpa, I don't think this is something they want you to wait for," I tried.

"Well, I don't give a rat's ass what *they* want," he snapped. "I've said yes to the damn operation, but I'll do it when it's convenient and that's that."

I knew it was pointless to push the issue.

I didn't have any overwhelming urges to surf myself. In some ways it felt like a relief, the way an addict must feel when they're finally clean. I realized it was probably a temporary state of mind, the after-effect of the accident—but I couldn't be entirely sure.

As we sat there, a little kid ran up and shoved several sheets of paper in our hands. Another flyer for the Montauk tournament— the tournament that refused to die.

195

"Is this the contest you did when you were younger?" Grandpa asked. "Says here it starts this weekend."

"Big whoop." I crumpled my flyer up and tossed it in the bin next to the bench. Suddenly I wanted to leave. Getting up, I walked toward the truck. Grandpa eventually followed.

Grandpa dropped me off at Toilsome and headed back to Easton General to pick up Gramma. I stumbled up to my room hoping for a nap, but couldn't fall asleep. I lay on top of the quilt with both Fluffy and Woof Woof clutched to my chest and pondered the idea of professional surfing. It still gave me heart palpitations. I would be a professional disaster—crashing and burning within days. Even the idea of drawing didn't excite me anymore. I couldn't conjure a single Wavehouse.

When I had first lain down, the sun was a bright slash across the bed. Now, it was dark out and my whole body was cold. The smell of Gramma's cooking seeped under the door. Trudging down the stairs, I heard them going at it in the kitchen.

"You can't wait, Tom!" Gramma shrieked. "I don't care about the money. We'll find a way to pay for it."

"You don't get it, Lorraine." Grandpa was trying to sound reasonable. "There is no money anywhere. That first operation near cleaned us out. The co-pays on this valve replacement are going to ruin us. And now this last disaster with Sara? She can't pay those hospital bills. She won't say boo, but I know the shop's not doing too well. We're gonna have to help out. This is gonna sink us into an even deeper hole."

Gramma was crying. I could hear her sniffle and moan. "You're going to die. I just know it."

"There, there, Lainie," Grandpa comforted. "I'll drink the piss milk and take my pills. I'll be fine, don't you worry."

"Just get out of the kitchen now," Gramma stammered. "Come on. Go. Go!"

I tiptoed back up to the top landing as I heard Grandpa grumbling his way toward his La-Z-Boy. I sat on the bed and waited another ten minutes before walking downstairs. I didn't quite know what to say or do. Everyone and everything in my world seemed to be falling apart.

Gramma and Grandpa were in the living room watching TV. Gramma was swooning and clutching her potholder to her heart. Grandpa was in full recline looking self-satisfied and smug. I noticed the flyer for the Montauk tournament had made its way home, and was lying on the table next to the TV Guide.

"Oh my," cried Gramma. "Amazing." Her eyes were puffy and red, but she looked happy.

"What are you guys watching?" I asked. The screen was filled with lots of ocean, a bit of sky and not much else. "What is this? One of your nature shows?"

"Just wait a minute," Grandpa said slyly. "You'll see."

Suddenly from the right corner of the screen a bright yellow dash appeared; then a flash of red and black. I realized what we were watching—me.

"You're lovely, Anna Marie," gushed Gramma. "Like a beautiful bird riding the wind in the sky."

The me on the TV took off and flew down the face of a nice, chunky wave. My legs looked like a pair of stilts, my hair pushed off my forehead in odd little peaks, and my hands looked like paws at the end of string beany arms. But once I got over my physical self-consciousness, I had to admit the surfing was all there. I was pretty damn good.

"Myra gave us this DVD. Dropped it off yesterday, before all hell broke loose," Grandpa explained.

"I can't friggin' believe her," I said and started to leave the room.

"Anna Marie, you come back here this instant!" Gramma demanded in a shaky, on-the-verge-of-tears voice.

Gramma didn't deserve any more pain from me. Obediently returning to the couch, I watched the Surfing Siren take on a few more waves. Gramma continued to watch me and sigh. I had assumed that I would need to wear a dress, or sing in the church choir, or join the cooking club to get those types of sighs. But go figure. All I needed to do was ace a nice ten-foot Secretspot left and polish it off with a confident cut back. Monkey paws and all.

That's when the Siren made it clear. She told me exactly what I needed to do.

I stood up. "I'm hungry. What's for dinner?" I left the room and walked toward the kitchen. I was going to need lots of fuel—physically and mentally—to get through what I had determined to do. Dinner had never smelled so good in all my life.

Chapter Thirty-Three

The next morning, the sound of a howling wind woke me from a deep sleep. It was seven thirty and I was drowsy and disoriented. By normal-person standards, half-past seven was a perfectly acceptable time to wake up, but by dawn-patrolling-surf standards it was wicked late. And I was now back on patrol. I had a mission, and only one day to prepare. My mother had risked her life to save me, and now she was in the hospital. I had to win this year's Montauk Junior Surf Tournament so I could get the money needed to pay Sara's hospital bills. And maybe enough to get Grandpa his heart valve operation pronto. They had all put themselves out for me. It was payback time.

And how totally psyched would Sara be if I could come home from Montauk a winner? Maybe that would make up for her broken bones and broken heart. "Hey, Sara. Guess what I just did?" I imagined myself telling her, all nonchalant and cool as a cucumber. Then I would tell her the great news and she would give me one of her killer smiles.

And at least Myra wouldn't be able to call me a scared little mouse. Though I was trying as hard as possible not to care what Myra thought about me ever again.

I had told my grandparents that we had made up and that I'd like to stay with Myra through the weekend. They thought it was a grand idea. Like every other Kendall's Watcher over the age of sixty-five, they thought Myra Berkowitz was the 'bee's knees.' I didn't quite know what I thought of Miss Paris Cafe anymore.

Right now, though, it was all about surfing. I needed to get back on top of my game, and only had until Saturday to do it. Changing into my surf gear, I made the bed, shoved my clothes into my backpack, and kissed my pet pillows goodbye. Then I rode the banister downstairs, starting the day with a wave-like slide, and tiptoed into the kitchen where I gobbled a banana and a corn muffin, and washed them down with a glass of milk. I left my crummy plate, banana peel, and filmy glass by the sink—I knew Gramma would be happy to notice that I had eaten a proper breakfast, even if she grumbled about the mess I had left behind.

The rainbow-colored windsock flapped away on top of the garage; gusts from the southeast were beating it silly. The waves at Secretspot would be a gnarly mess. When the wind was *that* strong and blowing from *that* direction, all it did was chop the ocean up like a giant washing machine. It would most likely be a total drag, but come hell or high water, I would be a hard-core surf-training machine.

I had an old, dinged-up board stashed in Grandpa's garage. I secured the board to the rack on my bike and rode to Secretspot at warp speed with the wind at my back.

At the beach, I sneaked a peek up at the Ramelle house. The curtains were all drawn and there was not a soul in sight. The ocean looked dirty and cold. Mushy peaks formed all over the place; the waves had no rhyme or reason. It would be like surfing in a slop sink. Waxing my board, I secured the leash to my ankle and did a few side stretches and forward bends to get the early morning creaks out of my body.

In the water, the familiar feeling of salty coolness washed over my feet. *Same old, same old,* I told myself. *You've done this a million times before.* But I had a brief flash of panic It took me a few minutes to talk myself off the scaredy-cat ledge, to remind myself that surfing in the dark had been a crazy-pants move, whereas surfing in the light of day—in manageable, if not perfect, waves was something I'd done my entire life. I lay on my board and off I went.

The paddle out was one big splash-fest. I got hit from the east by a nasty little bump that sent me in the opposite direction, only to get slapped silly by another little annoyance from the west. It stayed that way until I got outside the tricky break. Not a whole lot of fun.

The outside was equally nauseating. A stealthy southwesterly drift meant I couldn't relax in any one spot. *This is good practice,* I said to myself. *Imagine the people. They're what's gonna trip you up, not the waves.*

200

I imagined being bookended by my mother's surfer favorites, Kelly Garrison and Mindy Shultz. Eventually, a quasi-rideable three-wave set came through. In my mind, Kelly took off on the first wave of the set, and Mindy took the second. I would wisely wait for the last one, hoping there would be less whitewater frenzy behind it.

My wave wasn't huge, maybe five feet high, but it packed a surprising punch. As soon as I stood up, I could tell it would be a ride that required concentration. I faced a steep and sudden slide on a face that was as rutted as an abandoned train track. There was no getting into a groove with this wave; I could only endure the *bump, bump, bump* that traveled up my feet to my thighs, back, and chest. I imagined what my surf session might look like from the beach. Not pretty, that's for sure. *What kind of score would that wave have gotten me?* I wondered. *Probably a minus ten.*

"Goddamn wave," I snarled, as I repositioned my board to paddle back out. I was really testy, but realized that cursing the ocean got me nowhere. Blaming the waves for my incompetence was just bratty and stupid. "Okay. Sorry, wave," I sighed. "It's not you. I'm just having a bad day."

Whatever kind of wave came next, I vowed to accept it as gracefully as possible. The next wave was slightly better, larger and thicker, and the drop not quite so steep; it held its shape longer, giving me the chance to try a few maneuvers in the whipped cream wind-blown surface. I managed to carve a few edges, flapping around in a loony-bird-meets-orangutan style. During one upward move, a bump in the wave almost sent the nose of my board into the nose on my face.

Once I got back to the outside, I looked toward shore and spotted Sara standing by Pee Pee Rock.

"What the hell?" I said aloud. She wasn't supposed to be out of the hospital for at least another two days. Why was she back here at Secretspot? Sara saw me looking her way and raised her crutch in a wave.

I paddled in to shore and stumbled up the beach to where she waited.

"This place must go off big time with a northwest wind and southeast swell," Sara said.

With a crutch under each arm, and a cast on her left leg and right forearm, I could not believe she had come to the beach.

"What are you doing here?" I yelled.

"That asshole Rusty texted me saying he was leaving town and that it might be best for everyone if I got my car out of Amelia's driveway before she returned tonight. Can you fucking believe that guy? I nearly die—*we* nearly die—and all he's thinking of is covering his slimeball tracks. But he's not getting off so easily," Sara smiled. "I left Ms. Ramelle a note on her door telling her all about his two-timing ways. Old college buddy, my ass."

"But you're not supposed to be up and around yet!"

Sara shrugged. "I thought I would take a peek at the cove during daylight. Geez, it really is sweet out there. Damned shame that I can't surf for god knows how long." She looked out at the Secretspot surf like a toddler eyeing a bowl of jellybeans.

"You're supposed to be resting. In the hospital."

"Anna, I couldn't stay there any longer. I was going bonkers. It's the most boring place ever."

"It's a hospital, Sara," I groaned. "Not a beauty spa."

"I know," she sighed. "Okay. To be honest, I couldn't afford it. Our crap insurance only covered one night. And they had to let me out once I showed them how good I was on these suckers. I was speeding up and down the hallway like a total pro."

"How did you get here?"

"Mr. Shore picked me up at the hospital. He let me practice driving on the way here. What an old sweetie."

"Do Gramma and Grandpa know?"

She nodded. "They're not happy about it, but they're not making a big stink because I promised to stay with them for the next few days. Gramma wants to be all motherly and shit. Make me soup and muffins and god knows what else. I'm gonna get fat as a cow."

Sara, fat? Impossible.

"Don't worry," she said. "I won't be taking your room. The

doctor said definitely no stairs. So don't you dare tell her I took this little cliff walk."

"Sara," I moaned. "Don't push it. Especially with Gramma and Grandpa."

"No worries. Up there on boring Toilsome Lane, I'll be good as gold. Looks like I'm on a cot in the dining room."

"Next to Gramma's china cabinet?"

"Yep. Should be really interesting. I may have to break into her schnapps stash. I'll let you have some, if you want."

How motherly. "I'm staying at Myra's till Sunday," I lied.

"Grandpa told me that you and Myra had a falling out?"

"We did. But we made up." I lied on top of my lie.

"What went down between the two of you anyway?"

My mother was actually asking about something to do with my life, so I thought I should throw her one true bone. "Myra's the one who posted that YouTube video of me."

"Wow," Sara cried. "Really?"

"Really."

"Who would've thought? Your friend Myra Berkowitz, a crafty little operator. That's impressive."

Not the response I wanted, but I should've seen it coming. Now I wanted the true bone back. "No, it's not impressive. It was mean and devious."

"Oh come on, Anna, that's a bit harsh."

"Listen, you may live in a world of crafty operators, but I like my friends straightforward and honest." But here I was, also lying. The opposite of straightforward and honest. *I'm such a hypocrite*, I thought.

"Whatever. I'm glad you made up with her, especially now that you and Ceekay are history. You need friends in broken-heart times like these."

I thought I hated Chris, but when Sara mentioned him my heart ended up in my gut. "Yeah," I sighed. "I guess."

"And you probably need more of a mother, too," Sara said softly.

"That might be nice," I replied, even more softly.

"So, I was watching you out there," Sara began. "When you start getting nervous, you tend to let up on your back foot. Don't do that. Dig in deeper with the back foot and take your shoulders back, too. Otherwise you get too much momentum and lose the sweet spot. You have a tendency, when you're spooked, to ride it a hair too far forward."

Was this what "more of a mother" meant? Surf tips? My heart, which had returned to its rightful chest position, was again slipping southward. "Whatever." I shrugged.

Then, miraculously, Sara turned it around. "Anna," she said, eyes watery, sad, and serious. "Don't let your demons get the best of you. Don't be like me that way."

"Sara—"

"But *you*? You have it all, but you just don't see it."

I looked down at my feet.

"Stop holding back," she pleaded. "Just go for it, okay?"

I didn't know what to say. I suddenly wanted to tell her everything about my plan, but I worried about creating expectations that I might not be able to meet. And if Sara knew, and if I screwed up in Montauk a second time, I wouldn't be able to face her. I would have to go live under a rock in Japan.

"I gotta get back out there," I said. "Meghan will need me in the shop soon."

I turned back toward the waves when what I really wanted to do was climb up the cliff and carry my mother home.

Chapter Thirty-Four

From the outside, I watched my determined mother make her way up the cliff. I had to smile. Sara rocked those crutches like they were sports equipment, racing along the rocks like a speedster.

For the next hour, I focused on surfing, blocking everything else out, and letting the currents guide my moves and the swells direct me. We did okay together, me and my wave friends. I prayed they wouldn't let me down the next day at the tournament.

That night I went back to my own humble home, knowing Sara was up at Toilsome—already driving my grandparents crazy, no doubt. I gobbled a quick bowl of cereal with milk that was on the cusp of curdle, and scrubbed the bowl clean. Next I attacked the crusty remains of eggs, grease, and other unknown substances that had turned to cement on a pile of dishes in the sink. Once the kitchen was clear, I set up my makeover supplies. I had quite an evening beauty project ahead of me.

I couldn't take the chance of being recognized as either Anna Dugan or the Surfing Siren at the tournament. I didn't want to be Anna, in case I crashed and burned and reports of my failure made their way via the Eastern Long Island surf community gossip mill to Kendall's; and I didn't want to be recognized as the Surfing Siren because I wasn't entirely sure how I felt about my cyberspace alter-ego and all her public notoriety. If I aced the contest—which is what I intended to do—I would return home in a blaze of glory, but I preferred it to be a very private fire.

To that end, I needed to look as different as possible. I snipped my hair, trying to achieve a sporty kind of shag, but ended up with a just-released-from-the-insane-asylum crew cut. And it only got worse. Dying my hair wasn't something I should ever have attempted in the privacy of my own home. But what did the hair-and-makeup-challenged me know? I now know that going from black to blonde is not what hair stylists refer to as "a single process." It took four attempts to manage a weird mustardy shade. I almost died when I gazed in the mirror. I looked like an emaciated ghoul released from the House of Horrors. My hair stood up in tufts like mildewed wheat, and my seriously burned scalp felt like it was on fire. "Different" was an understatement.

I heard a knock at the door while I was cleaning up. I went to see who it was and then remembered my new look. Rummaging around in the hall closet, I found an old Yankees cap one of Sara's former flames had given her a couple of summers ago. I glanced in the mirror next to the closet and moaned. When Sara wore the cap, her long black ponytail was thrust through the space above the snaps, swinging in back all femme and come hither, but I looked like a plucked chicken with a saucepan lid on their head. *Stick me in an oven and grab a fork.*

Before opening the door, I called, "Who is it?"

"It's me."

My heart dropped. Myra. I wanted desperately to let her in, hug her, and apologize for being so mean, but then I remembered it was Myra who had started this whole thing by keeping secrets.

"What do you want?" I asked, trying to sound as cool as possible.

"I just wanted to make sure you were okay. You know, after the accident."

"I'm fine. You can leave now," I said, waiting for her to walk away. She didn't leave. "I said you can leave now."

"Come on, Anna." She was using the sensible Myra tone. "Let me in."

"I'm busy," I lied. I might've been acting like a baby, but I didn't really care. I wasn't ready to talk to her and that was that. "Now please, just go home already!" I pulled down the shade and left her in the dark.

The next morning, I rode to the train station and got on the five forty-five westbound train with my bike and board. Fortunately, it was an empty train and the conductor was fine with me and my various modes of transportation.

206

Two short stops later, I was in Montauk. I rode my bike to the center of town, then headed left on the Montauk Highway up to Ditch Plains Road, where I assumed the tournament would be. If I had any doubts, there were signs pasted on every telephone pole I passed: *This way to the 7th Annual Montauk Junior Surf Tournament*, and *MJST next right*. I followed the signs in an agitated daze, trying to psych myself up.

Just pretend you're out there on your own. The other surfers are buoys. Tune out any shit that comes your way...

Imagine all the people on the beach are animals, not humans. A nice big pack of friendly dogs, chimpanzees, baby bunnies...

Think of Grandpa. Sara. Gramma. This is for them...

BEEEEEEP! The sound of a car horn almost sent me careening into the bushes on the side of the road.

"Hey, watch where you're riding!" a girl's voice yelled out the window as a shiny station wagon sped past with at least five brand-new surfboards stacked upon its roof. I watched them make a sharp, dirt-blasting turn into the Ditch Plains parking lot a few yards ahead.

Oh great, I thought. *My competition. Can't I just turn my bike in the other direction and head back to Toilsome Lane, skitter upstairs, get under the covers with Woof Woof and Fluffy, and stay there for the rest of my life?*

Taking a deep breath, I righted my bike and continued on, making my own less splashy and dramatic entrance. The lot was filled with kids carrying surfboards, parents schlepping rainbow-striped umbrellas, and a bunch of teenage volunteers directing people to the sign-in table. All the volunteers wore white tee shirts with an awesome graphic of a girl surfer ripping down the face of a curling wave on the front, and MONTAUK JUNIORS RULE across the back. *Sara would love one of those,* I thought. *Note to self—if you win, you'll buy her one as a souvenir.*

As I locked my bike, I heard giggling behind me. Turning around, I noticed two girls whispering to each other and staring in my direction. They were probably twelve years old max, harmless and silly. But their giggling and staring made me feel like I was barely a tween myself. It was as if they were Kiara and her nasty sidekick all

207

over again.

Two deep breaths later, I realized the girls weren't even looking at me. They were looking at a toddler who had pulled his bathing suit down and waddled with the suit around his ankles. It was legitimately funny, and even I, in my panicked state, managed a few weak chuckles.

At the registration table, a rag-tag line of surf kids shuffled impatiently from foot to foot, waiting to sign in. They were mostly around three feet tall and between the ages of eight and eleven. Not a very intimidating bunch.

You can do this, Anna, I said to myself, *I know you can.* As I stood waiting my turn, I tried to keep my head down, avoiding eye contact with everyone and anyone. In one peek, I noticed the judges table together with a line of four chairs under a canopy, set up with the best view of the surf break. I imagined them sitting there, taking stock of my surfing from the shore. Writing notes, giving me scores. Giving me hives.

"Hi. Name, please?" asked the woman checking off names, taking tournament fees, and handing out jerseys. I raised my eyes. I couldn't be entirely sure, but I thought it was the same freckly woman with the friendly smile who had taken my name that horrible morning seven summers earlier. A little older, and heavier maybe, but still a nice person, not a threat.

"Um…ah…Ada Louise Huxtable," I muttered, gazing somewhere in the vicinity of my belly button. It was the name of the author of the Frank Lloyd Wright book that Myra had given me last Christmas, a gift meant to inspire me toward bigger and better things. I felt a lurch in my gut as I said the name. There I was, trying something bigger and better for the first time in my life and my best friend wasn't with me. It was easy to be mad at her while I was mired in my Kendall's funk. Here at the contest, not so easy.

Freckle Face wrote my name, or rather Ada's name down, then said, "That'll be twenty dollars, please."

I dug my crumpled twenty dollar bill out of my pocket and gave it to her. She told me the basic rules and then asked, "First time in the tournament?"

I nodded.

"I assume you're competing in Girls Ages 15 to 18?"

"Yes," I managed to say, in spite of wanting to shuffle away and take a seat under the Nature Conservancy table.

The woman reached into a bin by her side and pulled out a bright red jersey and handed it to me. "Well, here's something fiery to help keep that competitive edge burning. You'll need it with those girls. Good luck, sweetheart."

Establish eye contact, I told myself. *It won't kill you.* I looked at the woman and managed to smile back. "Thanks," I bleated, sounding like a lamb about to be slaughtered.

Wandering to the beach, I spotted a familiar face—Jimmy Flannigan. Clueless Jimmy. He'd had no idea that he had been a major topic of discussion lately—and a source of conflict. But today was all about surfing: not Myra, not romance—hers or mine. Nothing but waves.

"Hey, Jimmy," I said as I walked up to him.

He turned and gasped. "Anna! What did you do to your hair?"

"Shh!" I whispered. "I don't want to attract attention. I needed a change. That's all."

He stared at the top of my head as if I had grown horns. Lots of little, itchy yellow horns.

"What's wrong?" I challenged.

Jimmy finally closed his mouth. "Oh, nothing. I just didn't expect you here."

"Do me a favor, just for today, call me Ada," I said. "For luck. Don't ask questions."

Jimmy shrugged. "Sure. Whatever, Ada."

"And don't dare mention the Surfing Siren or I will break both your legs so badly, you'll never surf again," I whispered with as serious a look as I could muster.

"Whoa," his eyes got wide. "Okay…so you're competing?"

"I guess," I shrugged.

"Awesome!" he shouted.

"Quiet, Flannigan." I poked him in the ribs. "I'm trying to keep a low profile, remember?"

"With *that* hairdo?" Jimmy rolled his eyes.

"Whatever. Hey, have all the judges arrived yet?"

"All the local ones are here," he said. "But Ceekay isn't here yet. My guess is they'll announce him last minute and he'll make some splashy cool entrance."

"Ceekay won't be judging," I said.

"How do you know?"

"I just know. Believe me."

"Bummer. Ceekay is, like, *it*. But hey, look out there. This is gonna be a challenge. Those waves look like crap," said Jimmy.

I looked out at the break for the first time. Jimmy was right. Knee-high peaks, maybe waist-high at best, total mush piles with about as much power as a baby's wind-up toy. Small, weak waves were harder to catch than any others—it required a whole different level of skill to stay on them and do enough tricks to score points. I excelled on the big waves, the killers that few others would consider surfing. This small stuff? I might be out of my element. I started deep breathing, which I had heard was supposed to stave off panic.

"You okay?" Jimmy looked at me as if I was a fragile old lady who might need help crossing the street.

"Fine," I exhaled. "Just fine."

The reggae music playing on the sound system ended and a voice announced. "Attention competitors, friends, and families. We've finished up registration so please make your way to the beach for our opening ceremonies. The 7th Annual Montauk Junior Surf Tournament will begin in ten minutes. Cowabunga!"

"Come on Ann—I mean, Ada," said Jimmy. "Let's go."

We weaved our way through the crowd to the beach. Once there, we separated into age and gender groups, which sucked because Jimmy's optimistic chatter was a nice distraction that kept me from getting too jittery. Reluctantly, I gave Jimmy a quick wave and found my group—fourteen tall, tan, muscular beach babes. And me.

It came as no surprise that *she* was there. Kiara, my long-ago nemesis. She was impossible to miss, standing in the center of the pack like a queen bee. In my mind's eye I had imagined her the way I'd last seen her: twelve years old and a catty little whiner. I had done a good job of preparing myself for *that* imagined version. But this Kiara was a whole other beast; she wore her jersey draped down her back with the sleeves tied around her neck like Wonder Woman's cape. This Kiara had broad swimmer's shoulders, washboard abs, muscle-bound arms, and long legs that shouted, "Hey, look at us! We run ten miles every day, just for the fun of it!"

Kiara gave me a quizzical look. *Uh-oh*, I thought. *If she blows my cover, I'm toast.* Kiara sauntered over and examined me from my sweat-beaded forehead to my sand-clutching toes. "Do I know you?" she asked in a voice dripping with superiority.

I shook my head and looked at those toes as they burrowed deep.

"Well, do yourself a favor, stranger," she hissed in my ear, her breath hot and tinged with peppermint. "Stay the hell out of my way out there." Kiara walked away, the rash guard cape billowing behind her.

I shrugged.

The other girls stared at me. My face got hot; everything from my neck down felt like rubber. Then the whispering began. I caught dribs and drabs—

"Oh my god. That hair…"

"She's so, so, skinny…"

"Like a boy…"

"And what's with those baggy board shorts…?"

One girl came over. "Hi," she said cheerily. "I'm Deanna."

"Um…ah…hi," I replied. *Good girl*, I thought. *Keep it up.* Ada Louise can manage polite conversation, even if it's a stretch for Anna.

"And you are…?"

"Oh, um, yeah," I stammered like a fool. "Sorry. I'm Ada. Ada Louise."

Deanna narrowed her eyes, and I felt a jolt up my spine. Was my cover blown? She looked at me for a second longer and then said,

"Oh, never mind. I thought you were someone else."

"Heh-heh-heh." I laughed like a nervous imbecile.

Deanna stared at me like I was a total freak-geek. "Well, good luck, Ada Louise. See you out there."

She returned to the group. Thankfully, off my scent. The starting bell for our heat could not come soon enough. Waiting was excruciating. I wanted to get in the water and start paddling as soon as possible. Only problem was I might end up paddling my way to China, the contest be damned.

"Yo! Hey! Welcome everyone," a voice boomed over the loudspeaker. "Let's hear it for the 7th Annual Montauk Junior Surf Tournament!"

The crowd cheered, hooted, whistled, and clapped. Craig Wynn— an old-time surfer with bronzed, leathery skin, and stringy blond-gray hair—held the mike. Craig knew me well, and I worried that if he spotted me, there was a risk he would shout out my name with his typical exuberant enthusiasm. I shuffled my way to the back of the pack and hunched low.

"Well, the waves might not be perfect, but I know you groms are gonna still have fun out there!" he hollered. There were more cheers and barely controlled pandemonium. Craig continued, "Before we get started, I want to introduce you to this year's judges. First, coming to us from Gilgo Beach, the owner of Patsy's Pizzeria and Board Shop, a guy who provides those GB surfers with all that is necessary, the former Men's East Coast Amateur Longboard Champ, Patsy Romano!"

A beefy guy mounted the stage and waved at the audience. More cheering and clapping. I kept my head low as Craig introduced two more people, the freckle-faced woman from registration, and another briny, craggy-looking older man. Then Craig added, "And now, for the moment you've all been waiting for. I know you're all going to be super amped when I bring our guest judge up here. Soon to take his place among the greats, with chops as radical as Slater, Curren, and Machado. What a beast this dude is. And what a nice guy. Give a big shout-out for…" I lifted my head just as Craig

212

shouted, "...Kevin Morrisey!"

No Ceekay, no Chris. Even though I knew it wouldn't be him, my heart sank because I realized suddenly that in fact I did want to see him again after all.

The crowd cheered. Kevin competed in the Professional Men's circuit as one of the top ten surfers in the world. Not only that, but he was a homegrown hero—local surf royalty—living in a fancy Easton beach house worth gazillions of dollars. Even out-of-the-loop me knew who he was.

"And now for today's program," Craig continued once the frenzy died down. "This year we're gonna switch it up and let the big kids go first. So all you groms under the age of fifteen can chillax. Go play. But keep an ear out for your age group call. And don't eat too many of those brownies so generously donated by the Montauk Women's League, you hear me? Last thing we need is a bunch of belly-achin' surfers."

The younger kids dispersed, leaving the rest of us waiting by the water. I stole a glance over at the boys and spotted Jimmy. He gave me a wink. Maybe I should've registered as Adam, rather than Ada, and paddled out with the guys. I probably could've pulled it off since everyone seemed to think I looked more like a boy than a girl.

"In keeping with tradition, ladies first. So that means Girls Ages 15 to 18, you're on! First five in the water will be—" Craig listed five names, none of which was mine.

I was bummed because the sooner I got in the water the better I thought I would feel. The waiting was pure agony. I watched the first heat line up at the water's edge, Deanna among them. Kiara and a cluster of remaining girls sat down together a fair distance from me. *Good,* I thought. *Do me a favor and stay away.*

A bullhorn sounded and the girls ran into the surf, jumped on their boards and shoved off. Deanna led the way. She was a fast, strong paddler—a great asset in surfing, as it means you can sometimes catch waves that other people can't, just by virtue of getting there quicker. The other four girls weren't too shabby either. But the first set of waves would demonstrate who could actually surf.

Turned out they all could surf—Deanna, particularly well. She made the unpredictable barely there waves seem like even sheets of shiny ice, riding the meager humps with the grace of a figure skater. Deanna had a really clean cutback—super graceful overall. It was cool to watch. I even forgot that I was there to compete. It was only when the bullhorn went off and their heat was over that my heart palpitations and sense of dread returned.

The next heat included Kiara, and this time I was grateful not to be called. I wanted to see how she surfed.

When the bullhorn went off, Kiara wasted no time—she was out there in seconds, faster even than Deanna. I watched her shifting position over and over again, crowding out the other girls as she tried to read the oncoming set. It was as if a kid stood patiently in line, waiting for an ice cream cone and just as it was about to be handed to the kid, someone else ran up from behind and snatched the ice cream. That was how Kiara surfed—greedily paddling around the other surfers, positioning herself further outside, away from the shoreline, and stealing waves.

The line between 'Wave Hog'—someone who doesn't share waves—and 'Snake'—someone who steals them—was not always clear. Some might consider her surfing merely aggressive, but I thought it selfish. I had to admit, however, that she was outrageously fab once she caught a wave. Kiara surfed like a well-oiled machine, precise and determined, with not a move out of place. There was no way I could win against this chick. No way.

"Don't you just want to shoot her?"

I turned to my side. There was Deanna, looking bedraggled, tired, and soggy.

"Kiara's such a friggin' snake," Deanna continued, staring out at the water. "And she gets away with it every time."

Deanna trash-talking Kiara put me at ease. "Why?" I asked.

"Because, let's face it, she's the best surfer, even if she has the worst manners. My father says surf etiquette has gone to hell in a handbasket, even at these competitions."

"Hell in a handbasket," I giggled. "That sounds like something my grandfather would say. In fact, it is something my grandfather says. That and 'Don't get your knickers in a twist.'"

"What about 'Okie dokey, Pokey'? My father says that *all* the time. I mean, hello. Pokey? What am I? Gumby's horse?"

We laughed, and for a second I forgot about Kiara.

Deanna stared out at the break. "Ugh. Here she goes again."

I looked, too. Kiara was acing it, carving all over the place, without a glitch. She rode the wave as far as possible, squeezing out a few more yards in the ankle-high end-slop, like a ballerina on toe shoes, skittering off stage after her star turn as the Swan Queen.

"You're our last hope," Deanna said. She stared at me with a super serious expression.

I sank further into my sandy trough, bowed my head, and grabbed my knees. *Could I please just disappear now?*

"Don't worry," Deanna said softly. "Your secret's safe with me."

Chapter Thirty-Five

I know who you are, Surfing Siren," Deanna stated matter of factly. "I've watched you on YouTube, like, a hundred times."

"I don't know what you're talking about," I said, in the most unconvincing, jittery-sounding voice ever to be heard on planet Earth.

"All the other girls are too nervous about their own heats to pay close attention."

My cover was so obviously and totally blown. "Why didn't you tell them the truth?" I whispered.

She shrugged. "I dunno. I could tell you didn't want people to know. I mean, sorry, but nobody does *that*," she pointed to my head, "without good reason. Everyone's got secrets. It's not my place to expose yours."

I smiled at her. "Thanks, Deanna."

"Don't thank me, just win this thing, and hope I come in at least third. I've got an ego, too." She stared back out at Kiara. "It's just not as big as some others out there."

Kiara glided back to shore on her tummy without a care in the world, chin resting in her hands, knees bent and ankles crossed in the air. The other competitors followed—paddling and struggling behind her like defeated lemmings.

Deanna kissed me on the cheek. "*Merde*," she said. "That's French for 'shit,' but actually it means good luck." She stood and ran toward the returning girls, giving Kiara a brief pat on the back before kissing and hugging the others.

And then it was time. Time for doom. Craig called, "Now the last, but not least, five girls: Amy Adler, Corey Beacon, Eliza Carlson, Leah Gruenbaum, and Ada Louise Huxtable."

The horn went off, and the other girls dashed in. For a second I was frozen in fear—paralyzed. It was a disastrous *déjà vu*, with no Sara to push me in. Sara, jilted and duped, had tried to save me when I had needed saving, and my stupidity had left her with broken bones and a broken heart. *I have to do this for her, too,* I thought, *not just Grandpa, or Deanna.* Somehow I willed myself to move.

I don't remember the paddle out, if it was easy, hard, cold, or choppy. Once outside I was no longer shaking like a scared little rodent, but I wasn't exactly Miss Super-Chill either. The other girls paddled a few yards to either side of me and glared at me with a mix of fear and curiosity, as if I was a creature from another world. At least there were only four of them. Eight eyes total, as opposed to who knew how many on the shore.

The first wave set came toward us and there was a sudden frenzy of paddling and positioning. A girl to my right was set up best for the first wave, and everyone deferred to her. She caught the wave and rode it respectfully but without much grit. The second wave went to another decent surfer, and the third wave was mine.

I'd like to be able to say that I aced it; that I was one with the wave; that it was the beginning of a happy ending. But no—I messed up royally, and not because I was taking risks, but because my nerves were getting the best of me. Short of falling off my board, it was one of the lamest rides I had ever taken. I paddled tentatively, almost missing the take-off, and when I finally felt a bit of juice in the wave beneath me, I hesitated and stayed on my belly for a second too long. When I finally tried to get to my feet, it required extra effort and momentum. So instead of popping up, I sloughed up, one foot before the other, with a split second of both knees on the board. By the time I was standing, I was too far back, nowhere near the power spot of the wave. Humiliating, to say the least; a total loser ride, if ever there was one.

If I had a tail, it would've been tucked between my legs on the paddle back out. The two remaining surfers shook their heads at me and laughed as I re-positioned myself for the next set. Another set was already building and I was in a good position to take the first wave— my chance at redemption. *You can do this, Anna,* I said to myself. *You have to do this.* I paddled more aggressively this time, certain I would nail it, but one of the other girls weaved her way there first, and took the wave. As she glided past me, she called, "You're out of your league. Watch and learn!" She was the best of the bunch so far, but still not all that hot. Watch and learn? That pissed me off to the max.

I finally found a rhythm, disjointed as it was, and managed to catch a bunch of waves. But I had no idea how my surfing measured up to the competition. This second taste of public surfing left me with no sense of myself other than a deep-seated certainty of total lameness. Talk about inadequacy—I felt like a robot with loose wires, disconnected and all over the place. If competitive surfing was always this way, I never wanted to do it *ever* again. When the bullhorn went off and we all made our way to shore, I figured I had blown it, that it was time for me to pack up and leave.

I had started to do just that when Deanna ran up to me.

"What are you doing?" she asked.

"Leaving. I sucked." I hesitated, before adding, "Right?"

"Well, you weren't up to Siren standards, but you didn't suck. That last right you caught was brilliant. I love that little flick of the wrist thing you do."

"Really?" I had no idea. Truly.

She looked at me oddly. "Um, yeah. Really."

"Attention, lovely Surfer Girls Ages 15 to 18," Craig's voice boomed over the loudspeaker. "I couldn't be more impressed. Even those of you who aren't going to move on in tomorrow's final round were totally awesome. Let's hear it for these girls!"

The crowds cheered.

"Our four finalists," Craig continued, "are Deanna Adams, Kiara Callahan, Leah Gruenbaum, and Ada Louise Huxtable!"

No way! I thought. Every man, woman, and child roared. Deanna giggled. "See? Now we're up against each other, Ada Louise Huxtable. May the best surfer win." She gave me a quick squeeze and ran off to a man who must've been her father. I watched him lift her up and swing her around as if she were five years old, his expression bursting with pride and joy. Deanna had this great dad, and I had a smudgy image of some loser standing under a palm tree in Oahu. To each her own.

Chapter Thirty-Six

I wasn't out of the running—at least not yet—but still I left Ditch Plains Beach as quickly as I could. The last thing I wanted was to hang around and watch more surfing. Now I had a whole day and night to kill, to try and keep myself calm, and quash my growing feelings of crippling self-doubt.

There were no early trains from Kendall's to Montauk the following morning, so I was stuck in Montauk, whether I liked it or not. I spent the entire afternoon trying to convince one motel manager after another to rent underage, unsupervised me a room for the night. Finally, at 5 p.m., the owner of a tacky motel down by the fishing docks agreed to rent me a tiny mildewed, non-air-conditioned room behind the pool generator for a "fair rate"—if I paid cash. His idea of a fair rate and mine were two different things, but I had no choice and no place else to go. I forked over two hundred dollars, leaving me five to get through the following day.

I took my remaining five dollars to the Montauk Market and bought myself a day-old loaf of bread, a jar of peanut butter, a bag of carrots, and two green bananas. In the motel room, I made myself a pasty sandwich and ate it as slowly as I could. After I was done, I had nothing to do. I didn't want to go outside and risk being seen. Deanna might not be the only person who recognized me. I took out my sketchbook, hopeful that drawing would calm my nerves, but found myself blocked. Every stroke I made on the page I judged as harshly as a Marine drill sergeant might assess a new recruit.

Time for everyone's favorite brand of mindlessness, I thought, as I turned on the TV. I was good for about two hours, semi-absorbed in an old Bette Davis movie where she goes blind at the end. I cried but took some comfort in the fact that her character's fate was worse than mine. I flipped randomly through the channels and almost lost it when I saw *him*. Chris careened down the face of a killer wave;

219

then, in a flash, he pixilated into twenty-five mini-versions of himself in a variety of psychedelic colors. The screen then shifted to a very tight, round female butt wearing the skimpiest bikini bottom this side of the equator. The butt—and the body it was attached to—walked away, getting smaller and smaller, but wiggling and jiggling in a way that would have given Grandpa the major coronary he was trying to avoid.

"When you want to stay cool but kill it, use Ocean Breeze. She'll love it," cooed the sexy voiceover. Then, in a flash, Chris was back, his face filling the screen, smiling at the camera like a pig in shit. Whether the smile was for the bikini bottom or the killer wave, I couldn't tell. And while I wasn't blind like Bette, I still wasn't sure if Chris's snaggle-toothed grin, live or on the TV, was the beginning or the end of me.

I slept deeply in that mildewed, non-air-conditioned room, which surprised me given that I had been as upset, confused, worried, and nervous as any one person had a right to be. The clock radio woke me at half-past six, and I shot out of bed like a bullet, desperately wanting this day to be over already. I prepared a few peanut butter sandwiches to take to the tournament, and gobbled one before I left. Then I packed up all my gear and left my hellhole of a room.

Riding my bike toward Ditch Plains, I could hear the waves, and smell the salt spray in the air. I got there early, before most of the other contestants. The waves were clean—six- to eight-foot beauties in the early windless morning. By mid-morning an eastern breeze would give them a bit more texture and size. My surfer's heart couldn't help but sing.

Soon thereafter the beach was jammed. There were twice as many spectators as the day before, sitting on beach blankets and chairs, or standing in restless packs by the water's edge. I'd managed to get through the first day of the tournament without any severe panic, but now the stakes were higher than ever. And all those people watching! I braced myself for the usual heart palpitations, shortness of breath, sweaty palms, and faintness, but they never came. Even though I wasn't exactly comfortable, I wasn't completely undone— at least not yet. A series of images ran like a slideshow through my head and I found them oddly motivating—Grandpa sick in bed, Gramma hovering over him like a fretful hen, and Sara hobbling around the shop on crutches. This surf competition was the only way I could help them all, the only way I could give back to those who had given so much to me.

But just in case a sudden bout of Shy-Person-Type-B symptoms bubbled up, I avoided everyone, including Jimmy and Deanna. I found a spot between two dunes that kept me semi-hidden and waited for the damn contest to start. When 9 a.m. rolled around, everyone was getting restless. Finally, Craig got up on the podium.

"Morning, surfers," he said cheerily. "I've got some good news, and I've got some bad news."

The crowd rumbled.

"The bad news is that Kevin Morrisey can't be here today. He's been called away on an emergency."

The crowd rumbled more.

"But the good news is that that emergency is the birth of his fifth child, Rogan Ella, born at seven thirty this morning!"

Everyone clapped and hoorayed for the Morrisey family's good fortune. Even me.

"And there's more awesome news."

Everyone was quiet again.

"Since Kevin can't be here, we've found someone really special to take his place. Here he is, groms and gromettes, to gauge your moves, the one and only Ceekay!"

Chris walked up to the podium and fist-bumped Craig. Then he turned and waved at the crowd. Instinctively, I ducked as his gaze traveled toward me, wedging my head as deeply between my knees as I could without breaking my neck. *How is this possible?* I thought. *He's not supposed to be here. He's supposed to be off in Fiji with Inga Ward, breaking my heart.* This was too much. Way too much.

Finally the crowd stopped roaring. "Okay, then," called Craig. "Let's get this party started. First up, Girls Ages 15 to 18. Everyone down to the water!"

I had a choice: I could either crawl on my knees through the sand to my bike and flee—no one, except Jimmy or Deanna, would ever know the difference—or I could stay, woman-up, and take my chances. The waves were breaking pretty far outside, and the entry point was some distance from the judges' stand. Maybe, with my new hairdo, Chris wouldn't recognize me. But more importantly, I had to decide whether his being there would unnerve me more than I was already unnerved. To wipe out in a humiliating finale would be the kiss of death. I had roughly two seconds to decide.

I rose on weakened knees and walked unsteadily across the sand to join the others at the water's edge. I took my place next to Kiara, who wore her hair in provocative pigtails, and a bikini bottom that barely covered her butt. *Perhaps her porn star display will be a good distraction for Chris*, I thought. It seemed he went for that kind of thing. Her hairdo and butt would be way more appealing than my baby poop crewcut and baggy board shorts.

Kiara sneered at me as I hunkered low next to her. "Well, hello Spike. This is a surprise," she said. "I thought it was girls only."

I wished I could say something barby in return, but Kiara's jeering expression left me mute.

"Give it a rest, Kiara," sighed Deanna, standing on her other side. "Let's just get out there and surf."

The bullhorn went off. I may not have been ready with a quick response for Kiara, but her bullying manner made me angry. And anger was a good motivator. Now I had something to prove, not just something to win. I paddled my ass off, more aggro than ever before in my life, careening past all the other surfers to make it outside first. Once there, I sat up on my board, chest heaving and out of breath. I willed myself not to look behind me, back at the shore, back at the crowds, back at Chris.

The horizon was still, and I had a moment to catch my breath before the other girls arrived. Deanna paddled up next to me. "Holy shit. What are you, a cyborg? I've never seen anyone paddle that fast!" she laughed breathlessly.

I tried to smile, but my face was as rigid as a pie pan.

"You look freaked," Deanna said. "Everything okay?"

I gave her a thumbs-up.

"Yeah, right. I shouldn't probably tell you this, but you've set yourself up way too far east. It's gonna break over there." Deanna pointed to her right, where Kiara and Leah waited. "Guaranteed. This is my home break. I know it like I know the annoying mole on the side of my neck." She lay back on her board and paddled away.

Deanna was right. I could now see it coming. The first wave of the set was starting to form in a meaty, sweet blue hump. I poured the steam on, paddling madly again, this time to get closer to where it would break, but missed it by a long shot. Leah took it, popping up just as the wave squeezed upward to form a steep and challenging peak. The wave had such power and intensity that there wasn't much more she could do other than nail her stance, and keep upright till the end. She managed to make it without any flourishes and would score some big points just for taking off on that sucker.

Meanwhile, Kiara had been biding her time. She took the next wave, equally big but not quite as radical. This wave had a wider face and held up for longer, allowing for more maneuvers. Kiara barely had to paddle to catch it, before carving her way across the face of her wave with so much ease it was nauseating. As I watched her ace her way to the end, my chest deflated, flatter than flat, concave in total defeat.

The last wave of the set could've been mine; I was set up for it, but my heart, mind, and body were in no way prepared. The whole tournament idea was now officially the worst idea I had had in my entire life—next to falling in love with Chris. I was so paralyzed with my own incompetence that I let Deanna have the wave. Right before she took off, she yelled at me. I figured she was thanking me for giving it to her. I watched her pass and wished her well.

I looked back out at the horizon. Part of me thought, *What's the point? Kiara is gonna win this thing, and, in the meantime, Chris is here and my heart is in danger of bonafide exploding.* But I couldn't give up now, could I? It wasn't in my nature to let either one of them—lover or nemesis—undo me so quickly. Or was it? Then it came for me. The one and only answer. A super sweet ginormous wave. Deanna had been coaching me, not thanking me when she passed. She had yelled, "Outside! A big one! Go for it!" And so I would. I instinctively turned to take this beauty. Part of me was completely stoked; the other part couldn't believe I was doing this. I couldn't stop myself from noticing the crowds on the shore. *Just don't look*, I told myself. *Do what you do best and when the time to pop up arrives, do what comes naturally.*

My beginning was somewhat shaky. I was too far forward on my board, and my rhythm was off. If I didn't get it together soon, the ride would be a total bust, a waste, another embarrassment. I would nose-dive into oblivion. I got it together quickly and started feeling fine, back to my brand of normal. I went for the most stupendous bottom turn of my life, swooping down the face of the wave, riding there for a few seconds then flying back to the top in glory. I carved a few smaller arcs, thinking, *Yes! Maybe I could do this thing after all.*

But I couldn't help myself. I had to look at him. I could see the curly Wheaten Terrier mop of hair, the slightly stooped posture; the beautiful caramel-colored skin. He stood behind the judges table, while the others were still sitting. Even from this distance, I felt Chris staring at me. It took only a split second to destroy me.

I tumbled off the end of the wave in a wipeout more suited to a Laurel and Hardy skit than a surf competition. My arms flailed, my feet skittered out beneath me, and my butt landed with a bang on my board. After that I was sucked down deep, where it was all white foam and deep blue shame.

But my survival impulse was still pulsing. I pushed through to the surface and gasped for air. Now the decision was which way to paddle. Heading back outside seemed the safer option. Give myself more time to figure out how to deal with Chris—God, I still wanted him so badly; God, I hated him so much!—on top of the humiliation of my last move.

"Nice ending, Spike," Kiara called once we were all back outside. "That should cost you a few points."

"Whatever, bitch," I snarled. *Wow*, I thought. *I snarled!*

"What did you call me?" she paddled over.

"Wave hog." I couldn't control myself. Something inside me

opened up. I was like a dragon with an internal fireball gathering momentum, working its way up my gullet, then spewing out my mouth.

"Excuse me?"

"Bitch and wave hog," I said, very calmly. "Oh, and snake. You are the worst snake I have ever seen. You're a real slimy, snaky wave stealer."

Her jaw dropped.

"Close your fat trap of a mouth, Kiara," I added. "Or all the evil fumes will escape and poison us humans."

"You're such a loser," Kiara spat. "In all ways. You are *so* out of your league here. You couldn't surf your way out of a kiddie pool."

She might have been right. I wasn't really sure how the rest of the contest was gonna go down. But something was already shifting in me. Something big. Already I was talking to strangers. Smiling. Staying put when I wanted to flee. Shy-Person-Type-B-hood was shedding off of my teen girl skin.

"And you clearly have the intelligence of a flea," I cried. It was the kind of thing Myra might say, and for a brief moment the memory of my former best friend made my dragon heart feel faint.

The next set was upon us, and Kiara snaked her way around Deanna and Leah to nab the first wave. Once again she was close to perfect. But her bad sportsmanship was so blatant that it got my dragon up and going full force again.

"You are evil incarnate!" I screamed as she sailed away.

Deanna and Leah clapped. For me, not Kiara, which made me nervous and giggly but felt totally awesome. Then Deanna caught a nice eight footer, followed by Leah on a respectable six.

Once again, I had waited till the bitter end. This time there was no surprise fourth wave, giving me less opportunity to score points, and even more time to fret over whether I wanted to keep competing at all. I fixed my eyes on the horizon, hoping for a sign.

And then it came for me—a beautiful, perfect wave. A giant rogue. *Ten feet at least*, I thought. Holding up like a real regal queen. "Fuck, yes!" I yelled to no one and paddled to take it. I stood up easily and began surfing with complete and total abandon, having the time of my life. I was exactly where I had wanted to be, and from that moment on it was just me and the wave and our own glorious dance. My watery partner was blue bliss, easygoing but steep and fast. The rest of the world disappeared.

I milked it to the max, my ride ending very close to shore where the rest of the world was waiting to undo me again. After my kick-out, the crowd on shore cheered for me. I felt my heart race, moving toward panic mode, as I treaded water.

Then a boy's voice called out, "Go for it, Anna!"

Friggin' Jimmy Flannigan. Couldn't keep his mouth closed. Now everyone knew my real first name. And Chris would now know for sure what he already probably knew. I looked to the judges table and watched him try and leave—probably wanting to get as far away from me as possible—but Craig yanked him back.

As if matters couldn't get worse, or better, or more confusing, I saw Myra. She stood next to Jimmy with her silly cabbage hat plopped on top of her Brillo pad hair. What she did next was either the most brilliant or the cruelest thing she had done yet. She pointed at me and yelled at the top of her lungs, "It's her! It's the Surfing Siren!" And all of a sudden, all eyes were on me. Hundreds of eyes. I was bombarded with stares. And in that moment, frozen in fear, Sara's advice came rushing to the fore:

When you start getting nervous, you tend to let up on your back foot. Don't do that. Dig in deeper with the back foot and take your shoulders back, too. Otherwise you get too much momentum and lose the sweet spot. You have a tendency, when you're spooked, to ride it a hair too far forward.

And more important than anything: *Don't let your demons get the best of you. Don't be like me that way. Just go for it, okay?*

I turned back toward the outside. There was a set coming. If I were sane, I would grab my board and hold it steady. Or I could do more—I could go for it; no more demons; no more Shy Person Type B getting the best of me. I had a choice. I breathed deeply, hoisted myself on the board and paddled back outside like a lunatic, duck-diving under breaking waves that almost pummeled me to a pulp.

Chapter Thirty-Seven

Talk about a glorious re-do. I surfed with delirious abandon. The next wave was a ticket to paradise. It swelled up right where I wanted it to, as if Neptune had delivered it to me on a sea-foam platter. I plunged deep into the trough, imagining that I was ten years old again and that this was my first tournament. I imagined a young Sara standing on the beach, hopeful, happy. Proud.

I shifted directions and shot my way up the face of the wave to the very edge, skittering for a split second as if I were tap dancing on the lip, before heading downward again. I was all over my wave friend, up and down it as if I were a curvy, tickling feather.

The wave after that was pure bliss. A hollower, lovely thing. An aquamarine cavern. I didn't balk, or hesitate to experiment. I used my skill at stalling—maintaining my balance to get tubed—and hovered underneath the deep blue curl, running my fingers along the wave wall.

Wave number four was the crowning jewel. The ultimate wave of the day. Ten feet high and majestic. This gorgeous wall of water was so spectacular that when I was on it, I was more transfixed by its beauty than I was by the action of surfing. While I flew, and carved, and stalled, and spun, my sense of connection and rightness were as powerful as the wave itself.

When the bullhorn blew, signaling the end of the heat, I smiled like a demented fool and thought, *Today's fun may be over, but the real fun may have just begun.*

As we all paddled back in, Kiara couldn't even look at me. She knew she didn't stand a chance. Even with all her slippery aggro moves, I caught more waves fair and square, and surfed them better than she ever could. At the shoreline she stormed out of the water like an angry, sore loser.

As I stumbled up the beach on wonderfully wobbly legs—an

after-effect of an awesome surf session—I saw Myra next to Jimmy. She looked totally spooked, like she was waiting for me to lose it with her again, but my heart had softened. No way could I be mad at her anymore. I had just broken through a major wall, surfing my butt off in spectacular fashion in front of hundreds of people. I tried to make my way toward Myra, but as soon as my feet touched the sand I was bombarded by crowds of little kids hovering around me like I was Santa Claus giving out extra swag. Their parents wouldn't leave me alone either. They were all pats on the back and handshakes, saying "good job," "you're amazing," "what an inspiration," and stuff like that.

My newfound celebrity status was mildly uncomfortable. Unfortunately, surf success hadn't suddenly transformed me into a totally chill and normal person. I smiled and thanked them all, but it still required effort. Myra made her way over to me, pushing her way through the crowds to finally arrive at my dripping wet side.

"I'm sorry," we said at exactly the same time, then laughed at our shared moment in our own unique way—Myra sounded like a hyena with hiccups, and I like an old man with smoker's cough. We threw our arms around each other and both squeezed so tight that I was certain we had broken a few ribs between us.

"I'm getting you all wet," I snuffled into the fuzz of her hair.

"I couldn't care less," she snuffled back.

"I said such mean things to you. You must hate my guts."

"Impossible. No hating guts ever. Plus, I wasn't exactly the nicest person. We were both kinda bitchy."

"Thank you, Myra. I couldn't have done this without you, you sneaky girl, you."

"Don't thank me. It was all Anna Dugan out there." Myra held me away from her so she could look me straight in the eye, which was hard because we were both crying happy, relieved tears. "And I'm telling you, girl, I have never—and I mean NEVER—seen you surf so well."

"This is gonna sound so super corny, but you of all people will get it," I said, wiping the tears from my eyes.

"What?" Myra asked, wiping the tears from her own.

"I feel like one of those butterflies that's broken out of their stupid sticky, why-is-nature-so-cruel cocoons."

"Nature is a bitch."

"A total fucking skank," I agreed.

"But nature helped you rock out there on those waves. You were amazing."

"Aw, shucks," I grinned. "I messed up a lot in the beginning, though. That could matter. But wait a minute, how did you even know I was here?"

"I told her," Jimmy said. He had also made his way through the crowds, picking little kids up under the armpits and moving them out of his path.

"Huh?" I was shocked. "You?"

"Yeah, me," Jimmy said. "You guys are usually together all the time. I thought it was weird Myra wasn't here at the tournament with you."

Myra shrugged and gave me a look that said, I'm as surprised by this as you are.

Jimmy continued. "Plus, I don't know if you realized it, but you were talking to yourself—well, actually to Myra—before your heat yesterday."

"That's embarrassing," I cringed.

"Yeah. It was kinda weird. Mumble, mumble, Myra this, mumble, mumble, Myra that..."

Myra smiled at him. "Jimmy got his grandmother to give him my number so he could call me." Myra Berkowitz; the only sixteen-year-old in every Kendall's Watch senior citizen's address book. "I told him we were in a cold war, but I asked him to give me a lift here today anyway. I had to see you do this."

I gave Myra a knowing look. "Funny how things work out, eh?"

"Very funny." Myra cast a quick glance at Jimmy then nodded back at me. "Anyhow, I knew you probably still hated my guts so I tried to stay out of sight."

"But then I messed up when I yelled your name, so Myra ran over to shut me up." Jimmy gave Myra a flirtatious nudge. She smiled at him, and he grinned back. There was definite chemistry.

"No worries, Jimmy," I said.

"When I saw you out there in the water just standing there I couldn't help myself," Myra said. "I guess I outed you when I screamed Surfing Siren."

"Myra, you can't go to Paris," I started crying again. "You just *can't.*"

"Well, who knows," Myra sighed. "Judith is being all cagey about whether they even want me there or not. As usual, my needs take a back seat—like the way-back-rear-of-the-bus back seat."

"Do you *want* to go?" I asked. "I mean, I know I'm saying you *can't* go, but if it's what you really want to do, you know I'll understand. Sort of."

Myra tilted her head and placed her index finger thoughtfully to her cheek. "Pros? Paris and all things Parisian. Cons? Losing out on the last two years of high school with my best friend in a town I love, where I can do all sorts of vitally important things for the community, and—" she did a cagey chin nod towards unsuspecting Jimmy, "—maybe where I have some kind of 'future.'"

"Well, just so you know, whatever happens, I totally support you," I said.

"Besides, I have my own underwater Parisian Wavehouse to live in," she said. "At least, on paper. Which I snarkily never thanked you for."

"You're welcome."

"But if I stick around, you have to promise me that you'll go into the city with me at least a few times next year and expand your horizons. Enough with this myopic beach town routine."

"Sure," I said. "I promise. We can go to MoMa."

"Moe who?" Jimmy asked.

"MoMa," I said. "It's a place, not a person. It's short for the Museum of Modern Art."

"That's my girl," Myra sighed and we hugged like full-frontal Siamese twins until Craig's voice boomed over the loudspeaker. "Attention, everyone. Results are in."

I squeezed Myra's hand and forced myself to look over to the judges table. Chris was staring straight at me. He looked sorry and ashamed. But about what? About what he had done to me? Or because I hadn't even placed?

"Third place goes to Leah Gruenbaum, second to Deanna Adams, and the winner of the Girls Ages 15 to 18, who gets a nice prize of five hundred dollars and then qualifies at the end of today to win an additional $4,500 for Best Surfer Overall is the beautiful—"

'Beautiful,' that didn't bode well for me.

"—incredible Ada Louise Huxtable, better known as the Surfing Siren, but best now known as Anna Marie Dugan from Kendall's Watch!"

The crowd went crazy; little kids clawed at my legs like frantic puppies. I was stunned, relieved, and stupefied. Kiara hadn't even placed. I was happy—that is until Chris rose from the judges table and started to work his way toward me.

"Myra, I have to leave now," I said. "I don't want to see him."

She glanced at Chris, now off the podium and making his way across the sand. "Oh yeah. Him. Yikes."

"But you can't leave," Jimmy said. "What about the big prize?"

Chris was stopped in his tracks, I noticed, barnacled by the leftover groms who hadn't already attached themselves to me.

"Anna," Myra said calmly. "You can do this. You need to do this."

I knew she was right. If I wanted to stay butterfly-esque, I had to practice flying around with confidence. No fluttering straight back into my claustrophobic cocoon, I vowed not to let Chris or anyone else send me back there. It was a tall order, but at least I could try.

"Okay, but I may need you to do that thing they talk about in sports," I said.

"What do either of us know about sports, other than this one?"

"You know, run, run—"

Jimmy chimed in. "Run interference; is that what you mean?"

I nodded. "Yeah. Like, if Chris gets too close to me, you have to stop him."

"It's a long story," Myra told the perplexed Jimmy. "I'll tell you later. That is, if it's okay with Anna."

I shrugged. "Later is later. Right now, all I want is my money and my glory. But I *don't* want to talk to him. I may be able to tolerate other people—yay, yay, finally, hooray—but him? No way."

Chris had managed to extract himself from the groms and had a path toward us that was free and clear.

"Myra, now. *Please*," I said. Even though I had sea water cooling my skin, I could feel the prickle of nervous sweat begin to form on the back of my neck and under my arms.

Myra grabbed Jimmy's elbow. "Come on, Jimmy. Let's go do gushy." She dragged Jimmy over to Chris and started babbling. "OMG, I can't believe it! You're Ceekay! I am, like, a total fan! You were so awesome in that contest at, um, ah—" I saw her elbow Jimmy in the ribs to join in. *Poor but lucky Jimmy*, I thought. *He has a whole lot of Myra Berkowitz-style fun ahead of him.*

"The Billabong Invitational in J-bay," Jimmy added. "Outstanding, man."

"Yeah, yeah, that one," Myra chirped. She was doing such a great airhead imitation, I almost believed it myself. "You really kicked butt. You can say that in surfing, right? Kick butt? That's okay?"

Chris couldn't get a word in edgewise. He tried to get a peek at me but Myra was running perfect interference, expertly putting her cabbage hat in his line of view.

Craig came back on the loudspeaker. "Okay, so let's have those shredding girls up on stage right now to get their awards! Leah, Deanna, Ada. Or Anna—or should I say the Surfing Siren?"

Deanna appeared at my side and took my hand. "Come on, whoever you are. Let's go get our moola."

We walked to the podium and with every step forward I felt lighter. When we turned to face the crowd, I waited for sheer panic to overwhelm me, but other than some expected heart flutters, I was surprisingly fine. Deanna grabbed Leah's hand with her free one and together we lifted our arms up in a triumvirate of victory. The crowd cheered. I looked back to Myra, Chris, and Jimmy. Chris was leaving. I could see him making his way up the beach toward the parking lot.

Myra shook her head, her brow creasing in concern. She got it. While I might've been deliriously happy about my newfound comfort with performing, being betrayed by my first true love was something I might never recover from.

A half hour later, Craig made an announcement that "Ceekay was unfortunately called away for the rest of the afternoon, so the judges will have to proceed without him."

Called away by Inga Ward, no doubt, I thought. I hadn't a clue where my feelings about him would ultimately land. But I knew for sure that I was whole without him—more *me* than I'd ever been before, and it felt amazing.

I swallowed the cry that bubbled up. Surfers, families, friends, sand, ocean, and an incredible sky. I opened my arms wide and tipped my head back with my eyes closed. I took it all in and was better than fine.

"What are you doing?" asked Myra.

"I'm connecting," I said.

"Don't get all hippy-dippy on me now, you hear?" she warned, gently slapping one of my outstretched arms. "Surfer cool, I can take, but hippy-dippy, *that* I don't do."

"Oh Myra. You really have to take more chances," I joked. "You're like a scared little hermit crab, staying in its too-small shell."

"Ha, ha. Very funny." She grabbed my arm and twisted it behind my back, giggling.

"Ouch," I cried in mock pain. "You don't know your own strength! Lifting all those library books has really paid off, eh?"

Myra and I stuck around for the rest of the afternoon and watched the other heats. Jimmy rocked the Boys Ages 15 to 18 longboard division, scoring second place by walking his toes to the nose of his board at least five times.

All afternoon, I shook people's hands, made small talk, and smiled until my cheeks hurt. It was a chore, and I was not very smooth. I made a gazillion *faux pas*. Social grace would have its own learning curve, but I was finally up to the task.

At the end of the day when I scored the "Best Overall Surfer" and got that extra $4,500 bucks, I should've been jumping for joy. Sure, I was happy. I loved it when Jimmy and a few of the other guys lifted me up on their shoulders and paraded me down the beach to the shoreline, then tossed me back in the water. But I couldn't help remembering Chris's joke about me winning "Best in Show," and all the other moments we'd shared.

I had another ache in my heart as well. And this one was even bigger. I wished more than anything that Sara could've been there to see me compete. How stoked my kick-ass mother would've been seeing me charge those waves. Moms and dads all over the beach were celebrating their surfer kids. Now that the break was clear of competitors, some of the parents were out in the water, catching end-of-day glass-off waves themselves. Sure, I'd won the tournament. I had the trophy and the checks. But, as the saying went, "The best surfer out there is the one having the most fun." I would've had a lot more fun if Sara had been there then, strutting her stuff, artfully tossing her gorgeous hair, and rightfully taking credit—or at least some credit—for my success. I missed her more than ever and couldn't wait to get home and tell her all about it.

Chapter Thirty-Eight

Myra and I squeezed into the cab of Jimmy's truck for the drive back to Kendall's Watch. I had my trophy and two checks totaling $5,000 in my backpack. I stared out the windshield at the passing dunes while Jimmy and Myra chatted. At one point, I noticed with a smile that Jimmy had slipped his hand off the steering wheel to rest on Myra's knee.

I was exhausted, jazzed, and jittery. I felt as if I had lived a thousand lives in twenty-four hours. Forehead resting on the window, I worried about Grandpa. Five thousand dollars was a hefty chunk of change, but I wasn't sure how much Grandpa's surgery would cost. I also worried about Rusty's photos of Chris and me kissing at Secretspot being made public. I imagined headlines on every tabloid sold at the checkout of every grocery store across America: "Ceekay's New Hook-up Revealed: Kendall's Watch The Surfing Siren Anna Dugan," and "Ceekay and Anna Dugan Getting Hot and Heavy at Secret Kendall's Watch Break" or "What Will Inga Think?" And underneath that really embarrassing shot: "Hey, Where's Ceekay's Other Hand?"

I refused to let anyone—not Rusty, not Chris, not *People-friggin' Magazine*—make a fool of me. I had to turn this around.

Jimmy pulled into a parking space in front of The Shell Shop.

"Where do you want us to drop your board?" asked Myra. "My house? Your house? Up at Toilsome?"

"Take it to your house. I want to surprise my grandparents and my mom—in a big-ass way."

"Got it, boss," Myra giggled.

As I walked to the shop, Myra leaned out the window and called, "But Miss Uber Surfer, Social Butterfly? That hair of yours? We have, like, major remedial work ahead of us. Be prepared."

Meghan was busy unpacking the new shipment of Kendall's

Watch tees. The shirts looked great, the logo perfectly placed.

"Hey, Meghan," I said.

She saw my hair and gasped.

"Don't ask," I commanded with a stop sign hand. "Thanks, though, for getting started on those tees."

"No problem," she replied. "I was thinking that instead of displaying them here, we could trade spots with the towels. That way people would see them right away and we wouldn't get that, you know, crowding thing happening so close to the Shellys?"

The girl had it down. "Meghan. Don't ask. Just do."

She got to work shifting and sorting while I thumbed through the local phonebook, looking for the listing for Robert Tellings, Esquire. Bob was the only lawyer in town, or at least the only one I knew. I figured he might be able to help me with this photo debacle—it seemed like the kind of situation that required a lawyer. I didn't exactly know what it meant to sue someone, but somehow I thought that was what I should do. Sue Rusty and maybe Chris too.

I got Bob's answering machine. "Hey Bob," I said. "It's Anna. Anna Dugan. I think I need your advice. For something, um, about law. You know, legal advice. Not surf advice. Even though I'm sure you give good surf advice, too. So, like, if you could call me back at the shop, that would be awesome. Thanks."

I hung the phone up and sighed. Suddenly I was wicked tired. Showing up for oneself really took a toll on the old stamina.

"Meghan, I'm gonna go in back and do an inventory check. Call me if you need me." I was planning on taking a little nap on the pile of beach towels stacked in the corner. But worker bee Meghan was in high gear and I would have felt like a slacker telling her the truth.

I was starving. I fished out the last soggy peanut butter sandwich from the bottom of my backpack, scarfed it down and then dosed fitfully on my makeshift bed for the next half hour or so. At around four, I was woken by the Shell Bell jingle-jangle. I could hear the murmur of Meghan's enthusiastic sales pitch, but not her words. Then the storeroom door opened.

"Anna?" Meghan said tentatively.

"Yeah?"

"He was just here and said not to wake you, but he left something for you." Meghan held out a copy of the *Kendall's Kalendar*.

"Who?"

"Ceekay," she sighed. Seemed everybody but me was a major fan.

"What the hey?" I took the *Kalendar*. It had been folded intentionally to the TV listings. One item was circled in red marker. I read within the scarlet loop a few times before it registered. I needed to be absolutely certain, so I asked Meghan—who, like Myra, knew more about these things than I did—"Meghan? What does this *R* mean?"

She looked at the paper. "Repeat. Means the show was a repeat."

Live with Larry. But *not* live. Repeated. *Repeated with Larry*. That's when I noticed something else written boldly in the margin of the page:

917.555.9531. Don't lose it this time, please.

Chapter Thirty-Nine

I didn't need to call; I just needed to look out the window. Chris was waiting in front of the shop in his funky VW surf van. He got out as I approached and ran around to the passenger side to open the door. Man, was he pouring on the charm. I hesitated—still not exactly sure, still with many questions.

"Come on," he said. "I'll take you wherever you want to go."

"Whatever," I said and got in. Chris raced around to his side and then there we were in the car, together again.

"So," he said, nervous hands getting lost in snaggy curls.

"So," I said.

Our gazes darted around the car like ping pong balls colliding every few seconds, before I broke the awkward silence. "So, no Inga?"

"Nope. No clue where that ego on stilts is now, and I couldn't care less. That *Live with Larry* show you watched originally aired over six months ago. A lightbulb went off in my dense brain after you banished me from your store and from your life."

"Lightbulb?"

"You said, 'Fly off to Fiji. Go have fun in the sun. The waves are really sweet this time of year.' I remembered I had said something like that on *Live with Larry*."

"Wish you'd remembered sooner."

"I did, but you wouldn't let me anywhere near you."

"True," I sighed.

He shook his head. "What a disaster that dumb talk show was. When Inga said 'I can't let this one out of my sight,' it was the final straw. She was a controlling, nasty piece of work. After filming was done, I broke up with her there in the hallway at 30 Rock."

"So really, really no Inga?" I asked.

"Really, really no Inga," Chris nodded. "It suddenly dawned on

238

me that you saw that stupid show. They replay it all the time. God knows why. I think it's 'cause Clooney comes on after us, and there's always an audience for Clooney."

I nodded. Even I knew who George Clooney was. So even I had to agree.

"So I've spent the last hour racing around this town trying to find a newspaper with TV listings. Finally nabbed one off a guy sitting in that sandwich shop at the corner. He thought I was insane when I offered him twenty bucks for it."

"You are sort of crazy," I joked.

Chris smiled. "Yes I am. In more ways than one, thanks to you."

He leaned in to kiss me. But I edged away.

"Wait a second. You still stood me up. I came to Secretspot the morning after we, we almost, well, you know. And you weren't there."

"I fell asleep in the van, parked around the far side of the house under a carport. I knew Rusty was up at the house and I didn't want him anywhere near you. I should've told you sooner about Rusty being my manager, but I chickened out. Things were so great for us; I didn't want to spoil it. I planned on telling you, but I never got up the nerve. I was a selfish idiot."

"Not your finest moment," I agreed. "That was low."

"I know. That night I finally had the balls to call Rusty on all the stupid stuff he'd been doing 'on my behalf'—the other shady crap he was up to besides stalking you and cheating on your mother. I couldn't let it go on."

"Rusty Meyers," I shook my head. "What a complete a-hole."

"Anyway, I kinda lost it that night."

"What do you mean?"

"Well, I punched him in the jaw," Chris looked down. "The dude was bleeding. It was bad."

"Ah," I said. So it hadn't been a shaving nick on Rusty's pointy hipster chin after all.

"I haven't lost it with anyone like that in a long time. I've been in control of what you call my 'anger management issues.'"

"I guess he sort of deserved it," I said.

239

Chris shook his head. "No. Punching anyone—even a total asshole—is never the answer. But after that, I did what I really needed to do. I fired him."

"Good," I said. "I hope he rots in unemployment hell."

"I couldn't stay in the same house with that douche, but I couldn't leave knowing you would be coming back in the morning. I managed to stay awake in the van until about 5 a.m. before passing out. Slept right through the emergency alarm I had set on my phone for six, and woke up at half past nine. When I got to the beach, you were already gone."

Way gone, I thought. Then I remembered the worst of it all—the pictures. "What about the photographs Rusty took of us?" I cried. *Please have an explanation for this too*, I thought. *So maybe I can stop hating you as much as I love you, and go back to just plain loving you.*

"I had no idea he was taking photos or movies, of you, of us. He was so slick, he hid all that stuff away whenever I was at the house."

"Why should I believe you?" I sighed.

"Belly Flop, for real, I never knew how messed up Meyers was. I knew he was scouting someone in Kendall's, but I didn't know it was you until our dinner at Brinestellar's when you told me about what he was pulling with your mother. I didn't have to be a genius to figure out that she was his pipeline to you. When you showed up at Secretspot that first morning, Rusty didn't need to go searching anymore. You came right to him."

"So where are the photos?"

"No worries. I took care of that."

"How?"

"That morning, after falling asleep in the van, I found Rusty at his laptop and saw what was on the screen."

"Us?" I cringed.

He nodded. "Very much, um, us."

"Oh crap," I moaned.

"It's okay. I caught him before he sent anything off. I grabbed the laptop and threw it on the floor. Totally trashed it. Electronic crap flying all over the place. Then I found his cameras. Stamped on those suckers. Have the sore ankle to prove it," He held up a bandaged ankle.

"Ouch," I sighed.

"So totally worth it. I swore to that asshole that if any photos of you, or you and me together, ever surfaced, I would sue his ass for millions, and make his name mud."

"So I don't have to—" I started.

"Don't have to do what?"

I was about to say I didn't have to sue anyone, but decided that could be my little secret. *A tame one, in the grand scheme of things,* I thought.

We sat there for a moment, neither of us talking. "You could've told me that you were judging the tournament."

"Actually, it was last minute. Kevin called me at the crack of dawn to cover for him. I figured, why not? You weren't talking to me, but I hadn't given up hope, yet. I wanted to stick around here for a while longer, so I figured I could handle a pit stop at the contest, help a bro out." He reached over and mussed my hair. "And then, there you were at the tournament trying to hide your killer moves under that freaky do."

"You left early," I said, moving closer to him. "Craig is probably wicked pissed off."

He smiled his snaggle-toothed grin. "Nah. I told him my choice for 'Overall' before I left. Cast my most important vote. Like I said, 'Best in Show.'" He leaned toward me and we kissed.

I tried not to worry that I might still taste like peanut butter. But if I did, I think he liked it.

Chapter Forty

Chris and I had a whole lot of making up to do and the long front seat of his van was the perfect place to stay for a spell. Eventually, we headed to Toilsome Lane. I wasn't sure yet if I would invite him in. Having my family meet Chris might be too intense, too much too soon. It could cause a riptide of feelings that would sweep me into some way-too-emotional sea.

When we pulled into the driveway, I had decided. "Why don't you come in?"

"Okay," Chris said tentatively.

"Don't worry. Contrary to what you may have heard, my grandfather doesn't really bite, and my mother, though heartbroken and devastated, is in a cast and a sling and is so weak she couldn't spit at you, even if she wanted to."

"Well, that's reassuring," he sighed.

"Just kidding. Come on. Meet my folks," I said.

He followed me inside. It was the usual scene—Grandpa watching TV in the living room and Gramma clanking pots and pans in the kitchen. Sara's inflated air mattress was set up in the corner of the dining room. I took Chris's hand and led him to Grandpa first.

"Hey Tom-Tom," I called to the back of his head.

"What the fuck do you want? Can't you see I'm busy?" Grandpa snarled.

"Turn around, you rude old bastard," I said.

Grandpa pulled the lever on the side of his La-Z-boy, sat upright and swiveled around. "Jesus Christ, Mother Mary of God. What the hell did you do to your hair?"

"It's a long story," I said.

Grandpa scowled, looking over at Chris. "Who's this?" he asked suspiciously.

I took a big swallow. "Grandpa, I would like you to meet

Christopher Kahimbe. Christopher, this is my grandfather, Thomas Dugan."

Chris stepped forward and held out his hand. "Nice to meet you, Mr. Dugan."

Grandpa looked at me and I mouthed, *It's okay*. So Grandpa stood up stiffly and shook Chris's hand.

"Nice to meet you too, Christopher," he said—almost nicely. Then he turned to me, "Hey, Bobby Tellings just called here. Said you left him a message. What's up with that?"

Yikes, I thought. *Cover-up, come to me quick!* "Um, ah, I was just calling to see if he had an extra longboard for me to borrow. I think the waves are gonna get small again this week and I want something I can fool around with."

"You're surfing again?" Grandpa said. "Since when?"

I looked at Chris and sneaked a wink. "Since a couple of days ago. I'll tell you all about it when we're all together. You, me, Gramma, Sara."

Grandpa looked at me with his you're-up-to-something stare, but I did my best deadpan-back-at-you in return.

"Believe me, Tom-Tom, it's nothing to get your knickers in a twist over."

Eventually he gave up and yelled, "Lorraine, come in here. We have a visitor."

Gramma weaved her way from the kitchen. I cringed in preparation for her response to my freak show makeover.

"Oh Anna Marie," she sighed. "Your hair! How stylish! You look just like Twiggy!"

You never get what you expect, Anna Marie Dugan, I said to myself. *A very good thing to remember.* "Um, thanks, Gramma. I'd like you to meet my friend."

Chris smiled at Gramma and shook her hand gently. "My name is Christopher. But you can call me Chris, if you want to."

"I think I'll stick with Christopher. I've always admired that name. In fact, my brother's youngest child from his first marriage married a man and they—"

243

"Hey, Chris, you wanna stay for dinner?" Grandpa interrupted. "We've got enough food, right Lorraine?"

"Oh yes, we've got plenty." Gramma nodded.

"Sure," Chris smiled. "That would be awesome."

"Don't get too used to it," Grandpa warned. "Come have a seat. I'm watching a very interesting show. It's about the Wright Brothers. You know who the Wright Brothers were, don't you?"

"Sure, of course. Orville and Wilbur. I learned all about them when I was a kid," Chris answered. He walked over to the couch and sat upright on the edge like a good soldier.

"You're not much more than a kid now, mister." Grandpa shot Chris a look and saved a little extra to shoot at me. "Both of you. Just. Kids. And don't you forget it."

"Come, Anna Marie," Gramma said. "Give me a hand in the kitchen."

"Where's Sara?" I asked.

"Upstairs," Gramma sighed. "She just wouldn't sit still. She's refusing to sleep down here on the cot. Insisted on climbing those stairs all by herself. I almost fainted just watching her. And with your grandfather yelling at her the whole time? It was very upsetting."

Let the games begin. I thought of my soon-to-come announcement. $5,000!

"I have no idea how she plans on getting back down for dinner," Gramma added.

"I'll go get her," I said.

"Thank you, Anna Marie. I don't know what we would do without you." Gramma scurried back to her burning beans.

Sara was sitting on my bed, her casted leg raised with Fluffy supporting her foot. Woof Woof was wedged behind her lower back. "Hey you," she said without looking up. "This one is really cool, but what's the deal with the funky roof?" She was examining the loose Wavehouse sketches I'd left behind. I should have been upset—my privacy being invaded and all—but I wasn't. Sara called my drawing "cool," and that mattered much more. I looked over her shoulder.

244

"The roof is curled like a radical lip, but it's open so you can still see all around," I said.

"Maybe you'll design me a real house one day," Sara said, as she paged through my drawings, shuffling and examining them like they were treasure maps.

"Um, sure. Yeah. If you want me to." I shrugged, trying to seem nonchalant about the fact that my mother, of all people, was talking about me doing something besides surfing one day. I noticed a pile of used tissues on the floor and something small, silver and shiny—the ring. Residue of Rusty. Sara hadn't let go of that asshole entirely, at least not yet.

I also noticed, peeking out from under a copy of *Surfer Magazine*, the photo of Clueless Sperm Donor—the non-magic talisman, the who-knows-why image of a guy she barely knew, but clung to in her loneliest moments. The photo that I too sometimes looked at for clues about love, life, men—the works.

But for now everything was good, or at least better than it had been. Tonight was only a night for good news. "Come downstairs," I said.

For the first time she looked directly at me. Sara had obviously been crying, but her face was less swollen, and her bruises were healing. "Holy shit, Anna. Your hair." She started to laugh, which made me happy, even if it was at my expense.

"I know, I know. Come on, let's go downstairs. I have some really good news."

"Well, fuck knows we could all use some good news. But those stairs are a bitch. I may need a little help."

I offered her my hand just as her phone went off. Alanis Morissette's "You Oughta Know," one of Sara's favorite break-up selections. She lifted the phone off the pom-pom quilt and smiled when she saw who was calling.

"Steve Mezzi," she sighed, as she shifted her hips and turned her back on me getting ready for a breathy, flirty phone call. Maybe to arrange a revenge hook-up with the poor unsuspecting schmo, to make herself feel better about Rusty. Like *that* was gonna work. Like that *ever* worked.

I turned to leave the room.

"Whoa, Blondie," she cried. "Where the hell do you think you're going?"

I turned back—her phone was off; tossed on the bed, and she was smiling at me with both arms wide open. She'd screened a guy call! For me? Maybe. If so, another first. Or maybe it was because she still needed my help getting downstairs.

But I like to think it was just for the me-ness of me.

Chapter Forty-One

You call *him* good news?" Sara shot daggers at Chris with her steely glare. As far as she was concerned, he was a heart-breaking demon, the disciple of Rusty Meyers, another bad boy who needed to be obliterated.

Chris stood and smiled when he saw us, but his polite manners did little to reassure my lioness mom. Sara was ready to pounce. It was a good thing that I still had my arm tight around her waist, having just stumbled Siamese-twin style with her down the stairs. We'd nearly face-planted because Sara refused to take it slow.

I squeezed her tighter. "Don't freak, Sara. He's a good guy."

"Fat chance." She glared at Chris as if she wanted to bite his head off. "Once a cheater, always a cheater."

Poor Chris looked terrified. No doubt he'd already been given a thorough interrogation by Grandpa while I'd been upstairs. Now he had the wrath of Sara to contend with.

"Come on," I coaxed her. "Sit down. I'll explain everything."

"What. Ever." Sara wiggled out of my grip. "I'll get to the damn couch myself." She grabbed her crutches from beside the bannister and swiftly maneuvered around Grandpa's massive chair, past the bulky coffee table to the far end of the couch. Like a gymnast, she vaulted up and over so she could sit as far from Chris as possible. She tossed her crutches to the floor, and clunked her cast down on the coffee table to form a barrier between them. "You're not winning any brownie points standing there, dude," she grunted at Chris without looking at him. "Sit down already."

Chris opened his mouth as if to say something, but chose not to. Instead, he wisely did as Sara directed. The poor guy looked more upright and stiff on the couch than if he'd remained standing.

"Enough already," Grandpa barked once Chris was seated. "Anna, tell us what's going on."

"Just a sec. I want everybody here. Gramma," I hollered. "Can you join us? I need to tell you all something."

"In a minute, Anna Marie," Gramma's sing-songy voice called back from the kitchen. "I'm just about to sear the top of the peach pie."

Knowing Gramma, one minute meant ten minutes and I couldn't risk subjecting Chris to more of Sara's dart-ray stares or Grandpa's intrusive questions. I ran to the kitchen and grabbed Gramma just as she was about to stab the top of the pie. "Gramma. I need you *now*. The searing can wait." Once again, I had my arm around a waist, this time escorting Gramma to the living room where a very uncomfortable silence had descended.

Chris stood again as soon as Gramma appeared.

"Oh my," Gramma tittered and smiled. "What a gentleman."

Chris would have to move closer to Sara if Gramma was to have a seat, but it looked like Sara wasn't going to accommodate anyone.

"Geezus, Sara," snapped Grandpa. "Move your damn leg. Your poor ma's been on her feet in the kitchen since 3 p.m."

Sara groaned and lifted her cast so Chris could sit between one Dugan woman who thought he was a slime-bucket and another who thought he was Cary Grant.

I began pacing in front of them all, at a loss for how to start.

"Come on," Grandpa growled. "Just spit it out. Whatever it is."

"No offense, sir," Chris said softly. I was stunned to finally hear his voice. Pleasantly stunned. "But give her some time. She's got some really cool stuff to tell you." He looked at me and nodded, "Go on, Belly Flop."

"Belly Flop?" Sara shrieked. "What kind of a dumb ass thing is that to call my kid?"

"Sara," Gramma hissed. "Don't be rude to our guest!"

"Could everyone just shut up?" Grandpa yelled. "You're the ones giving me that heart attack everyone's so scared I'm gonna get!"

I had to do something before all hell broke loose, and it would have to be show rather than tell. I raced to the hallway, got my backpack, and dashed back. Opening my pack, I pulled out the trophy and placed it on the coffee table next to Sara's foot. Then I took out the two checks and handed one to Grandpa and one to Gramma.

Sara grabbed the trophy and examined the inscription at the same time Gramma and Grandpa read the endorsements on the checks. For the first time I could remember in my entire life, they all said exactly the same thing at exactly the same time.

"Holy shit!"

Yes, even Gramma.

Then there was silence again, but this time it was loaded with excitement. My family looked at me, their eyes jazzed, but confused. Sara was the first to speak.

"You won the tournament? This weekend?"

I nodded.

"How did I not know this?"

"I wasn't sure I could go through with it and if I bailed I wouldn't have been able to stand disappointing you, yet again."

"Oh Anna..." Sara sighed.

Grandpa cleared his throat. "So let me get this straight. You got out there and surfed in front of all those people?"

I nodded again.

"In Montauk?" he asked.

"Uh-huh," I shrugged.

"And you didn't freak out?" Sara asked.

"Well, I kinda freaked out. But I worked through it. I had to."

Sara looked confused. "Whaddya mean, you had to?"

"I had to for you. For all of you. You're my...my...heroes." Suddenly I started to cry. Like, *really* cry. Even more gushy than at the beach with Myra. Happy tears, relieved tears, historically pent-up tears; tears making up for lost time; tears that had been too proud to show their vulnerable little wet selves before.

"Oh baby," Sara sighed. She put the trophy down and held her arms out to me. "Shove over," she barked at Chris. "Make room for Belly Flop."

I made my way around the coffee table to hug my mother. Now there were four of us squeezed on the couch like sardines. I rested my head on Sara's shoulder and bawled like a baby as she patted my spiky-haired head. No one said a word, for a change.

Eventually my heaving stopped. I raised my head and saw that everyone else was also a bit waterlogged. I'd been bawling so loud that I hadn't noticed. Even Chris had little salty tracks down his caramel cheeks.

Grandpa took out his handkerchief and dabbed at his dripping eyes, then blew his nose foghorn loud. His face was as red as a tomato. "Okay, enough of this sappy shit. What do you mean you had to do this for all of us?"

"You've been taking care of me my whole life," I said. "All of you. And now *you* need some taking care of." I looked up at my mother. Her eyes were like dark tidal pools. "I know having me wasn't part of your original life plan. And I know that sometimes I can be a snarky little bitch. Or a scared one. But you've still shown up for me when it mattered most. And you just risked your life to save me. The least I could do was put my stupid shy ass on the line to win the tournament and help pay your hospital bill."

"Oh Anna," she started. "You didn't have to—"

I held a finger up to her lip to shush her, and kept talking. "Don't worry. I did it for me too. For the first time, I didn't let my demons get in my way. I just went for it. Like you told me I should."

"Left foot and shoulders back?" she asked. "Digging in that rail?"

"Yep," I said. "Charging. It was insane. I might be into this competing thing after all."

Sara sat bolt upright. "Really? Because you know the Long Beach Junior Invitational is in September. I think sign-up starts—"

I held my stop hand up. "Whoa. I said I *might* be into competing, not I *am* into competing. Don't get ahead of me."

"Okay. Okay." Sara took a deep breath. "Whatever you decide to do, just know that I have always been proud of you. Even when you were a snarky bitch, or when I was one; or when we both were together." She nudged the trophy with her cast. "You didn't have to win this. You could've bailed and you'd still be my hero. I've got your back, you little weirdo. Always."

Then my mother was the one bawling with her head on my shoulder. As I patted her much nicer head of hair, I turned to Grandpa and said, "And you. Enough with the tough guy routine. Don't be a pain in the ass. You need to have that heart operation whether you want to or not. This money can pay for it. Or at least help pay for it."

"You can do whatever you want with your money," Grandpa grumbled. He leaned back in the La-Z-Boy with the foot rest flipped up and stared at the ceiling.

Meanwhile, Gramma was a petite gray-haired, peach-scented volcano about to erupt in geyser tears.

"Mrs. Dugan, are you okay?" asked Chris.

"Fine, fine, Christopher. Thank you for asking." Gramma nodded and tried to smile, but when she did she looked like a demented Halloween jack-o'-lantern. I knew that the sheer relief of knowing her Tom-Tom might have his heart mended had undone her.

"Can I get you anything? Something to drink, maybe?" Chris's voice was so sweet and gentle that it left me wanting to drink him.

"Well, there might be a bottle of schnapps somewhere in the kitchen," she squeaked in a quaky voice. "Perhaps on the countertop, near the sink, but I can't be sure, it's been so long since I've had any."

"Okay, I'll go see if I can find it for you." When Chris left the room, Gramma broke down in sobs, which caused Sara to lift her head off my shoulder and look over at her mother.

"Ma," she said. "Who are you kidding? You're a mess."

Gramma sniffed. "Well, maybe I am a bit overwhelmed. This is all too...too...wonderful!"

In a flash, Sara was down the couch sitting with Gramma in her arms. I'd never seen them so much as shake hands before and here they were hugging, with Sara cooing lovingly in Gramma's ear.

Grandpa yanked on his La-Z-Boy lever and jerked into an upright position. He looked over at his wife and daughter nuzzling each other like a couple of puppies, and a few more tears dribbled down his tomato cheeks before he turned to me and smiled.

"Look what you've gone and done, missy," he said.

I smiled back. "Funny what a little risk-taking can lead to, Tom-ster. Maybe you should try it."

"Okay. Give it a rest," Grandpa sighed. "I'll take your money and have your goddamn operation. Happy?"

I nodded. "Over the moon."

"And also—" he grunted.

"Also what?"

"You're my hero, too. The best thing since sliced bread."

Of course that got me crying again. And Grandpa, too. By the time Chris returned with the schnapps the whole living room was a blubberfest.

Grandpa grabbed the glass out of Chris's hand as he walked by. "Give that drink to me, kid. My wife's over there getting what she's always wanted. Me? I'm about to have my chest cracked open. I need that schnapps more than she does." Grandpa downed it in one big gulp.

Chapter Forty-Two

 I can't believe you're making me do this," I muttered, as Myra and I rode our bikes up the Secretspot path.

"No one's making you do anything, Anna," Myra reminded me. "We told you last night if you weren't ready, you didn't have to come."

Ah, yes. The night before. Myra and Chris in Myra's living room. Peas in a pod. Planning a morning rendezvous at Secretspot, while Jimmy sat across from them nodding his head like a bobblehead on a trucker's dashboard. Planning my future. Not letting me get a word in edgewise. Chatting away like old friends while we all waited for the gobs of black hair dye combed through my fried blonde mess to dry, adhere, stick—whatever it is that hair color is supposed to do.

Myra was right, I didn't have to go. But of course I went. "I'm not making any promises," I reminded her. "I may just watch."

"Whatever. I'm just glad you agreed to put on the new gear ahead of time."

Myra had gone all out, buying me a skin-tight black rash guard and super-short red board shorts that barely covered my bum.

"They're a present," she had claimed last night. "My make-up gift."

She held them up, and Jimmy and Chris, sitting side by side on the couch, clapped and whistled.

"See? That's exactly why I *can't* wear them," I had protested.

"No," Myra asserted. "That's exactly why you have to wear them."

Now Myra peddled ahead of me, pure Wicked Witch, while I kept my pace snail-like. I finally got to the end of the path where the sky opened and the blue ocean shimmered in the orange sunrise. Jimmy—the only other surfer besides Sara who knew exactly where to find our special break—would join us later that morning. He had to supervise the pool-cleaning guys at the motel. Jimmy was

253

sworn to secrecy, but surfers were a relentless bunch. One whiff of a mystery wave and they couldn't control themselves. It was only a matter of time before the hoards discovered Secretspot.

Even if it stopped being a secret, this spot would always be beautiful. Myra had already parked her bike and was organizing her supplies. I leaned my bike on Pee Pee Rock and walked to the cliff's edge.

"Hey, Belly Flop!" Chris called from below. "Look what I have for you." He held up a beautiful new light-green surfboard with a white stripe scoring the center, a double-edged tail, and two fins.

"I hope that thing doesn't have 'Ceekay' plastered all over it," I yelled.

"Nothing. Totally blank. But one of these days *your* name will be plastered over surfboards worldwide." He flipped the board over; the top of the board was my favorite shade of my favorite color—a brilliant sunshine yellow. Either the boy had great instincts or he'd done his due diligence, and either way, I was impressed. Scampering down the cliff-side path, I arrived breathlessly on the beach.

"Don't push it, pro-boy," I warned, playfully poking Chris in the chest.

"Sorry, I can't help myself," he grinned unrepentantly.

"You know after I take that thing out—*if* I take it out—it will be covered in dings," I said.

"You can do whatever you want with it. It's yours." He deposited my new board on the sand and proceeded to wax his own.

Myra came up beside me and sighed. "He is so phenomenally sweet."

"It's true," I agreed. "Even Sara thinks so now."

"I'm glad you got to explain the whole camera chaos to your family, and the misunderstanding about Inga, before one of them hauled off and punched him."

"Luckily they were so overwhelmed by the news of my big win, they were a captive audience. Plus Chris was so great with them, especially Gramma. She wants to bring him to the church to meet the biddies."

"Oh my god! For real?"

I nodded.

"Now that is something I refuse to miss," Myra acknowledged with a grin as she unpacked her equipment.

"I'm heading in," Chris called. "You do what you want, Belly Flop. The board is here. And by the way, you look redonkulously hot." He turned away, grabbed his own board—another new beauty—and raced to the water.

I watched him paddle, duck-dive, paddle, duck-dive and paddle his way out past the break. Effortlessly, as if he was a kid playing in a bath. He sat out there for a moment until his first wave arrived. It was ginormous, swelling up out of nowhere to the size of a two-story A-frame. Chris paddled into it, and suddenly appeared on top. He popped to his feet and headed right, staying high near the lip; then he catapulted downward in a beautifully timed free-fall before turning back up in a wide graceful curve. For a moment I thought he was going to bail, cut his losses and head over to the other side. But no, Chris was a pro. He continued to slip 'n slide the wave as if it were the easiest thing in the world. As the wave petered out a good hundred yards farther down the shore, after he had aced a perfect backside aerial, he shot back over the crest, plopped down on his board, and paddled back out for more.

"Oh, what the hell," I sighed. Chris had already waxed my beautiful new board, so all I needed to do was attach my leash and dive in. I stared out at the ocean and a twinge lurched in my gut, almost making me sob. Everything was changing and it gave me pause. *Change is good*, I reminded myself. *For everyone, including me.*

"Anna," Myra called from her rock. "You sure you're okay with this?"

"I'm sure," I said. Maybe I wasn't fully out of the shy-girl cave, but at least I was hovering by the entrance, or rather, the exit. "This time, please, none of those arty close-ups of my body parts. Just me surfing, plain and simple."

"You got it," Myra grinned. "Now go for it, BFF," she added, waving her camera. "Don't you love that? BFF? Best Friend Forever,

Belly Flop...Flop. Multiple meanings. It works for everyone."

I attached the leash, picked up the board, and paddled out to Chris. He nodded calmly at me when I arrived, then resumed his silent study of the horizon—the wave-waiting game. We were together in what Gramma might call "companionable silence." Until I broke it.

"So, do kids ever do independent studies when they're on these pro tours?" I asked.

"Independent studies in what?"

"I don't know." I pretended to think. "Maybe learning to speak Mandarin, or the history of, say, Uzbekistan, or maybe studying, like, drawing, or maybe, um, architecture?"

"I know one dude who does some archeology thing. He's always going off with his notebook and camera to check out some temple or famous ruin."

"Really?"

Chris shot me a snaggle-toothed smile. "Really." He pointed toward a beautiful hump heading our way. "Looks like you got out here just in time, Belly Flop. Here it comes, big and steep, just the way you like them."

"You sound like my mother," I called, as I paddled to position.

I could barely hear Chris cry, "I hope sounding like your mother is a good thing."

Well, it's not as terrible a thing as it used to be, I thought, as the wave pulsed nearer. And then it was me on top, heading down the steepest face, dicing and slicing the wave with my board. The wave broke behind me, roaring at me, chasing me, playing with me. It caught up to me and I stalled on purpose, letting the best part happen. The wave curled around me as I continued to ride. I was deep. Everywhere was water, except straight ahead of me, where I saw an open window to the sun, the land, the sky, my life. I was in the Wavehouse. I was home.

Acknowledgements

Thanks to:

The East End of Long Island and the people who live there, for inspiring this story.

The generous surfers I've shared waves with, here, there, and everywhere.

Jaynie Royal, editor and publisher extraordinaire, and everyone else at Regal House who helped my *Wavehouse* dream come true.

Zoe Sandler, agent amazing, for her savvy and support, making sure I'm taken good care of out there in the big, bad publishing world.

Alison Seiffer for nailing it with cover art that belongs in a museum.

Traci Inzitari, who helped shape *Wavehouse* early on, and to whom I will always be enormously grateful.

My father Jack Kaltman, a true waterman who instilled a love of all things ocean-y in me. I miss you every day.

Family and friends who have believed in Anna's story for years; we are finally in the Wavehouse. We are home.